June Days

Lisa Keifer

Copyright © 2022 by Lisa Keifer

First paperback edition: 2024

ISBN: 979-8-9906604-1-0

All rights reserved.

This is a work of fiction. Names, characters, places, and incidents are either the product of the author's imagination or are used fictitiously. Any resemblance to actual persons, living or dead, events or locales is entirely coincidental.

No portion of this book may be reproduced in any form without written permission from the publisher or author, except as permitted by U.S. copyright law, or for the use of quotations in a book review. For more information, address lisakeifer@lisakeiferauthor.com

Cover design: Sarah Kil Creative Studio

Editor: Joanne Lui

Note to the Reader

This book references illness of a parent and cheating.

Chapter 1

Lucy

I AM, AS IT happens, not only a hopeless romantic, but a helpless one. I love despite everything. Doctors could probably classify a whole new disorder based solely on me. It would certainly involve a new type of rehab or group, like Romantics Anonymous. I can just hear my introduction now: "Hi. My name is Lucy, and I'm addicted to romance."

I love to love, to be in love, to be showered with love. Once I fall, I'm all in. And I *always* fall.

Therein lies my downfall.

I definitely see the irony in how it happened in the exact same place we met the previous year. This location was one of my most favorite spots in the world. It's where I felt the most comfortable, the most secure, and the most at peace. My family and I visited this place—our home away from home—every summer, from the time I was a toddler all the way up to my early teen years.

Then came the summer I was thirteen. We didn't pack up and go in June. We didn't pack up and go in July either. It was our first summer vacation away from the only place I ever wanted to be. To be away from the cabin felt like being away from home, even as I lay in my bed in the place I grew up.

By the time I was eighteen, enough was enough. My sister Kenzie and I started a new tradition of traveling to the lake on our own every weekend in June. Once I became a teacher, I still went every weekend. It didn't matter that school didn't end until June was almost gone.

It was one of these trips with Kenzie at the start of the summer that pivoted my life in a direction that I, the hopeless romantic, never saw coming.

Even at twenty-five, the lake was still like home to me. In fact, it was better in some ways, because home consisted of an adorable yet outrageously expensive one-bedroom rental in what had to be the most populated part of my tiny town of Syracuse Falls, New York.

That late June day, the trees were in full bloom. The verdant grasses had reached a shade of perfection. Even the clouds seemed fluffier and brighter than in recent months.

Kenzie and I had driven from our cabin to the state park to meet a few friends before they spent the night at the cabin with us, as they were at the lake a day before we were.

Near the six of us, a group of teens tossed a football around. Adults and children alike built sandcastles and flew kites, and some even swam in the cool, fresh water. It had been such a bitterly cold winter that we were obviously all grateful for this magnificent change. Everyone and everything felt happy and alive. Laughs and smiles emanated from all the people I could see.

And there he was.

A man about my age. A very, *very* cute man. He sat comfortably in jeans and a blue T-shirt just snug enough to see there were muscles underneath. A tan hoodie lay on the sand next to him. The sun-kissed blond streaks in his darker hair matched the warm sand beneath us. He scratched at his dark, stubbly beard with a wide grin on his face aimed at his friends, and I nearly had to force my lungs to work in order to breathe. It was like I had found my very own Prince Charming.

But I was familiar with these sensations. Honestly, I felt them almost all the time when meeting new guys, or seeing a random guy in the store or even hearing what sounded like a cute guy on a customer service line. None of those relationships had lasted long, though. It was beyond disturbing when the men I dated behaved worse than the third-grade students I taught.

I made my way closer to this man on the beach. Little by little, I nonchalantly took a few steps here and there. I "needed" to look at a shell I saw half-buried in the sand. Our Trevor asked if I wanted another bottle of water since I'd finished mine, but I waved him off. I was already a little too far away to reply.

As I moved more in the direction of the super-hot guy, I feigned interest in what turned out to be a soaked, rotten stick. No matter how slow I moved, I had to keep going. It was like a force was pulling me to him. All I could do was obey.

Finally, I was close enough to catch his attention. His amazing baby blues locked on mine, and we smiled. He had nonchalantly stood up and moved his way toward me, I saw, because he was no longer where I first noticed him. While gazing at him, nothing existed except him and me. All else faded into the background as he and I slowly walked even closer to each other.

"Petey Boy!" a male voice called.

Hot Guy turned his head in that direction before we had a chance to speak. His gorgeous, muscled body, however, still mostly faced me.

"What?" he called to the other man. His smooth, baritone voice practically gave me goose bumps.

I looked to see who he was talking to. There was a group of two guys and three women, all of their eyes on either me or Pete—or maybe Peter. I wasn't sure yet.

"You ready to go grill?"

Pete or Peter shook his head. "Nah. You go on without me."

The other man waved him off, and no one really replied.

"Should I call you Petey Boy, too?" I asked when he turned back to me.

He grimaced. "Please don't. Pete is fine."

Yes, you are, I thought, but of course I couldn't say this. "Hi, Pete," I said with a grin.

He grinned back with his perfectly crooked smile. "Hey."

"Luce?" Kenzie called.

I didn't turn to face her. I only wanted to look at Pete.

"Luce," she said again, much closer this time based on the sound of her voice.

It took a lot of willpower to glance away from Pete to my sister. "What?" I asked her, trying to keep an annoyed tone out of my words.

She brushed several dark blonde strands of hair out of her face. "We're ready to go back for lunch."

"And?" Whoops. That tone came out anyway.

"And," she answered, drawing the word out, "you and I brought your car here. They don't have room for both of us in their vehicle."

Oh, right. I couldn't see a way out of this. "I'm sorry, Pete," I told him. His upturned mouth had straightened by the time I looked back at him. "Will you still be here if I come back?"

"I'll wait all day if I have to."

This about weakened my knees to the point I couldn't stand. My lungs also seemed to have devised a scheme with my heart, which immediately copied its friend and sped up to a level I wasn't sure I could handle. As my cheeks begin to heat with a blush, I laughed to myself, knowing my whole body was conspiring against me.

Of course, my brain didn't want to be left out. It seemed to forget how to form words or what they even were.

"I'll be back as soon as I can," I finally managed to tell him, my cheeks hot.

Kenzie and I were halfway to the parking lot with our friends when I stopped my feet. I dug in my pocket, then held out my keys to my sister. "Go without me. I'll see you when you come back."

She slowly reached for the keys. "Are you sure? You don't even know this guy."

I laughed. "We're at a busy public beach. I have my phone if I get into trouble. You worry too much."

"You don't worry enough." Then she walked away, catching up with our waiting friends.

Without waiting to see them leave, I shifted my body and headed back to Pete, hoping he would keep his word. Sure enough, he was still in the area I left him. One of the women and the man who called him Petey Boy were also with him, having what looked to be a funny conversation. They were all laughing and smiling.

Pete took a few steps away from them when he saw me. They moved closer, too. Pete's feet carried him all the way over to me, stopping maybe six inches away. "Luce, this is Miles and his fiancée Corkie."

We said our hellos. All the while, I tried to fight the spread of tingles from hearing Pete call me Luce. Only some family, my besties, and maybe one or two previous boyfriends ever called me that. Everyone else was happy to call me Lucy.

Corkie pulled on Miles's arm. "Let's let them be."

He didn't really acknowledge her. "What about Drea, Petey Boy? You promised her a rematch on the grill today. Loser cleans up."

Pete grimaced again. He turned his eyes my way. Then he suddenly lunged forward and grabbed something. When I looked, I saw an errant football in his hands. Based on where his hands went, it must have been just a few inches away from hitting me.

"A head's up would have been nice," he said to the teen who came over to retrieve it.

"Sorry, man," the kid said in return.

I didn't really care about the head's up. Prince Charming, who turned out to be Prince Pete, had just rescued the damsel in distress, aka me. I was head over heels already.

"Hey, Lucy." My sister's voice.

Why was she calling me again? Didn't she leave?

I swiveled around. "What's wrong? Everything okay?"

"Fine," she told me. She held my keys out to me. "I found your spare in your glove box. Trevor and I will bring your car back soon. I'll lock it and text its location to you."

"Why would you leave then come all the way back here?"

"Because Trevor agreed with me that you shouldn't be here without a vehicle."

"You really do worry too much," I said with a chuckle. But I appreciated the effort she put into keeping her little sister safe.

"You staying?" Miles asked Pete in a harder tone as my sister left again.

I realized more than just my body was conspiring against me. No one in this park wanted Pete and I to have a decent conversation except the two of us. Well, I knew one of us did for sure. I held my breath in hope for the other.

Pete reached over and moved the stray hairs that were blowing in front of my face. "I'm staying," he replied, though it felt like he wanted me to hear it first, before them.

I exhaled softly. My wish came true.

Corkie and Miles returned to their other friends. Pete stepped closer to me. Only a few inches separated us.

"Guess you forfeit!" a woman's voice called out. We both glanced over. She looked to be around twenty-five—my age and Pete's, too, from my best guess—and was simply gorgeous in a bikini top and short shorts. I wondered if they ever dated or slept together, but not for long. It didn't matter. He was clearly more interested in me.

Finally on our own, Pete led me over by the railing, under the shade of a tree. We sat on the sand, the soft warmth radiating into us as the stories flowed out. We didn't talk about boring things like jobs. I wanted to know about his life outside of his obligations. Who wanted to think about work when they were on vacation? Most people I knew went to the lake to forget about what would be on their desk or in their inbox. The park didn't even offer Wi-Fi.

"You seriously cheered for Gatsby and Daisy?" Pete asked after we got around to one of my favorite books. He laughed like he just couldn't believe it.

"Why not? They just had a little growing up to do."

Pete gave a slight nod. I took this to mean he agreed with me.

"And the affair?"

"Never should have happened," I replied quickly, "but she married the wrong man. That's what makes it so tragically romantic."

Pete gave a laugh along with a handsome smile.

As we continued to chat, he moved closer to me and again tucked a stray section of hair behind my ear. Right then, I knew there was no going back. There was no turning around and away from this place I now found myself. The air was suddenly sweeter, the breeze warmer.

"Shall I compare thee to a summer's day?" he began.

Then.

Oh then.

He recited the whole damn sonnet, much to my—quite physical—delight. It turned out that he knew all my favorite sonnets by name. We shared a love of baseball and bluebirds, football and finches, and camping and cardinals. He was my athletic, intellectual, nature-loving dream guy.

Pete's eyes watched my face, then he brushed some sand off my hand after I repositioned myself. "I love how the sun dances on your hair, but the light in your eyes is so much more intense."

I wondered how he could see that, a thought I questioned aloud.

"How can I not?" he told me as he moved ever closer to my side. "It's the most alluring part of you."

I wanted to kiss him right then, kiss the beautiful mouth of this beautiful man with a beautiful soul. Instead, I kissed his cheek and rested my head on his shoulder as he wrapped his muscular arm around my waist. We stretched our legs out beneath us, my jeans the only things between his lower legs and mine. The spice of his cologne blended so perfectly with the sweetness of my perfume that it felt like we really were in paradise.

Never once did I think about hunger or thirst or time until the sun had suddenly set. Only it wasn't exactly sudden. We'd talked the entire afternoon and evening. It was time to go back to the real world.

Pete stood and offered me his warm hand. He also offered me his hoodie, which I eagerly accepted and put on. The temperature was yet another thing I hadn't paid attention to until I was already cold. We ambled over to the parking lot, the moon and stars acting as our celestial guides. At my car, we paused, both unwilling to let the night go. I moved my eyes over him, wishing I hadn't let go of his hand so soon after I stood from the sand. He was tall but not too tall, the kind of height that was perfect for me to tiptoe up to for a smooch or be gracefully dipped in a dance. I could see both in our future.

The soft breeze lightly kissed my skin as Pete kissed my hands, quick and gentle.

"Parting is such sweet sorrow, that I shall say good night till it be morrow."

I honestly giggled. "That's supposed to be my line. Unless you would rather be Juliet."

Pete put his hands on my hips, nearing his body to mine. "I'm going to miss you, Luce."

Then he leaned down, his eyes watching my mouth before moving back up to my eyes. His hands continued sending tingles through me as I moved so close to his face, I could feel his warm breath on my skin. I gave the slightest nod then gently connected my lips to his.

Pete gave a whisper of a growl and slid a hand to my lower back, pressing me into him. I could feel his heat through his sweatshirt, which impressed me even more. I parted my lips just enough to feel a little bit of Pete inside me. This sparked a bolt of desire that burned all the way down to my toes.

Then we slowly released our hands from their tight grips on each other and pulled back.

"Where are you staying?" I asked in a hushed tone.

My arms were wrapped around his shoulders. The scent of his sexy cologne was all around me with his sweatshirt on. The only thing I wanted to do more than kiss him was hold on to him forever. "You have a campsite here?"

"Yes, and it's not nearly close enough to you." He smiled, but there was a sadness to it. "Do you have to leave so early tomorrow morning? We won't head out until late afternoon."

"Kenzie and I both have work stuff, or I wouldn't even think of it." The day before had been the last day of school, but there was never a break, it seemed. Summer school loomed already. "But we'll see each other soon. Syracuse Falls is practically down the street from you. Besides, living in different towns is nothing to two people who really want to see each other."

"Mmm, and I do," he whispered, his face so close, I could almost feel his beard on my skin. "How about dinner tomorrow?"

"Like a date?"

"A date that destiny arranged."

Oh my, how right he was. It felt like we were exactly where we were supposed to be.

"You want to date me?" I asked again, gently tightening my arms around him.

He gave a soft chuckle. "I want to date you. I want you to be my girlfriend. I want to spend all my time with you. What do you say?"

It was exactly the kind of speech I always wanted to hear. It was the thing I always dreamed of. Prince Charming falling for me as hard and as fast as I fell for him. It was the single most enthralling moment of my life.

"No," I replied quietly.

Chapter 2

Lucy

PETE'S SMILE HELD, BUT his face scrunched up. "No?" He couldn't hide the surprise in his voice.

I was shocked, too, honestly. He gave me my dream. Just handed it to me on a silver platter. But I couldn't accept it.

"Please understand," I added. "I so desperately want to say yes. But I think we should take our time getting there."

"Take our time getting to the date? Like doing things before we go to dinner?"

"Like getting to know each other better first."

"Isn't that what we did all day?"

"It is, and it was amazing. That's why I think it would be best for us to start out as friends first."

"So we'll still see each other?"

"Yes, as friends. *Not* platonic ones," I felt the need to remind him. "It isn't like we can't flirt with each other. We just won't officially date yet. Or kiss or do anything physical."

He took a moment with his eyes closed before looking at me again. "How long?"

"Six months. Well, how about *almost* six months? Until the beginning of December."

Pete let out a sharp breath. "I can't say I completely understand."

"But you'll do this for me?"

He smiled again. "You bet. So I'm guessing that means, as my friend, you won't want to come to my tent with me?"

"You'd be right." Well, he was so wrong about that, but I'd resolved not to anyway.

"You mean I can't. . ." He finished the rest of the sentence as a whisper in my ear.

My cheeks burned, while the rest of me tingled. I hadn't expected dirty talk so soon. "I don't think you're supposed to speak to your friends like that."

He stayed close to my ear, his breath soft on my skin. It was as fast as mine, too. "That's a no?"

"For now."

Pete moved back just a bit, and we made eye contact. "And later?"

I ignored the urge to bite my lower lip. "Just you try keeping me out of your bed when the time comes. Right now, though, I think it's time to go."

"One thing first." He asked for my phone number.

I couldn't believe I'd forgotten that part. There was no way I wanted to do what my bestie Gwenn once did to her boyfriend and make Pete find me without it. My other bestie Lourdes wouldn't have even considered talking to Pete at all, I'm sure, so I was at least ahead of where she would be.

"You won't change your mind?" he asked as I reached into my pocket for my keys.

I moved my eyes back up to look at his handsome face. "I want to. I really do, but it wouldn't be right. Rushing into a relationship has only led to heartache for me. So has rushing into other things," I added, before he mentioned anything about friends with benefits. "I hope you can understand that."

Chapter 3

Pete

I UNDERSTOOD. I DID. I just wasn't sure how I felt about it. Before I saw Lucy, I'd been on the beach with friends, including a couple women I had a good time flirting with—Drea in particular. That grilling contest was going to have heat coming from more than just the burning coals. We'd already gotten to a point, especially after our first competition in which she smacked my ass a few times, that if I'd just said to Drea, "Let's go," she would have met me in either tent, naked and ready.

There was just something about Lucy as she watched me move closer to her on the beach before I said her name for the first time. Like she couldn't wait to hear anything and everything I had to say. Considering she did just that the whole rest of the day, I thought it was a given that she'd love to go out with me. I thought she'd be as ready as Drea.

It was rare that I fell for a woman who didn't want me back. Wanting me but not agreeing to date me? This was new territory.

"Good night, sweet Lucy," I told her as she kissed my cheek.

She moved to take off my hoodie, presumably to give it back to me.

"Keep it," I told her. "At least until we see each other again."

"You leave me no choice," she said with a grin.

I watched her get in her car and drive away, then I returned to my campsite, assuming I'd find my friends there.

"Where you been, man?" Alec asked once he saw me.

They all sat around a blazing campfire.

"And why are you back?" Miles asked before I had a chance to reply. "Did she turn you down?"

I hated that he knew this with every fiber of my being. I bristled at his words. "Not exactly," I told him.

Miles laughed. "She turned him down," he said to the rest of the group.

Corkie made some sympathetic sound. Drea looked smug. Miles kept laughing.

"It's not like she told me no," I lied. Well, it didn't feel like a lie. "She wants us to get to know each other better before we date."

"You hear that?" Miles said to the group. "Poor Petey Boy fell for that."

"Did you not see them at the beach?" Corkie asked him. She looked over at me. "That woman had hearts in her eyes watching you. I think taking things slow is a good idea. Even if it is an odd concept for you."

She was right. Never in my dating history had I ever been friends first with a woman for an extended period of time. Maybe a weekend at most. Like Drea. We'd only known each other a few days. We had mutual friends in both Alec and Corkie. I had actually been waiting for that grilling contest between Drea and me to take things further. Use it as foreplay, with all the innuendo we could handle. I knew Drea could take it.

However, I wasn't sure how much Lucy could handle, or how much I could handle keeping my hands off her. I'd already stroked her hand and held it and kissed it. I'd kissed her incredibly soft, sweet mouth. I wanted to kiss her and hold her and stroke her everywhere else.

All that wasn't to say I wasn't capable of waiting. I knew I was. Well, I knew I was going to do my best and certainly not beg her for it.

"You'll have her wrapped around your little finger soon enough," Drea told me.

I hated the way she said this. I was a little cool without my sweatshirt, so I got up for a few moments and added a log to the fire before returning to my chair.

"Among other things," Miles added with a laugh. "Or maybe not!"

"So, are you going to date anyone else while you get to know her?" Corkie asked.

I shook my head. "I don't think so. This is really important to Lucy."

Miles shook his head, too. "Giving up other women for one chick who isn't even your girlfriend? Doesn't make any sense. Why would you agree to that?"

What else was I supposed to do? I wanted to show her I wasn't like the assholes she'd previously dated. I said as much to my friends.

Then Miles laughed and sent me a smirk. "Oh, but you are, Petey Boy. You just haven't admitted it to yourself yet."

I ignored him and grabbed a water out of the cooler next to me. "What did I miss while I was gone? Did Miles burn the burgers to a crisp again like last night?"

"If you'd cooked with me, that wouldn't have happened," Drea said in a sultry yet crisp tone.

If she and I had started that contest together, we never would have made it to the cooking part. I think she knew that, too, based on the way she looked at me with her sensuous, dark eyes. They contained a different kind of glow than the one Lucy's had.

Miles put his hands up. "Blame last night on the shots of vodka, not on me."

Drea and the other woman in the group, Tess—who worked with Miles, Alec, and me—both ignored Miles and kept their eyes on me. Tess was also Corkie's friend, and enjoyed telling me how much she liked being able to see me both at work and play.

I guess it was play. She and I flirted, too, but never seriously. I was never interested in dating her or having any kind of relationship with her. Unlike Drea, Tess gave me a look with an expression that said maybe all that flirting between us was about to end.

"Hey!" Miles suddenly exclaimed.

I glanced over to see that he was eyeing me. "What?" I asked.

"When are you going to see that woman who will never sleep with you next?"

Drea laughed.

I shook my head. "You're wrong, man. It'll happen when Lucy's ready."

"Dude, she blew you off. Can't you see that?" He was still laughing, but I knew he was serious.

Corkie asked him to fix the fire, as the log I'd added had fallen a bit to the side. Not enough that it needed fixing, but this was an easy thing to distract Miles with. He often acted like he was the king of fire. He acted like he was the king of a lot of things. And he didn't let up.

"I don't think she's ever going to want you," he said loudly.

"And I don't think that's any of our business," Tess told him. Corkie and Alec agreed.

Despite reassurance and support from my friends, Miles was still getting under my skin. I hated both of us for it.

"She'll want me," I told him. "She already does."

"Prove it," he snapped back.

"How?" I was genuinely curious.

"I bet you can't get her to sleep with you—and by sleep with, I do mean have sex with."

Corkie took in an audible breath. Unlike her, Miles's antics never surprised me.

"Did she give you a time frame?" Tess asked me.

"Six months. Nearly."

"It'll never happen," Miles pushed.

"Forget it, man," I told him. "I'm going to bed."

My other friends said good night as I stood from my chair. I walked over to my tent across the way and crawled in, quickly zipping it behind me. Corkie somehow managed to get Miles to shut up, but his voice was still in my head, screwing with me.

I already liked Lucy more than I thought I would. The idea of only being friends with her for six months sucked, but the idea of pushing her and losing her from my life completely sucked even more.

I was going to be her friend. I was going to be the best damn not-platonic friend she ever had. She was worth it.

Chapter 4

Lucy

"ARE YOU FEELING OKAY?"

"I'm fine, Kenz," I told my sister.

"You sure? Because a gorgeous, kind, intelligent man asked you out, and you turned him down."

"I didn't turn him down."

She raised an eyebrow at me.

"Okay, I did, but not in that exact way. It's a 'not right now' answer, not a full-on no."

"But it's so not like you."

This had me unsettled.

"Let's get going," I said. "I still have to psych myself up for summer school, and I'm not one hundred percent prepared."

"Are you ever?"

"Yes, I am," I replied quickly, not liking her snarky tone. Though she was just eight years older than me, Kenzie had always treated me like I was still a kid and she was the only adult.

I zipped my large white-and-yellow-striped bag and carried it out with my sunny yellow suitcase to my car. I'd already loaded up my toiletry bag, my purse, and the picnic basket I took on every trip to the lake, whether I planned on using it or not. Kenzie had packed up her stuff before breakfast. Our friends had already left, but since they grew up on a farm—or still ran one, in Trevor's case—they were used to super-early hours.

The sun was barely up. It was surprisingly muggy and warm. I wondered how Pete slept last night and if his dreams were as full of me as mine were of him.

"Back to the ho-hum," Kenzie said after locking the cabin's front door. We'd already secured the back door. I watched the wind blow around her long blonde hair. She shoved it all into a high ponytail before asking, "How well do you think Pete will fit in with your everyday life?"

"As they say, only time will tell. But I hope it's a perfect fit."

She gave me a smile. "Me too, sis."

We walked the short distance to my car and climbed in. Our patch of land was so small that, even though my car was up by the cabin, near the lake, the car was also practically on the curve of the road already. It was the type of lot that would have been bought out for pennies by rich people years ago, along with the neighbors' houses, and torn down to make room for a ten-bedroom, five-bathroom monstrosity that would have completely destroyed the quaintness of the area. It was one of a few holdouts whose owners never thought of all those dollar signs, though my parents had sold of plenty of side acreage in the past when in need of money.

Even though I knew the cabin was still only worth pennies, relatively speaking, I couldn't care less about that.

I was so grateful my parents had chosen to hold on to this property they no longer had a use for. My brother barely had a use for it, either. But my and Kenzie's love of the place was enough for our mom and dad to keep it, and that warmed my heart.

Though I obviously stayed alert while driving and chatting with my sister on the way back to our town, I easily could have closed my eyes and known exactly where the turns and stops were. The drive was practically second nature to me. Only construction detours threw me off course.

I couldn't help thinking that every mile farther down the road was a mile farther away from Pete. Of course, this was a little ridiculous since Pete told me he lived in Syracuse, which meant he'd have to drive closer to Syracuse Falls and to me anyway, instead of staying by the lake. I just felt like I was missing something during that drive.

Well, I was. I missed Pete.

All I could do was hope that he missed me, too.

Chapter 5

Pete

I FORCEFULLY RAN A hand through my hair. I couldn't listen to him say it one more time.

"Babe, stop messing with Pete," Corkie said as they took their tent down. She was busy folding the top tarp.

"I'm not messing with him. The guy acts like he's some kind of a Lothario, but now we know it's a lie." Miles turned to me again. "You choked, Petey Boy. It's okay to admit that."

I tossed my tent poles into the trunk of my car before facing him. "I didn't choke." I kept my voice calm and smooth, but inside, I was stiff and growing warmer. I'd wanted to chuck those damn poles through the window just to release some of the tension building up in my body.

"What would you call it?" Miles pushed some more.

"Respecting her wishes?" Corkie offered.

"Bullshit." He turned to her. "If she really wanted him, she wouldn't make him wait. You didn't make me wait. Drea wasn't going to make you wait," he added to me.

I didn't think we needed to drag Drea into this, especially after seeing her smug, silent expression as she loaded her bag into Corkie's trunk. Then Miles said yet again how I'd choked.

I snapped.

"Lucy will be mine soon, and so will your money," I told him as suavely as possible.

I could see Corkie stop what she was doing, her arms immediately hanging at her sides as she stared at me. Unable to resist, I looked over in Drea's direction. She scowled at me and kept packing up her stuff.

"You're on, Petey Boy!" Miles said with glee as he came over and grabbed my hand to shake it.

"You sure about that, Pete?" Alec asked, his tent and bag already loaded into my car.

"Yes, he's sure," Miles answered for me then let my hand go.

Except that wasn't my answer.

I was only sure that I'd completely and absolutely messed up. That, and there was no getting out of it, as far as Miles was concerned. He'd never let me back out.

What the hell did I do? I couldn't breathe, even with that stupid, phony grin plastered on my face. I'd screwed up so, so freaking much. There was no way else to look at it.

"Just tell him you changed your mind," Alec said later as we drove to his apartment in Syracuse. I was dropping him off before heading to my house.

"Right. Because Miles is so reasonable."

"You know he's going to make your life hell about this."

I knew it. That's why I knew I could never let Lucy meet Miles again. There was no predicting what he'd say or when.

Alec must have been thinking the same thing, because then he said, "You can't let them hang out together."

"I would never. Certainly not now."

"So what are you going to do? How are you going to explain to her why she can't meet some of your friends? She already saw them at the beach."

That was a good question, one I didn't have an answer for.

When I got home, after dropping Alec off, I decided to text Lucy. Since her sister had to be at work, I assumed Lucy would be home. I wasn't sure exactly where home was except somewhere in Syracuse Falls. I doubted I'd ever gone to Syracuse Falls except to drive through it on my way somewhere else. It was some tiny little village that never meant much to me. Before Lucy.

She didn't text me back. I found myself missing her already. That was new. I never missed the women I'd just met. I did all I could to make them miss me, not the other way around. The most I felt was a physical craving, but never anything emotional. Lucy had brought a lot of new things into my life, and I smiled, liking her more for it.

Chapter 6

Lucy

AT HOME, AFTER DROPPING off Kenzie at her house, I carried in my luggage but decided against unpacking. None of it had to be put away immediately. We'd packed what leftover foods we could in the freezer since our brother Dominic mentioned wanting to stay at the cabin next weekend. He hadn't stayed there as an adult in more than five years, so we wanted him to at least not have to worry about much while he was there. Kenzie kept all the food that couldn't be frozen, since I didn't want any of it. She was probably already at our parents' house picking up her daughter Hayzel.

I sat outside on my patio chair next to my tiny glass table, working through the lesson planning I needed to go over to help prepare myself for teaching the upcoming summer school sessions.

This wasn't the first time I was going to teach summer school, yet I felt immense pressure because of it. Because I worked in a tiny school district, I at least got to teach in my own classroom and didn't have to come up with a list of supplies I needed to haul with me, but this didn't help the unease.

By the time late afternoon rolled around, I was even more frazzled from the last-minute choice I made to use a different hands-on activity with the puzzle-like pieces I had for the comparing fractions portion. I scrambled to find my packet of paper lunch baggies.

I searched all the supplies I kept at home, including those in my bedroom, hall closet, and kitchen. Even in doing so, a thought kept nagging at me that I left the packages in my classroom. I had no choice but to go get them in order to finish the preparations.

Before leaving, I pulled out my phone, remembering I'd wanted to tell Pete I was home, but it was off. Once the phone powered up, I saw I missed a text from him.

Thinking of you

Thinking of you, too. Hope you slept well.

I had to stop myself from babbling on with things like how much I missed him and liked him and couldn't wait to see him again. Flirting was allowed, but I didn't want to scare him off.

When he didn't reply right away, I walked to my car to leave. I couldn't spend all day texting with him. There were still other things needing my attention. Lourdes and Gwenn would be super proud of me for putting my work ahead of a man, I knew.

I was just pulling into the elementary school parking lot when my mom called.

"Kenzie and Hayzel are still here, and Dominic's coming here in a little while, so we thought it would be nice if we all had dinner together," she said.

"Oh, I'd like to, but I'm at school right now. Not quite where I'd like to be in my summer school preparations."

"Honey, you have some time until it starts. Give yourself a break."

Which sounded great except for the fact that both my siblings would harass me about not being ready ahead of time. "Can we do family dinner tomorrow night?"

"Of course, sweetie. I think your brother should be able to finish his work in time for dinner. He's starting a new build this week. A four-bedroom over on Azalea." Pride seeped into every word she said about my brother and his construction company, but she did the same about me and also Kenzie. Not one of us was ever a disappointment to her, as far as jobs were concerned. "Don't spend all day working on your lessons. Remember, you've earned this hiatus."

Mom knew all about how important summer break was for teachers since she was married to my dad, though he liked to teach summer sessions more often than not. Obviously, I hated that as a kid but definitely saw the appeal as an adult with bills to pay. I also never let it keep me from the best place on Earth.

After fetching the paper bags and also a few other things, I returned home. My mom was right. I had earned a break. Instead of jumping back into work, I texted Gwenn.

How's the new assistant working out?

I can see why it's taken me so long to find a good one. I don't think she's going to be around much longer.

This wasn't good news. Gwenn was a real estate broker running her own tiny brokerage. Without someone to help her, she had to be in charge of not only all the legwork for clients but also open houses and social media and anything else essential to effectively running her business.

You can't keep doing everything on your own. You did that for months and almost completely burned out because of it.

What choice do I have? Unless you know of an awesome assistant you can recommend.

I wish. Sorry.

I added a sad-face emoji. It sucked seeing my friend struggle after so much misfortune in her life, most recently a horrifying plane crash she and her now-boyfriend Rhett survived.

Already finished your end of the year stuff?

Naturally :)

Never doubted you for a moment. lol Summer school prep all ready?

Not yet, but you know me. I'll still find things I want to change even after the session begins.

I was keeping track of all I needed to do in my planner. I had sections for everything: school, personal events like dinners, parties, and the like—even town meetings. My planner not only had what I needed for summer school sessions, it also had reminders for when I needed to look at this year's class roster and make name tags, a seating chart, and a cute birthday chart. I preferred my lesson plans on paper as well, though the official plans were electronic.

Not everything can be perfect.

Says the woman who has been trying to find Perfect Assistant 2.0 ever since Taytum left.

I think your students will be out of high school before that happens, based on the interview candidates I've seen. But Rhett just got here. TTYL

I told her to say hi to her boyfriend for me. It must have been difficult for them to live apart, with Gwenn in Syracuse and Rhett in Auburn. Pete was practically in the next town to me. It felt like a million miles. I already wanted to drive into the city to see him, and it hadn't even been twenty-four hours. I didn't even know when I'd get to see him again.

Chapter 7

Pete

MONDAY MORNING MEETINGS.

I hated Monday morning meetings, especially the early ones. It usually involved customers full of desperation and begging for hope I couldn't give them. Even though I knew waiting over the weekend was probably not easy to do, I also knew starting the beginning of a new week this way wasn't any sort of relief for them.

Working in the mortgage department had always terrified me, and yet it was the best move for my career. Not so much for my emotional state during the workday.

"Kerrick, Nadine," I said to the Larkins as they sat across from me at my desk. They were in their mid-fifties, I knew thanks to the information in their file, though Kerrick looked a few years older than he was. "I want this to work out. When I was assigned to your account—"

"After Lewis retired," Nadine reminded me. Her tone had me questioning whether she blamed me for this.

"Yes. After Lewis retired, I—"

"And after that bank bought out ours, with no warning."

Except I was here at this bank before the merger. I couldn't say this, however. Nadine was on a roll, and I wasn't about to do anything to add to her annoyance with me.

"There was plenty more than a little warning, Naye, and it didn't affect us as much as you think it did," Kerrick said.

"How didn't it? I'd like to know, because—"

Her husband interrupted her. "Do we have to go through this again? I think Pete here was saying something."

"Yes, we do, Kerrick. Pete needs to know that we didn't expect a merger. I certainly didn't. And a new bank comes with new rates, which is why our mortgage payment requirements have skyrocketed for the past few months."

I didn't feel comfortable interrupting the bickering, but by this point, I needed them to focus. Nadine wasn't even accurate about most of it. I cleared my throat. The Larkins both looked at me again, neither speaking.

Finally, I could continue. "I noticed that you've settled the debts as much as possible and used every program available to you."

"We are just asking for an extension. Not dissolution of debt or repayments. We intend on paying every cent owed. We just need a little more time before we have to start making payments again." Kerrick's voice trembled, and I swallowed hard.

I knew the history. This man had struggled through health issues for years, and paid the price in high medical bills. Forced into early retirement, without enough money in the fund to pay for what he needed. Nadine had to quit her full-time job as his health deteriorated because his condition was unpredictable as to when it might worsen, and they didn't have the money for a home health-care professional.

After adjusting my tie, which felt like it was way too tight, I continued. "You mentioned possibly needing bankruptcy to get out of this enormous hole you're in due to Kerrick's medical bills." I paused, giving them and myself another moment to breathe.

I needed to be calm and not in any way emotional when I spoke next. It was hell having these conversations with our customers, but I found myself caring about these two particular customers more than I did any others. I didn't know why my new boss had chosen me for this account, and I felt like any misstep on my part was going to let a lot of people down.

I looked at the Larkins and continued. "If you do consider bankruptcy, please know that while the debt itself might be cleared, the lien on the house will remain in place."

"Which means we'll still have to pay," Nadine said with a rough voice.

I gently nudged the tissue box on my desk in her direction, but she pulled a few out from her purse. She dabbed one at her damp eyes.

"Yes, you'll still have to pay," I replied. "I have the ability to grant you a ninety-day extension, which I will absolutely do."

They both audibly breathed out in relief. Unfortunately, I wasn't done yet. Nadine was about to speak, but I had to put my hand up to stop her.

"However, once that time is up, my hands will be tied. If you do explore bankruptcy, I can't guarantee what the bankruptcy trustee will allow as far as you keeping your properties, especially outside of your main residence."

"You mean the cabin on Oneida Lake?" Kerrick asked, accepting a clean tissue from Nadine.

He wiped his own tears as I spoke.

"That's right," I told them.

Both of their faces dropped a little further into despair. Based on Lewis's notes, apart from losing their residence, I knew this was the last thing they wanted.

"Oh, Lucy will be crushed if we lose the cabin."

I froze. "Lucy?" My voice almost sounded like I was being strangled.

She nodded. "Our daughter. She's been going to the cabin every summer for years."

Oneida Lake. The same lake where my Lucy and I met at the state park.

"We used to take our kids there when they were children," Kerrick added, "until my heart decided to wreak havoc."

It couldn't be.

Then Nadine pulled something up on her phone and turned it to me. And there she was. The woman I was in a not-platonic friendship with. The woman I would have gotten naked with the day we met had she been into it. Her parents were my customers.

I heard thunderous alarm bells going off in my brain. Though inadvertent, this was the most compromising thing I'd ever done in my job. I hadn't even been in this particular office more than a few weeks since my predecessor's retirement.

I tried to breathe and maintain a sense of calm—or at least give the impression that I was calm—as Nadine continued, blissfully unaware of my torment.

"She's a third-grade teacher. Living on her own now after having roommates for years. Cute little house in Syracuse Falls. She's single. In her twenties. Gorgeous, isn't she?"

Gorgeous wasn't good enough to describe Lucy.

Kerrick put a hand up to gently push Nadine's hand and phone down, and I watched Lucy's smiling face disappear until I couldn't see her anymore. I refocused on Kerrick. "Naye, stop trying to be a matchmaker, sweetie. I'm sure Pete can find his own dates."

"But she's single now. She's always in a relationship. This could be the perfect time to introduce them."

"No!" I said quickly, then I cleared my throat and forced a non-freaked-out, congenial, businesslike smile. "I appreciate it, but that won't be necessary."

I already knew her. I knew her and wanted her, but I couldn't say these things.

"Easy, Nadine," Kerrick said. "We have enough problems. Don't want to add a conflict of interest for poor Pete here."

And what a conflict of interest it was. I mean, shit. How the hell was I going to keep my job, keep working with the Larkins, and keep Lucy? Shubin, my boss, was never going to allow all three. I was screwed.

"If we can just get back on track here," I implored.

It was too late.

"You're a very nice man," Nadine told me with a smile.

"Wife of mine, our daughter can get her own men. She's very good at it. Based on her track record, it won't be long until another fellow comes along." Kerrick said the last sentence to me, as if I could relate to having a daughter like that.

I couldn't, but I myself was often guilty of this in the past. It was the very reason I—mostly—understood why Lucy came up with the six-month rule, in order to give us a chance. I found myself wanting to hear more stories of her without it seeming like I wanted set up.

"So, this teacher daughter of yours. . ." I paused, hoping they'd think I forgot her name.

"Lucy."

"Right. Lucy." Just saying her name made me feel warm. "Lucy is attached to this cabin you have?"

"Oh yes. When we stopped going, it nearly broke her heart." Nadine looked over at Kerrick, mindful of what she'd just said.

Lucy hadn't mentioned her father's health problems or her parents' financial ones. This led me to believe maybe she didn't know. Now I was privy to something I was bound by my ethical code to not discuss with her, or at least to not disclose to her if she didn't already know. Yet another damn secret, one I felt equally as bad about.

Kerrick turned to me. "We can't ask our children to help us. Not that any of them are able to help, mind you. They all have their own debt and bills. Losing the place our daughter loves most will feel like defeat."

"I understand that. I do. But losing your home will feel worse."

There wasn't much else I could say. I had a feeling I wouldn't be able to persuade them to sell the cabin. Lewis had tried and was immediately shot down more than once. Their argument was always that the cabin wouldn't cover the mortgage or even the debt, and they were right. It was a small, outdated cabin in need of a major overhaul, situated on a tiny strip of land that for some reason was not in a big money-making part of the shoreline, perhaps intentionally by the homeowners who lived there. But that extra money could help alleviate some of the crunch the Larkins were about to feel.

Lucy Larkin.

I wished I'd known. My gut reaction told me I never would have worked on her parents' account if I had been aware. The more I thought this, however, the more I knew it was wrong, or at least inaccurate. I already wanted to help the Larkins before I knew their connection to the new woman in my life.

I tried to keep her out of my thoughts for most of the day, focusing on each customer and account that needed my attention to the best of my abilities. I did pretty well while I was at work. It was easy when there were live people in front of me and not just a file or a computer screen. At home, it was a different story.

I kept seeing Lucy. Lucy at the beach with me. Lucy softly kissing me good night by her car. Lucy on her mom's phone.

Kerrick had hit the nail on the head. It was an immense conflict of interest. Any aid I gave the Larkins could be misconstrued as favoritism or nepotism. If a coworker or customer reported me, all hell would break lose faster than I could refute it.

It was simple. I had to make a choice. There was no other option I could see that made sense.

But I couldn't give up Lucy. It didn't matter that we'd just met. I was drawn to her more than I'd been drawn to any woman before. And I couldn't give up my job. I'd worked hard for my position. Lewis had entrusted his accounts to me for a reason. It would be madness to give all that up.

This left me with giving up any hope of helping Lucy's parents. Then again, those worries were still swirling. Would she take their losses out on me? Would she ever want to progress our friendship into something more?

No matter how I looked at the situation, I could only ever come up with one solution.

Chapter 8

Lucy

"YOU FEELING OKAY?" LOURDES asked, her blue-green eyes watching me. She'd taken a break from readjusting the alstroemeria in the ready-made bouquets by the front door.

Lourdes took over Blooming Cascade Floral Design—the family flower shop—when her grandmother's health began to deteriorate as dementia slowly took control. Even though she was now a florist, Lourdes never failed to use the training she received when earning her psychology degree to help Gwenn and me get to the root of our feelings.

"Kenzie already asked me that," I replied, sniffing a snapdragon she'd brought from the back cooler to add to one of the bouquets but then set aside.

"That isn't really an answer," Gwenn said from her spot next to the door nearby that led to Lourdes's workroom.

During designing time, Lourdes's work tables were covered with ribbons, flower frogs, foam, shears, vases, and vase weights like pebbles, as well as the actual blooms and greenery. Since she was out in the shop, with the door to the back open, I could see that her table was clear, save for a couple empty vases that she planned on filling later.

I didn't want to acknowledge Gwenn's words. Both besties had me on edge. "I'm fine."

Gwenn and Lourdes shared a mutual look of confusion. When they looked back at me, Gwenn's gray eyes also contained a hint of worry.

"How do you explain not jumping off the deep end with the guy you described as the best man you've ever met?" Gwenn pressed. "You once couldn't understand how I didn't straddle Rhett when I had an injured leg."

I had said that to Gwenn about her and her boyfriend, back when they were still strangers. My situation with Pete was completely different.

"I know it doesn't seem like it would make sense, me not sleeping with Pete. But I just want to be courted. I want to take my time and be friends with a man first before jumping into a relationship or a bed with him. I've never done that before. My track record proves that's been a disaster."

Lourdes didn't respond to my jab of self-deprecation. Gwenn gave me a sigh.

I continued, serious this time. "I don't want that disaster with Pete. I want what I know it will be: true love."

Gwenn and Lourdes were quiet.

"Just because I've said that about other guys doesn't make it any less true about Pete. I feel it in my core."

"I hope you're right," Lourdes said with a kind smile.

"December will be here before you know it," Gwenn added.

I moved toward the loose blooms in the DIY bouquet section of the shop. Well, a "pick your flowers and our staff will quickly tie the bouquet together" kind of DIY. There was a bucket of bright pink flowers with fringed petals. The blooms were in water to keep them fresh. I gave them a sniff. The scent was almost spicy.

Lourdes motioned to them. "These dianthuses were supposed to be for this past weekend's weddings, but they weren't delivered until yesterday."

"Not a great Monday for you today, is it?" Gwenn asked. She and I both understood what the day following a late delivery was like for Lourdes.

"No, and I don't want to talk about it. Just need to advertise that they're available and get them sold. Marcy's already put up social media posts, so that should help."

"At least they look really pretty in the baskets," I said. And every flower looked fantastic in the vases Lourdes had for sale, up on shelving along the short wall nearest the DIY flower baskets. The vases were mostly clear glass, as well as colorful tinted glass.

Lourdes also had included a few ceramic selections in various colors and delicate floral and geometric patterns. My favorite was the white ceramic vase with a soft yellow decorative border along the top. If I ever got married, I wanted to use those with sunflowers or daisies. I wasn't sure yet.

This was one of my last free Mondays before summer session started. There was no way I was going to spend it with anyone but my friends, but all the romance of Lourdes's flower shop had me missing the man I told myself I wasn't going to discuss with anyone today. If the six-month agreement was going to hold up, I couldn't focus on him all day every day like I would have done in the past. I needed to not think of Pete for a while. Maybe it was a good thing I had plans with my family for the upcoming Fourth of July instead of with Pete.

Maybe.

But a big part of me doubted it.

Gwenn got a new text on her phone.

"Time to go back to work?" I asked.

She didn't reply. Instead she read out, "'Why is the owner selling?' Aw, man. That's a topic I never wanted to get into."

"Why? What's wrong?" Lourdes asked.

"This house has been for sale off and on for the past three years. I'm actually the owner's fifth broker."

I accidentally let out a soft gasp.

"Right?" Gwenn said, clearly feeling my shock. "The owner initially refused to disclose the leaky faucets, the 'tiny bit' of mold in the basement, and the weird flickering lights that I truly believed desperately needed to be looked at by a certified electrician. They said it was just a bad light fixture. Anyway, they also didn't want to fix the problems or even sell the house as-is."

"So they wanted to sell it as a perfect house?" I asked in horror.

"Yep. Pretty much. With much cajoling from me, they changed the faucets and cleaned up the mold—well, it looks like they cleaned up the mold—but I don't think the lights have been fixed. I haven't had a showing recently enough to go there, and the owner hasn't agreed to any open houses. I wish I'd taken the advice of another broker who told me to stay far away from this mess, but I am desperate for a sale right now. It's been way too long."

"And now you have to tell prospective buyers."

Gwenn sighed. "I need to prepare myself for that first before answering."

"Well, I'm just about done with this," Lourdes told us, a sigh lingering around in her voice, too, though I suspected she was trying to hide it. "Simone," she called to her worker over at the counter. "I'm taking a break."

Simone smiled and told Lourdes to take as long as she needed.

My phone beeped with a new text of its own. It was from Jade, our friend who owned the cutest boutique in the Falls. Well, it was the only clothing boutique but no amount of competition could ever have been better than Jade. She was texting to tell me she'd found the cutest saffron paisley maxi dress that I had eyed online and asked her about.

I sent a text back promising to stop by once I got paid again.

Jade

> There's also a short, ruffled peasant skirt in a pale cream if you'd like. It'd go really well with that butter-yellow wrap top you bought last summer.

Unfortunately, I could only buy the dress. I hated having to tell her so, but with college debt and other debt, I couldn't blow all my money on clothes, no matter how fabulous they were. Even with only buying the dress, I knew I'd have to skimp a little for a few weeks to be able to afford it. My teacher's salary never went as far as I needed it to.

Gwenn, Lourdes, and I walked from the flower shop down to Button's Diner, where Kenzie worked. It was time for "cheer me up" pie, and there was no better place in the world for that than Button's.

"A lemon meringue, a cherry, and a chocolate," I said to Kenzie by way of a greeting when we walked in. Of course, I also gave her my "help your little sister out" grin.

She rolled her eyes but still smiled. "Coming right up."

We sat at our favorite booth, the three of us—best friends who all had gray clouds looming overhead. Yet none of us wanted to talk about it. Mine wasn't a gray cloud so much as an emptiness I knew they would tell me I shouldn't be feeling so soon.

"How are your parents?" Gwenn asked, her eyes on me.

"They're okay. Dr. Randall thinks the medication regimen plus all the healthy choices Dad switched to are doing the job well enough right now. He doesn't expect him to have a setback anytime soon."

"Oh, that's good," Gwenn said.

Both besties smiled at me.

"How's your grandma?" I asked Lourdes.

She shook her head. "Gam-Gam isn't just getting worse every week. It feels like every day. Her memory is pretty shot. At least she still has all her faculties and can manage well enough with supervision."

"Your mom still taking extra jobs to pay for the home nurse?" Gwenn asked.

Lourdes nodded, tears brimming in her eyes.

Okay. This wasn't working either.

My sister came over with the tray of pie. I looked up at her.

"Oh no," she began. "Don't even tell me you don't want them now."

"We'll have them to go, please," I told her softly.

A look of annoyance flashed on her face, but it was quickly gone, especially once she'd glanced at Lourdes's paling complexion. "Be right back with that." Kenzie gave us a kind smile and was off.

Gwenn's phone beeped. "Oh," she exclaimed. "Wait, what?" She silently read something. "I have to go."

"Everything okay?" Lourdes and I both asked.

"It just might be perfect," she said with a laughing tone. "I think I sold a different, mold- and electrical-problem-free *impossible* house."

She caught Kenz on the way out, taking her pie and handing my sister some cash. Kenzie walked over to Lourdes and me. She handed us our takeaway pies and we quickly paid her. I also left her as generous a tip as I could for the moment, knowing my sister was just as behind in her bills as I was. It was a little something she and I did for each other whenever possible, though it was harder for her to give me cash since I didn't have a tip-based job.

After Lourdes and I walked back to her shop—leaving our pies in her back cooler, the one no one used but her—we headed on to the community garden. Both our moms were on the board that governed the garden, as was Lourdes. My bestie was pretty much the one in charge, doing her best to live up to the legacy of her grandmother, who started the garden years ago.

The community garden was really a safe haven for both Lourdes and me. She and I easily found solace among the flowers, fruits, vegetables, and herbs we grew there. Though I wasn't in my gardening clothes, I still knelt down on the dirt and helped her rip out the weeds that had already started to sprout in our newly planted broccoli bed.

Though we loved the look of the rainbow of flowers, the best part of the garden was all the produce we grew and gave away to anyone in town who needed a little help. Those fresh fruits and veggies were literal lifesavers in some cases. All anyone who worked at the garden asked was that perhaps some of those who received the fresh produce pay it forward and volunteer at the garden, even if only for a few hours once a year.

Lourdes and I were not the only volunteers today, so we silently commiserated with each other as we worked. If there was a better way to spend a late June afternoon, in this moment, I didn't know it. I probably wouldn't have believed it, either.

After an hour of weeding, Lourdes returned to the flower shop and I headed home. I promised to pick up my pie later in the evening, once I'd done a little gardening in my own little yard. An hour in the sun had me longing for more.

That "more" turned into four hours. I only stopped when I got a text from my mom.

Family dinner canceled. Dad not feeling great today.

His heart?

Not this time. I think he just overexerted himself today. Rescheduled for same time tomorrow.

Okay. Tell Dad to rest and I love him.

I'll tell him. Love you, sweetheart.

Love you, too.

When I initially saw the words "family dinner" and "canceled" together, I immediately assumed it was probably my brother's fault. It usually was. He was never as into family bonding time as the rest of us. The fact that it was my dad worried me.

He'd said just the other day how good he felt. Mom said it, too. I hoped and prayed it wasn't because they were trying to hide another setback. They'd done that in the past to "protect" us, but as my siblings and I were adults now, we didn't need protecting.

I got a text from Gwenn later that night saying she really was about to sell a house. I squealed in happiness for her. Then Lourdes texted and said working in the garden had lifted her up out of her funky mood, so that made me smile as well.

Things were so great with my friends. While I wished the same were true for my family—and I couldn't even say "at least we have our health"—I could at least look forward to tomorrow night's dinner. We were usually the best when we were all together.

I didn't have to wait long for my day to brighten. Pete sent me a message later, to my surprise, and we spent half an hour texting before falling asleep. I ended the day floating on a cloud. Things were only going to get better. I knew this without a doubt.

Chapter 9

"Are you stupid?" Tess asked me in a whisper-screech as she nearly shoved me into my office.

We'd been standing in my doorway Tuesday morning. I was still reeling from finding out Lucy's parents were my customers. A night full of doubts had me second-guessing my initial plan to keep all three: Lucy, the Larkins, and my job.

"Oh, come on. You and I both know Shubin will freak when he finds out. I can't keep the Larkins' account. I have to tell him that."

"*If* Shubin finds out. Pete, you are an expert at being discreet. Unlike Miles. You need to teach him your ways." She raised her eyebrows at me.

Shit. "He's telling everyone about the bet, isn't he?"

Tess gave a tiny, sardonic laugh. "I mean, taking a bet that you'll have sex with the woman who asked you to wait six months was a terrible idea, but you do you. When I left you all that morning, I never thought you'd agree to it."

"I know, I know. I'm an ass. But now that I'm in it, I'm stuck." I scrubbed a hand through my beard.

"Look at it this way. You can't do anything in your professional capacity to help your not-quite girlfriend's parents, but giving them a thousand dollars of Miles's money could help nudge them closer toward not losing everything. Though that would be a sleazy, shitty thing to do, and I doubt she'd ever forgive you," she added with a shrug.

I hesitated, and therefore didn't answer.

Tess gave a sardonic laugh. "Seriously, though, Pete. Think this all through. Okay? Forget about the bet, because that is not the issue right now. You can deal with your conscience later. Telling Shubin about Lucy and her parents is not the answer. You don't know for sure if dating Lucy would be a conflict of interest. You aren't even to that point yet. Don't put that on Shubin's radar. Don't sacrifice your career."

"Come on, Tess. You might be able to convince a newbie it's not a conflict of interest, but you and I know better."

"What good would it do passing her parents' account to some-one else?" Tess asked. "You ever stop and ask yourself why the account went to you when Lewis retired? Any one of us could have gotten it, but Lewis wanted you to have his accounts. Don't make Shubin regret trusting you."

I also needed to find a way to keep Lucy from regretting trusting me, too.

"I will say this, however. Do not let Miles know what's going on. He hasn't made the connection between Lucy's parents' account and the woman you have a wager about. If he figured it out, he would have said something to the rest of us. I only know because you told me. Let's keep it between the two of us."

Tess left to go back to her own office since lunch was now over. I sat at my desk, then pulled out my phone to re-read my texts with Lucy from last night when I couldn't get her out of my mind.

Still awake?

I wake up early every day, but far too often, I'm still a night owl at heart.

So when I can't sleep at night?

I'm available for texting or talking.

Or sharing my favorite relaxing playlists.

I'll even sing you to sleep if you want me to, but I can't guarantee it'll actually sound good.

This made me smile, just as it did the first time.

You'd sleep better with me there to hold you.

Again I say, I don't think friends are supposed to talk to each other like that.

But we're not platonic, remember?

She sent me a heart in return. Then she added a winking emoji.

Definitely not

So I can tell you anything I want?

Anything

> I miss you.

> That's not dirty talk.

I shifted in my chair, still smiling at the thought of her. So she did like the dirty talk. This made me happy and hopeful. I made a mental note to use it in the future. Until then, I had to balance it all just right.

> It's real talk.

> With real feelings.

> Would it help if I sent you some naughty emojis?

> LOL

> I miss you, too.

> When can I see you again?

> I have a family dinner tomorrow. Was supposed to be today, but Dad didn't feel too good.

That was the first time she'd mentioned Kerrick's illness to me, and only in an offhand way. As much as I wanted to ask how much exactly Lucy knew, I couldn't pry. She would have wondered what all the questions were about. I continued re-reading.

Also, my stupid brother was being an ass again and "forgot" about dinner, anyway. He is impossible sometimes. He's only three years older than me, but has always acted like he gets to be in charge of everything.

The day after? I know you're busy on the holiday.

I was, too, but it didn't stop me from wishing we could spend it together.

Dinner? Lunch? Coffee? Breakfast? Spontaneous non-platonic sleepover? (Pajamas required, sorry.)

I loved her sense of humor. Though we both knew we couldn't agree to a sleepover just yet, I asked her for a dinner date. She quickly replied yes, offering to meet at my house so we could spend time alone before going out. She even offered to bring dessert if we wanted to have more time alone after our meal to get to know each other even better.

Already, I knew she was amazing, but she was more than just one word could describe. I simultaneously couldn't wait to make love to her and also hear her laugh in person again. One was going to take a lot longer to have a chance at than the other. I couldn't let myself do anything to hurt this woman.

After a few minutes, I was on my feet again, knocking on Tess's office door. She called me in.

"I'm exactly the right person to help Lucy's parents. So how do I do this without getting caught? I know how to be discreet, but this is different."

"You came to the right woman," Tess told me with a smile. "I already made you a list."

"Thank you." I sighed in relief.

Then she added, "By the way, you know about that unwritten but still relevant loophole concerning the merger, right?"

I didn't.

"Technically, a different department authorized their extension. You can even call Williams and ask him about it. If you use it, you won't be in trouble if found out by Shubin."

"So I can give them more time?"

Tess smiled. "You can give them more time."

Chapter 10

Lucy

PETE AND I HADN'T known each other for a full week yet, but I dove right in with an invitation I hoped he wouldn't refuse.

> Care to join me at family dinner this weekend?

It took an excruciatingly long time for him to reply.

> I wish I could. Sorry. We'll have dinner another time, okay?

Well, it was worth a shot. We already had to skip the dinner he invited me to after my sister needed an emergency babysitter and my parents were out with friends.

"Lucy, this salad is delicious," my mom said later.

My immediately family sat around my parents' outdoor dining table, enjoying yet another pleasant al fresco meal.

I thanked my mom, then Dominic asked Dad what he marinated the steaks with this time. Dad was more than happy to share his recipes, but sometimes he made my brother wait for it.

"Well, there was some garlic. I think. Was there garlic, Naye?" he added to Mom.

Mom just smiled and ate a bite of her meat.

"Garlic. Got it. What else?" Dom said to Dad.

51

"The other day, I saw this chef add grapefruit juice to his marinade, and I thought, 'Hey, that's a wonderful idea!'"

"I don't taste any grapefruit," my brother said to him.

"Oh no. I didn't add it this time. Wouldn't have worked with the rest of the ingredients."

Dom let out a big sigh, but underneath, there was a hint of a chuckle. "Which are?"

Kenzie and eye made eye contact. It took all I had not to bust out laughing. By the tremors in her body, I could tell she was fighting the same urge.

Then my niece said, "Could you please pass the green beans, Aunt Lucy Goose?"

I choked a little on my food and began coughing, but the rest of the family broke out into a huge peal of laughter. Once I quickly recovered, I asked, "Okay, who put you up to that?"

Red-faced, Hayzel immediately pointed at Dominic. "Uncle Dom did! He said you'd think it was funny!"

My brother laughed even harder. So much so that it took him a good thirty seconds before he could reply. "Go easy on her, Luce."

I fake-glared at him.

"It's not my fault it sounds so cute coming from a kid."

"She's not the one I'm mad at." And yet I laughed harder, too. "Oh gosh. No one's called me that since I was eleven."

"And it was high time it came out of retirement," Dom told me, his eyes glistening with tears from laughing too hard.

Once we'd all finished with dinner and dessert—and my brother had his new recipe—Mom and Dad asked us to join them inside the house. This was a little odd considering we would usually watch the sunset or play a game or something outside.

My siblings and I eyed each other, well aware of the nervous expression on Mom's face. We sat down silently in the living room, Kenzie, Hayzel, and I on the sofa and Dom in Dad's favorite chair.

"What's going on?" Dominic finally asked. My brother may have been born in the years between Kenzie and me, but he most definitely did not have any signs of middle child syndrome. Of the three of us, I thought Dominic's personality was the strongest. He was no wallflower or people-pleaser or black sheep. Dom was direct, even if a little brusque.

Mom and Dad glanced at each other for a moment, then looked at the four of us with strained smiles that quickly faded.

"You all know about Dad's health issues," Mom began. "Unfortunately, the medical bills have become a little too burdensome."

"What do you mean?" my sister asked. "Burdensome how?"

Dad cleared his throat. "We fell behind in our mortgage payments."

I shook my head. "But you don't have much time left until the mortgage is paid off. There shouldn't be a problem, right?"

"Sweetheart—" Dad stopped to take a breath. Mom rubbed his arm, then slid her hand down to hold his. "We took out a second mortgage a few years ago after we were unable to get any other kind of loan. We still owe on both mortgages as well as the loans and the medical bills. And now our mortgages are in foreclosure."

I was speechless. Dominic heaved a sigh and rubbed his face roughly with his hands. Kenzie put her hand to her mouth but said nothing. Hayzel looked at all of us, her eyes wild with confusion.

"What does that mean?" she asked.

"It means Gramma and Grampa are losing their house," Dom told her.

"And possibly other things. Like the cabin," Mom added with a whisper.

Wait. The cabin? My cabin?

This wasn't happening.

There was no freaking way my parents were losing everything. I'd heard wrong.

Right?

"How long has this been going on? How long have you been struggling and not telling us?" My brother's voice was sharp, but also a little hoarse. "As long as you waited to tell us about Dad's heart?"

Mom and Dad looked at each other again before Dad opened his mouth to speak. "While we want you all to be aware what's going on, please know your mother and I are doing everything we can to fight foreclosure. We will find a way to pay off our debts. Don't worry, okay? We will figure this out."

"How can you say that?" Kenzie asked.

No one answered.

"Will you live with Mom and me?" Hayzel spoke up.

I looked over at her. I used to be so angry for not having known for years about my dad's health issues, but seeing my sweet little niece, I realized how lucky I'd been to have been shielded. She was younger than I was when I'd found out. Now she had this added to her worries.

Hayzel continued without waiting for a response. "You can have my room if you do. I can sleep on the sofa. Or will you move in with Uncle Dom? His house is big enough, right? Aunt Lucy doesn't have any room in her house."

While my parents gently reassured her—and all of us—that nothing bad was happening any time soon, I sat there on my favorite spot on their sofa, feeling like I'd been punched in the gut. It didn't matter what my parents said. We were officially at the point of wondering where they were going to live if the house got taken. It was a very real possibility.

"Would they take the cabin to sell it?" I asked suddenly, though I thought my mom had been in the middle of saying something.

"It would have to be sold to cover the mortgage debt, yes," Dad told me. There was a quiver to his voice.

"But it won't cover the mortgage entirely. It won't cover hardly anything. Developers haven't eyed that area in a while. Not since everyone refused to sell ages ago," I said.

"Doesn't mean their interest wouldn't be piqued again," Dom piped up.

I ignored this. "So nothing you could sell would cover the mortgage entirely?"

"Unfortunately, no," Mom replied, wiping her wet, reddened eyes with a tissue Kenzie offered her. "We need a miracle for that."

Chapter 11

Pete

IT WAS FINALLY THE weekend, and I couldn't be more relieved. Not only did I spend a lot of time during the week looking up the information Tess gave me on how to help Lucy's parents, but I also spent a significant amount of time researching what to do if I happened to get fired because of all this. It was hopeless, as far as I could tell. If I skirted the ethical rules, I would have no way to salvage my job after being terminated. That sent an ice-cold chill through me.

Miles was certainly no help. He made a point of loudly discussing the bet whenever we were together. I wasn't sure if that was to embarrass me due to him feeling like my lack of effort at Lucy's body made me less of a man in his eyes or what, but I was already tired of this shit.

"Lower your voice," I said to him more than once Friday, to which he laughed.

"No one cares, Petey Boy. It's all in good fun."

He expected me to chuckle in return. I refused. There was nothing funny about it. "What has Corkie said about this bet?"

There was fire in his eyes, but he smiled. "She knows it's in good fun, too."

I doubted that. Corkie was too smart. She was just never one to threaten a break-up with him over his antics. I half wished she would. Maybe that would put him in a place of, oh I don't know, acting like a real human being and maybe even an actual friend, not just the facade of one.

"Corkie also said it isn't fair for me to tell you Drea's been missing you big time, but I told her you're a big boy and can handle that information."

His eyes shone, letting me know he was telling me in hopes that I might contact Drea for a hookup and lose the bet. At least Miles knew enough to realize Lucy would never sleep with me if I had Drea first.

I ignored this and walked over to refresh my cup of coffee. There was amazing coffee in my office, much better than this stuff, but if I preoccupied myself with a task, there was a chance I could have enough time to think of something to say to Miles without him throwing it back on me.

I couldn't remember having struggled so much in our friendship before, but that was also before such an amazing woman entered my life.

"Seriously, Pete," Miles said, actually lowering his voice down to a reasonable level. "Why are you even bothering with Miss Priss?"

I scoffed, immediately ruffled at his description of Lucy. "Not every woman needs to be easy. Challenges can be good things," I told him. "And you don't have to have sex with a woman first in order to develop feelings for her."

His chortle had me regretting those words. "Pete, you are not a 'falling in love' kind of guy. Let's face it. This wager is the only way you're going to get anything from this woman. Get it, enjoy it, and move on, just like you always do."

Thankfully, Nella, my assistant, came into the break room get me for an important phone call. Once we returned to my desk, I realized there was no call. I raised my eyebrows at her.

She waved me off. "Syl said you might need some help."

Thank God for gossipy assistants, especially the one who worked for Miles. I gave mine a smile. "Thanks, Nella."

I took Nella's advice and avoided Miles the rest of the day.

Lucy and I didn't end up being able to see each other the entire week before this first day of July. She had family dinners and ladies' nights with her friends. I couldn't go to any of those family meals. There was still the complication of Lucy not having mentioned her parents' mortgage troubles or her father's health in any way. I also had enough to occupy my mind, though it sucked being away from her. I spent an evening playing baseball with Alec and a bunch of our friends, grateful for the much-needed distraction.

Since it was Saturday, I'd decided to give myself a little break from all the worry about Lucy, the Larkins, and Shubin. Early in the morning, I helped George, my elderly neighbor, with his yard work. While he didn't have any issues weeding his small flower pots, running a lawn mower was no longer an option for him. In the winter, I also shoveled his sidewalks, but with this being July, I didn't need to worry about that anytime soon.

Thing was, George liked starting the day extra early, even on the weekends, so we were done with all the work by seven o'clock. The sun had been up maybe fifteen minutes longer than I had.

"Hungry?" George asked as we sat drinking coffee at his small patio table.

The birds were still chirping their morning songs, something George had always liked to listen to, especially after his wife Candace passed two years before. They were both kind people, and I did everything I could to help George, just as I did when Candace was still alive, including setting him up with a window-washing company once that chore got to be too much for him.

I thought carefully about what to say. A simple "yes" would have had him offering to make me something to eat, which wouldn't be fair to either of us, honestly. Candace had been the chef in their marriage for a reason. But telling him "no" would've led him to joke about giving me more chores just so I could work up an appetite.

While I'd always laughed along with him in the past, today I wasn't in the mood. I had other plans for the rest of my day, and they didn't involve plotting out a brand-new garden area, which I knew George was considering. I had already raked the grass clippings, weeded the large flower pots and all the flower beds, including those that surrounded the house up to the front by the street, and swept off the front porch and back patio.

"How about I order us some breakfast sandwiches from that place down the street?" I offered, pulling my phone out of my right pocket after wiping off my sweaty hands on my black athletic shorts.

"Sausage and bacon, extra cheese," George said with a smile. Health food be damned.

I already had that included in the order on my phone. I added a bacon, egg, and cheese sandwich for me and small fruit salads for both of us, just in case.

"So, how are things going, Pete?"

"Things are okay." I couldn't lie and say "great." Only one thing in my life fit that description.

As if able to read my mind, George asked, "How's the dating scene these days? Haven't seen you bring a lady home in a while."

It had been a couple of months since I'd "entertained a lady at home," as George would describe it. And now with Lucy, I had no desire to meet anyone new.

I told George about Lucy, including my newfound connection to her parents, as well as succumbing to the bet with Miles. George was as trustworthy as they came. He was also pretty damn wise about a lot of things, including predicaments like the one I found myself in. He actually ran his own company for thirty-seven years. It was a regional shipping company that offered same-day delivery before it was trendy. If I could trust any outsider with this kind of information, George was definitely it.

After a few minutes of contemplation, during which I slowly drank the last of my coffee, he said, "Pete, I've known a lot of people in my life. Men like you who are stand-up guys, but who also perhaps let their egos get the better of them from time to time."

I acknowledged this description of me when he paused, though it was a bit painful to admit the "letting my ego get to me" part. I'd been kicking myself for a week because of it.

"I know you'll do the right thing in the end. Even if you think this is something you can't get out of—even if that's true—I know you'll find the right solution."

An hour later, once we'd finished eating and George decided he wanted to sit in his swing and read the newest bestseller that caught his eye at the discount bookstore, I was on my way to part two of my day. I was about to have the best day of my whole week.

Chapter 12

Lucy

It was a late Saturday morning, the first one of July and exactly one week since Pete and I met. I'd been putting my clean dishes away, but at the sound of my phone and the contents of my non-boyfriend's text, I ran to the door. He stood there with a smile and a bouquet of flowers that I recognized came from Lourdes's shop. Too bad she wasn't working today.

I squealed and wrapped my arms around him without planning to. Still holding my flowers, Pete lifted me up slightly and spun me around before gently setting me on my feet.

"What are you doing here?" I asked, flushed. "We didn't have a non-date planned today, did we?"

"I wanted to see you," he said, without adding more.

It had been a week. I wanted to see him, too. So much so that my mind went blank about everything else. "You've never seen my house before."

"Friends go to each other's houses." Pete laughed. "I won't mind seeing your lingerie strewn about. You don't even have to model it, though I wouldn't be opposed to seeing that. As a friend, of course." Then he winked with a broad grin.

This made me laugh as well. "You're right. Come in."

I welcomed him into the house, leading the way to my kitchen. I needed to find a vase. Only Pete wasn't as close behind me as I thought.

"Wow," he said, his voice coming from the living room.

"What?" I called, checking under my sink. I knew I had two taller vases that would be perfect for the pink daisies.

"It's all yellow."

I filled the vase, then snipped the ends off the flowers and added them. Then I rejoined Pete in the living room. It wasn't actually all yellow. The walls and shelves were, as was the cabinet for my electronics. The rest was white or shades of tan.

My whole house looked basically like this, to be honest. Lots of yellow, some white, and a bit of another color, mostly tan, green, and teal. It had been just over two months since Gwenn texted me the best message, leading with *I found the sweetest, coziest little rental for you.*

She was right, of course. It was the best home I'd had since I lived with my parents. I was allowed to paint anything I wanted should I be able to afford it, even if it all ended up yellow, including the exterior. The house also had pink rosebushes, to which I'd added yellow ones, and a picket fence that I knew looked best in its pristine white. My old rental hadn't allowed any leeway of any kind, and while this place was a bit more expensive, it was nothing close to double the rent, which I was going to have to pay if I'd stayed in my old place, since the owner decided to sell.

"I like yellow," I told Pete, smiling at my butter-yellow wall in front of us.

"I can tell. You wore it the day we met, and you're wearing it now. But dang." He laughed again.

"Do you not believe in living in your favorite color?"

"I'm not sure I even have a favorite color."

Now I laughed and stepped closer to him. He smelled almost woodsy and spicy. I loved how familiar I already was with his cologne and the way he looked in my living room. I wanted to see him in the rest of my house, too. "Did you make any plans for us?"

"Is hanging out with you not enough?" But the smile that accompanied this was so smoldering, I about melted. I was shocked his beard hadn't been singed off at some point.

"That sounds perfect, except my sister is supposed to come over soon. She mentioned some yoga thing in one of the parks in Syracuse. I don't know what time exactly."

Pete didn't say anything, but his crinkled expression told me he didn't like the idea of meeting my family.

"It's just my sister. You've seen her before."

"Yeah, but not officially."

"Friends meet their friends' families, and it doesn't have to mean anything."

"Except that isn't true in our case, is it?" He raised an eyebrow at me.

"I do like the idea of keeping you all to myself for a little while."

"So I should go?"

"Probably. But come back if you can."

Pete took my hand in his and kissed the top of it. Then my front door opened again. Kenzie and our friend and childhood neighbor Charisma walked in.

"Hey. I hadn't expected you this early," I said to my sister as she shut the door behind them. Pete still held my hand.

Charisma said hi, then looked over at Pete. Neither of them moved.

"Oh! I'm sorry," I said. "Pete, you've seen my sister Kenzie."

They greeted each other.

"And this is Charisma. She lived next door when we were kids. Her dad actually still lived there until a couple years ago."

"Nice to meet you," Pete said to her.

Charisma nearly choked based on the sound she made. "Meet me? Are you kidding?"

Pete was motionless.

"What's going on?" I asked, looking back and forth between them.

Charisma looked a little flushed. I inadvertently tightened my grip on Pete's hand.

"See you, I mean. It's nice to see you again," Pete corrected in her general area without looking directly at her. At least at first he didn't. Then they made eye contact. "It's been a while."

"I guess it has. Too long," Charisma replied. She shook her head almost imperceptibly then gave a smile. "It's nice to see you again, too."

"You know each other?" Kenzie asked, on alert. I could see that in her face. I felt the same down to my bones.

"We dated. A *long* time ago," Charisma told us.

All I could do was move my eyes to all their faces and watch their reactions. I couldn't move the rest of my body or speak. Then I finally found my voice. "You *dated*?" It came out as a squeak.

"It's okay," Charisma laughed. "It really was a long time ago. And it was so not a serious thing. A few dates here and there. No biggie."

"So it was no big deal. Okay. Can we move on from this now?" Kenzie said.

That shook us all back to normal. My sister and Charisma came farther into the room. Kenzie sat on the sofa, while Charisma leaned against the bamboo chair.

"I should go." Pete turned to me and grinned. Then he kissed my hand again, letting his mouth linger against my skin. "Have fun with yoga. I'll call you later."

I leaned up and kissed his bearded cheek, but I wasn't ready to let go. My hand was still in his. "I'll walk you out."

"So, that was a little awkward," Pete chuckled once we were out by his car.

"What happened?"

"I don't know. My mind just blanked. I hope I didn't hurt her feelings."

I smiled. "Charisma has never been one to hold grudges. I'm sure she's fine."

"But are you?"

I considered this. "You had sex with my friend."

"A long, long time ago, before we ever met. Are you okay with that?"

"You were never in love with her?"

He gave a quick head shake. "Never. I don't recall us seeing each other that much, anyway."

"I just—" I wasn't sure I could say the rest.

"What is it?"

"Well, I once lost a guy to a friend who previously swore she had zero interest in him. Not Charisma. But that just isn't something one easily forgets." Not when you fall in love as hard and fast as I did.

"I'm not leaving you for Charisma or anyone else. And I'm okay with waiting for as long as you want me to."

"All right," I finally said. "Then I'm okay, too."

Pete and I finally had to let our hands go. But he scooped me up for another twirling hug. Once he set me down, he kissed my shoulder next to my tank top strap before digging his key out of his pocket and making eye contact with me again. "See you later, Luce. I'll miss you."

We both bit our bottom lips.

I loved that we both recognized that would have been our moment to kiss. "In time." I blew him a kiss instead.

He did the same to me, then got in his car and drove away.

Just a little more time. But it had only been a week, and it was already so hard to hold out.

Chapter 13

Pete

I WASN'T SURE I'D ever been so glad I knew how to put on the charm. I shouldn't have lied about not remembering her, though. How did Charisma know Lucy? I wanted to ask, and yet I thought maybe it didn't matter. Maybe Kenzie was right. The past was in the past.

Maybe.

Though I left Lucy's house, I was too worked up to go home. I drove down to the local gas station to fill up my tank, since it was only a quarter full, and also to buy a soda. As I sat in my car after finishing and paying, I texted Alec.

What's up, man?

Doing anything today?

Nope

No Lucy?

She's not my ball and chain.

Though Miles would probably be happy to know that. As much of an ass as Miles could sometimes be, I couldn't for the life of me figure out why he'd been so determined to corner me into that wager. He didn't need the money. Winning the bet also wasn't going to win him any respect. It wasn't going to win me any, either.

Didn't say she was.

Drea text you yet?

Drea? No. Why?

Idk man. Thought she might.

Which meant she put him up to that. I went through my texts again. None from Drea. I mean, I knew she wasn't happy about me meeting Lucy, but to drag Alec into this mess was too much.

Drea isn't my ball and chain either.

You didn't hear it from me, but Drea can be a little vindictive when she's pissed. Watch your back.

Got it

How about we forget these women right now and take in a game at the bar?

Mets game is on in an hour. Meet you at Orville's in thirty?

Alec brought along his brother Henry and also asked our friend Chace to join us. There was no talk of Lucy, Drea, or even Miles. Only strikes that were outside the zone, ground outs that should have been easier than they were, and the team's prospects for the next couple months before playoffs.

Alec and his brother delved into the same disagreement they always had about whose dream starting line up was better. I laughed, unable to control myself. It was all in good fun, anyway.

A ball game and a few beers with my buddies was exactly what I needed to forget my women troubles for a while. So long as I could avoid Drea and Charisma, I figured life would be a lot easier for me. There was no reason things couldn't be smooth sailing from then on.

·♥·♥·♥·♥·♥·

When I heard my phone trill with a text while lying in bed, I couldn't wait to read what Lucy had to say. I'd missed her texts earlier asking me to hang out, though I was already with the guys by that point.

I rolled to my side and reached to grab the phone off my nightstand, but accidentally knocked into it, sending it flying to the floor. After pushing myself up and off the bed, I found the T-shirt I'd removed not too long ago. Once I finally had the phone in my hand and could read the new message, I wished I hadn't.

Time to talk?

Whether Drea was asking if I had time or if it was time, I didn't care. I didn't have much to say to her. I chose not to reply, but it wasn't long before another message came.

Haven't won the bet yet, have you?

Hasn't been long enough, not that it matters. Why do you care?

You and I would be having a lot more fun right now than you and this other chick are. I guarantee it.

Again, I hesitated in replying. Drea seemed primed for a fight. I wasn't ready to go there. I'd spent all evening chilling out with the guys, completely drama free. I was unwilling to let her ruin that, but she persisted.

Did you even want me before you met her?

Whoa. Now this I hadn't expected. Drea and I hadn't even known each other that long. I thought we'd both been comfortable with the casual flirting. How was I supposed to know it meant more to her?

I wasn't sure I could charm my way out of this one. In thinking about it, my charm was what had gotten me into trouble in the first place. Before answering, I checked the time. It was almost midnight. Lucy was still awake. Drea was still waiting for a reply. I did the only thing I could think of.

You never gave me the impression you wanted a relationship. I thought we were both good with the whole maybe/maybe not vibe. It didn't seem to matter to either of us.

She didn't text immediately in return like she had previously. In fact, she didn't text back at all.

I couldn't stay awake any longer, so I sent a good night text to Lucy and lay back down to sleep.

Chapter 14

Lucy

"OFF ALL THE DOGS, downward-facing dog is by far the worst," I whispered to my sister as she, Charisma, and I were nearing the end of our yoga in the park.

The drive there had been *interesting*, to say the least.

That's exactly what I did, too. I couldn't seem to come up with any good lines of conversation, not even anything anecdotal like the weather. No one mentioned Pete at first. I figured they probably weren't even thinking about him anymore, but he was the only one I could focus on.

"Have you mentioned the kayaking trip to Trevor yet?" Charisma had asked Kenzie in the car. "I'd like to go before school starts again."

"I did, but he didn't really seem all that hopeful about being able to get away. I think it'll have to wait until after apple season. He's really busy with the harvest right now, especially since Apple Fest is almost here."

"He's the boss. Even though it's a family farm, he does still have workers. He can leave for a few days if he wants."

My sister shook her head. "We go through this every year, Char. Trevor likes to be point man for the harvest, and he's never missed the festival. I can't ask him to skip out this year."

Kenzie and Charisma talked on about the trip they wanted to take, which I'd been invited to but turned down. I wasn't in the mood to stay anywhere except the cabin. Pete played just a tiny little part of that. Okay, who was I kidding? Pete played a huge part in that. I met him only because I'd been staying at the cabin. As if I didn't love that place enough, meeting Pete added a whole new appreciation for it.

Of course, I wouldn't have minded staying at Pete's place, but then that brought into play a can of worms I wasn't ready to tackle. It was because of me that I wasn't able to actually sleep over with him.

"So that was funny, with Pete," Charisma had suddenly said when we were almost to the park.

I'd sat up in attention but said nothing.

Kenzie, meanwhile, gave a laugh. "Right? I don't think I've ever seen a guy so embarrassed about a slip up before."

Charisma laughed, too. "Poor guy. I shouldn't have given him such a hard time. I was flustered at first, too. But I'm sure he didn't mean it like it came off, Lucy." She turned to me. "Next time you see him, tell Pete it's totally okay. No hard feelings."

I smiled. It was a genuine, relieved smile. "I'm so glad you said that. I'll definitely let him know."

My sister's voice brought me back to the present. "I don't mind downward-facing dog. I can do this flow in my sleep."

"Not all of us spend hours at the gym on our days off," I said.

"It's only because of the hours at the gym that I can spend my shifts on my feet all day long," Kenzie countered.

"Point taken," I replied quietly, holding myself as steady as possible.

The instructor moved on to the next flow, while my brain kept returning to that morning. Pete surprised me in more than one way, not all of it good.

Once I was home from a late, light lunch with Kenzie and Charisma after yoga, I immediately pulled out my phone to text my sexy non-boyfriend.

> Still around? Done with yoga. It was better than I expected!

> Maybe we can go see a movie or have a drink or watch the sunset together?

> Let me know :)

It was hours before Pete replied saying he was already busy hanging out with friends and watching a baseball game at the bar. By that time, I sat with my own friends at our favorite coffee house, discussing the pros and cons of Gwenn expanding the regional boundaries of her real estate business.

I didn't receive Pete's good night text until after midnight. Too late to call just to hear his voice. Phone still in hand, I curled into my soft bed, feet sticking out from the sheet just enough to keep from getting too warm in the night. Dreams of Pete had roasted me nearly every night, and I thought it was safe to assume tonight would be no different.

> Would love to see you soon, too. Good night and sweet dreams.

Against my better judgment, I added a few kissing-face emojis. But if that was the only way I'd be able to kiss him for the next six months, I wasn't going to pass up the opportunity.

·♥·♥·♥·♥·♥·

During my slow Sunday morning a week later, I made my self comfortable on my sofa with a warm cup of cinnamon-flavored coffee. I picked up my phone from the coffee table when it dinged with a notification as I skimmed through an article on my tablet from the *Syracuse Falls Sentinel*. The article discussed the pros and cons of bringing about a vote for my sweet little school district to be swallowed up by the neighboring district.

I moved my eyes from the tablet screen to the phone screen, but had no idea what I was looking at. Well, it was a new message, but it made zero sense.

Who was Miss Havisham?

I mean, I knew who she was. *Great Expectations*. Charles Dickens. But why would someone name themselves after a tragic nineteenth-century character and direct message me about an unknown man?

And what was it all about anyway?

He's a liar.

That was the entire message.

I called Gwenn.

"What does it mean?"

"I have no idea. Is there anything of interest on their profile? Maybe something that might give any clues?" Gwenn asked.

"Nada. There aren't any public posts at all." I shifted on my sofa, carefully reaching over for my laptop and regretting not having placed it next to me before sitting down. Yoga with Charisma and Kenz had been fun, but I was achier than I'd expected afterward.

While on the computer, I pulled up "Miss Havisham" in my messages and went to her profile again. "The profile picture even looks like a stock photo," I told my bestie.

"That's not good."

I agreed. It would be impossible to find clues in a stock photo.

"Maybe it doesn't mean anything. Maybe it wasn't for you."

"Doesn't that feel a little like grasping at straws?"

"I guess. But who is 'he'? If the message truly is meant for you, that could be any man in your life. Dominic. Pete. Haven't you been fighting off the annexation?"

I confirmed this. I'd been fighting it with my dad for a while. The most we'd had to do so far was create a few petitions and speak at both the school board meetings and the town meeting, but we were preparing for much more to come. On the other hand, Charisma was all for annexation. She considered our sweet district to be stagnant. *Stagnant.* We needed change, according to her, but what we really needed was for people to care enough to invest time and money in our district so we could grow. Some residents seemed all too happy to write us off.

"Your principal promised to do everything in his power to make sure nothing happens that isn't the best for the kids. Maybe it has to do with that. He might go back on his word. And you know people in this town have very strong opinions about the school district being annexed into a larger one," Gwenn said.

"I was just reading a story about it in the *Sentinel*. It hasn't reached the point of being ready for the ballot, thank goodness, but that doesn't mean it can't happen." I sat and thought a few moments. "You think the message is from one of my coworkers?"

"It's possible."

Honestly, this was the only explanation that made sense to me. "I'm with you. I think maybe someone knows something but is too afraid to go public."

Gwenn gave a slight laugh. "I know I would be, based on the division the annexation battle is going to cause. You and your dad have been at it for a while."

On the one hand, I should have been relieved to have most likely figured out who the weird message was from, or at least what it was about. On the other, the idea of coworkers conspiring against each other didn't sit right with me. Neither did the idea of possibly having to go against my principal if he, in fact, was going to choose the wrong side in the struggle.

I made a mental note to ask my coworker and mentor Sarah her thoughts on the annexation now that I was thinking about it. Since she was a sixth-grade teacher and farther away from my third-grade hallway, I didn't get to talk with her as often as I wanted to.

"Thank you so much," I told Gwenn. "I don't exactly feel better, but I am so relieved to at least have a better idea of what this is about."

"Are you going to respond?"

"I don't think so. If this person went out of their way to hide their identity to send a mystery message, I highly doubt I'll get any real answers from them."

"Let me know if you get any more weird messages. This might not end with one."

I promised her I would, then she told me about looking into going as far north as Baldwinsville to expand her business.

Pete called later, asking to come over. Obviously, I jumped at the chance to see him again. When he mentioned not having remembered being in my town until coming to see me, I knew it was the perfect time to show him around. We began with one of my favorite places in all of Syracuse Falls.

"How often do you come out here?" Pete asked as we wandered around the community garden.

"As much as I can." I told him all about the history of the garden and how much it meant to all of us in town. "We still hold the monthly dinners in the summer using as much as we can from the garden and from local producers. The number of guests has dwindled a lot in recent years, but it's still one of the best things to do in the Falls during summertime."

"You know, I've lived in Syracuse all my life. I still can't believe I've never come to this town intentionally except to pass through."

"Never?"

"The closest I got was Quill Bridge. When I was fifteen, a bunch of us went there—for what reason, I can't remember. Someone brought spray paint, which I didn't know until they suggested defacing it."

I gasped. "Are you serious?"

"Yep." He immediately shook his head. "I didn't do it. Didn't let them, either. It wasn't easy, but I wasn't the only one saying it was a bad idea, so that helped."

"I know Syracuse is a big city, but it still amazes me that we grew up so close to each other and yet so far away, in a way. Totally different worlds. And you've been camping up at Oneida Lake for a while, haven't you?"

Pete's hand brushed against mine as we slowly wandered around the bed of zucchini. I opened my hand more and allowed him to grasp hold of it as he said, "Since I was a kid. I guess that's just the genius of fate."

My cheeks grew hot as my breath quickened a bit. Pete believed in fate, too? "What do you mean?"

"We could have crossed paths at any time, from childhood to now. It seems there was a reason we saw each other that day of all days."

"The best day in June." I grinned.

"The very best." He gave my hand a gentle squeeze. "Speaking of childhood, what made you want to go into teaching?"

"Well, you know my dad was a sixth-grade teacher, before he couldn't work any longer."

Pete nodded.

"He had such an impact on those kids." I gave a small smile, thinking of all the stories I'd heard about what an amazing instructor Dad was. "Dad is beloved everywhere he goes, but the extra respect he earned both in and out of the classroom. . . he's awe-inspiring. Always has been. I wanted to make a difference like he did. I wanted to help mold our future leaders, make them strong and kind and caring as well as smart and savvy. Teachers have a big influence on children, one that shouldn't be taken for granted. They can help change children's lives for the better."

"You're right. They do. And I know you're a good one." Pete softly rubbed my arm for a moment.

"It's also about the kids. I love seeing their confidence grow, not only in the subjects we cover, like math and reading, but also—and especially—in themselves. I do my best to lift their spirits when necessary. And like most good teachers, I really encourage them to ask questions. That's how they grow."

My non-boyfriend smiled. "It sounds like you love your job."

"I really do. I learn from my students, too. They remind me to be empathetic and kind, even if they don't use their words to say so. They also show me that what seems like a big deal might not be and vice versa. I have a few coworkers who disagree with this, but sometimes I let the kids take a moment to get their giggles out. We stop what we're doing and take a few moments to laugh and enjoy it. It sounds silly, but it helps them refocus and be able to concentrate better."

"That doesn't sound silly at all," Pete said as we paused our steps by the tomatoes.

"Each child is so special. All the work of earning a degree, finding a place to student teach, the hours and exorbitant costs to get to this point and what it takes now—it was never easy, but I do think it's so been worth it."

Pete leaned over and kissed the tip of my nose. Then he squeezed my hand as we continued walking.

During a rare lull in our conversation, I contemplated telling Pete about the odd DM I'd received from Miss Havisham, but thought better of it. He wouldn't have any idea what it meant, and if it was about the annexation as Gwenn and I believed, there was nothing Pete could do to help.

"Where have you been, Kenzie?" I asked my sister as she walked up to the front deck at Mom and Dad's house later that evening. "You were supposed to be here an hour ago."

I had come to my parents' house after Pete reluctantly went home. Pete and I had toured the whole town, including my classroom—which I'd thankfully cleaned up, because summer session was in full swing, and sometimes that was more obvious in my room than in anyone else's. By the end of our walk, I could tell he was clearly in awe of my sweet little town, and that warmed me even more.

Of course, we were stopped by people I knew asking how I was and eyeing Pete, clearly wanting a complete dossier on him. Pete was more than a little overwhelmed by all of them, but he seemed to take it in stride, even after the fifteenth set of eyebrows raised at our insistence that we were only friends. Luckily, no one pushed the issue.

Kenzie opened the front door, sniffed the air, then closed it again. "Relax. Mom hasn't even started dinner yet."

I didn't want to pick a fight, but it was unlike my sister to be late for anything. She was the "reliable" one, which wasn't to say I couldn't be relied on, though she too often insinuated that she felt this way about me. "So why are you late?"

"My gym in Marcellus was closed due to a water leak. I decided to try the one over in Auburn."

"That's a long way to go for a workout."

"Not really. I didn't mind. I've already tried the one in Syracuse and wanted something different."

"But it's a franchise. Don't they all look the same?"

"Not exactly."

Mom stepped around from the backyard to join us on the porch. "Kenzie! When did you get here?" she asked, greeting my sister with a hug and cheek kisses.

"A few minutes ago. Do you and Dad need any help for dinner?"

"Dad's firing up the grill. We decided on al fresco tonight." Mom continued on down toward the sidewalk. "I just need to get my serving trays back from Mrs. Hanover." And off she went.

Al fresco dining almost always happened with my parents. None of us particularly liked being inside if we didn't have to be.

"By the way," Kenzie said, turning to me, "I met someone today who I think your friends know. Edin Marchant."

I sucked in a breath, suddenly feeling both hot and nauseous. "Rhett's ex? Please tell me you didn't talk to her."

"I didn't know who she was until I spoke with her. And why shouldn't I? She was really nice."

"Kenz, that's how she gets people. She's a genius manipulator. An evil genius." Rhett wasn't just my bestie's boyfriend. His dad died from heart failure when Rhett was a kid. Though my dad was thankfully still alive and relatively well, I felt a protective kinship with Rhett. The knowledge of my sister befriending the woman who set out to control Rhett's life didn't sit well with me.

Kenzie scoffed. "We chatted on the treadmills. How manipulative could she be doing that? Besides, just because she was like that with Rhett doesn't mean she's like that with everyone. Romantic relationships are a totally different dynamic that outsiders can't always understand. You, of all people, should get that."

"I do, but Edin tried to manipulate Gwenn, too. She's not a nice person." I looked at my sister expectantly.

Kenzie rolled her eyes. "You seriously want me to not be friends with her because of something she may or may not have done to someone else? How would people ever be friends with anyone if we all judged the way you do?"

"I'm not being judgmental. I'm being honest."

"Honestly, sis, she seems like a good person. I think she's my new gym buddy. We really hit it off. We agreed to meet at the one in Marcellus next week for a yoga class."

"How can you act like this is no big deal?" I knew what I told Pete about seemingly big deals turning out to be benign, but that was so not the case this time.

"Because it isn't. I'm not going to stop talking to her just because you say so. If my opinion of her changes, it'll be my decision whether I continue developing a friendship with her, not yours."

"I'm not saying it should be my decision. I'm just saying that she's a terrible person. That alone should make you want to stay away from her."

"Lucy, everyone except you seems to have gotten over those things Edin did. I'm sure she had a good reason for her behavior."

"I highly doubt Gwenn is over it. I doubt Rhett is, too."

"Isn't he friends with her again?"

"Well, yeah, but—"

"But what?" my sister interrupted.

"But you can't do that!" I was out of breath and feeling more than a little hot and light-headed. My hands hurt from clenching them.

"What can't Kenzie do?" Mom asked as she walked up the porch steps to rejoin us, three brightly colored plastic serving trays in her hands.

"Befriend Rhett's ex-fiancée," I told her.

Mom thought about this for a few moments. "Maybe that's something for Gwenn and Rhett to work through."

"Meaning you should stay out of it," Kenzie added. "The past doesn't matter. So who cares?"

I did, for one. The past absolutely mattered when it involved vicious bitches trying to destroy my friend's burgeoning relationship.

"You're all about giving people extra chances. You do it all the time with the men you date. Why not now?"

"What else is new with you?" Mom asked Kenzie, steering us away from our heated discussion.

"I'm selling my birthday necklace."

Mom and I both audibly sucked in a breath.

"You definitely can't do that," I told my sister.

"What don't you want Kenzie to do?" Dad asked as he walked outside carrying a tray containing four glasses of lemon iced tea. He began handing a glass to each of us.

I looked at him. "She can't sell her diamond necklace Aunt Maria gave her."

Dad's eyes widened, and his curious expression faded as his mouth dropped. "Kenzie, what's going on?"

"Hayzel needs a cheerleading uniform, and my car needs new tires. I don't have any other way to pay."

"Shouldn't Cal at least cover the uniform?" Mom asked. "I'm sure he'd pay for the tires, too. That is Hayzel's main mode of transportation."

Cal was my sister's ex-husband. He abandoned them when my niece was just a baby. One day, Kenz went home and found him and his clothes gone. He'd left everything else. He also sent a text that said he couldn't do it anymore. By "it," I assumed he meant marriage, and especially parenthood. Kenzie never went into much detail about it.

"He won't give it to me." Kenzie's voice cracked. "He doesn't give us anything."

"But you said he did." Dad's voice was equally unsteady. "All those years of nothing from him. The last time he was in town, you told us you confronted him and he gave you child support money."

I knew the reason why she'd lied. After that goodbye text, Cal never contacted them again. Not once. Hayzel was now nine, so it'd been more than a while. Saying I hated the man was too much like going easy on him. I despised the very thought of him. I cursed his every breath. And yet Kenzie still clung to both her love for him and her hope of him returning one day.

She cried a little harder now. "I didn't want you and Mom to worry."

"Oh, honey." Mom dabbed at her now-damp eyes. "We'd give you the money now if we could."

"So would I, Kenz." I patted her arm for a moment. I'd already given up the great dress Jade had found for me. When she kindly asked me if everything was okay, I explained how I was no longer in the market for any new purchases for the foreseeable future.

"I know, and I appreciate it. Thank you, all of you. But it is what it is. None of us are in a good place financially right now. No sense in crying over a necklace," Kenzie said as she dried her own eyes. It was more than just the necklace, but apparently, none of us felt the need to say this.

I took a sip of tea in order to try and calm myself. "Maybe Kenzie's right," I said.

Mom looked at me with furrowed eyebrows.

"Not about the necklace. Hopefully, it won't get to that point. But maybe we have other things of value. We could hold a garage sale. Raise some funds that way."

"That can take weeks to organize," Kenzie told me.

"Elementary cheer practices don't start for a month," I said, ignoring her pessimism. "How long can your tires hold out?"

"Maybe that long."

I thought she wanted to sound hopeful, but her words came out more like a question.

"Maybe we can ask Rhett to take a look at them for you," I suggested. "In the meantime, I'm sure we can all find enough things to sell for both you and Mom and Dad."

"Sweetie," Dad began, "I appreciate your wanting to include us in this, but it'll take a lot more than a garage sale to raise the money we need to keep the house."

And the cabin, I wanted to remind him, but that wouldn't be fair. "It's a start. If we can earn a decent amount, maybe the mortgage company will see how hard you're trying and not foreclose. Maybe then they'll let you go a few more months before having to start monthly payments again."

"They've hit their limit," Kenzie reminded me. "They signed papers agreeing to something. They need to keep the agreement."

"But they can't right now. We have to at least try to help them keep the house and the cabin."

"What is with you and that cabin?" Dom asked as he walked up the back steps to the patio. "They sell the cabin, and they might keep their house. Why would you risk trying anything that loses them their *home*?"

"Selling the cabin doesn't guarantee keeping the house, and you know that," I told him. "It's a small cabin with barely any land. It hasn't been updated in a long time. And don't tell me developers want to knock it down and build there. Why not try something else before letting it go?" I turned to Mom and Kenzie again. "We could put big-ticket items in the sale."

"Unless you have a mint condition, rare Babe Ruth or Jackie Robinson baseball card stashed somewhere, it's only going to end up a failure," Dominic told me. "Can't exactly sell a car."

"If we had a spare one, we would," Mom told us.

"I'm selling my necklace from Aunt Maria," Kenzie told Dom.

"Kenz, no," I implored her.

"Anything left over from selling it can go to Mom and Dad's house fund."

I still thought it was a bad idea, but I knew when my sister was determined to do something, and thought better of arguing with her.

"Do you have anything you can sell for the cause?" Kenzie asked our brother.

"Probably not, but I can check."

"You said it was going to be a failure," I told him with a sly grin.

"And I believe that. However, I'm also willing to do anything I can to help, even if it's futile."

Chapter 16

Pete

"It's absurd," Lucy said, her voice rising at the end. "Kenzie's being unreasonable, and she calls me the unreasonable one."

"Luce, Edin deserves to have friends. She at least deserves the chance," I told her once she'd explained the situation to me.

Honestly, I didn't care all that much about this Edin chick, but I did care about Lucy's feelings. Based on what I knew about Lucy and her sister, I thought they were both being too hard on each other. I couldn't tell if Lucy was more surprised or annoyed at my words.

"Edin can have friends who have no connection to Gwenn or Rhett."

"Your sister isn't exactly close to either of them, is she?"

"No, but she's connected to them through me."

"A proxy of a proxy seems a little flimsy."

I'm not sure she heard me. She continued ranting. "It's like Edin is obsessed with Rhett and Gwenn. She just can't let them go."

"Ba—" I stopped in horror. I'd almost just called her "babe." I needed to fix it. Fast. "*Blaming* Edin for everything won't help the situation, Luce. And I know you don't want to hear this, but you seem a little obsessed with her. Do you understand that?"

Chapter 17

Lucy

I IGNORED THAT LAST bit. My heart and mind were too giddy. Was Pete about to call me "babe"? This completely threw me off.

Babe!

It took only a couple weeks of being friends for that to almost slip out. The next five or so months were going to be brutal. I wanted to call him "babe" back. I wanted to rush over to his house in Syracuse, wrap my arms around him, take him to his bed with me, and do all kinds of fun, naked things with him.

I lost track of what we were talking about. Instead of trying to get back on track, I asked, "When can I see you again?"

"Not until Saturday."

"Can't. Mom and I are helping out at the community garden all day. Lourdes and Gwenn are going to be there, too."

"I'm assuming after school is no good."

"Not right now," I reluctantly admitted. "Sunday?"

"Lunch?"

I smiled to myself. "It's a non-date." We said good night and hung up.

I wondered how long I should wait before I "accidentally" called him babe in return.

·♥·♥·♥·♥·♥·

"When do we get to meet Perfect Pete?" Gwenn asked as she handed me a blue-handled spade.

We were in the community garden, gathering vegetables to make available for the town residents to pick up. Well, Lourdes and I were gathering vegetables. Gwenn was side-eyeing the dirt and bugs and wishing we were having this conversation elsewhere.

"As soon as you want to," I replied.

"We definitely want to," Lourdes said, "but we aren't sure what kind of expectations to go into this meeting with."

I stopped working for a moment, letting the spade rest against the soft soil in front of me. "Expect him to be amazing," I said dreamily.

"And will the royal carriage fetch you for your next non-date?" Gwenn asked.

I shook myself out of my daydreaming stupor. "What carriage?"

My friends laughed.

"That's how you make it sound, Luce," Lourdes said. "He isn't royalty, and neither are you. This is the real world. You can't keep calling him Perfect Pete."

"Hey, that was Gwenn's name for him, not mine."

"You know what I mean," Lourdes replied. "Gwenn and I are so proud of you for not jumping in headfirst this time."

I agreed this had turned out to be an excellent decision on my part. "Kenzie has already seen Pete a few times, and Charisma met him once, but I never worry about their opinions. You two are the ones who usually have issues with the men I date."

"The last one you fell in love with ghosted you after only a week. We have a right to dislike them," Lourdes told me.

"Pete's different. At least, I think he is. That's the whole point of this experiment."

"To see if he can live up to your fantasies?" Gwenn suggested.

"To see if I'm wrong in wanting to date him. And to see if he truly deserves me."

"Has he met the rest of the family yet, or is he still balking at the idea?" Lourdes asked.

I didn't want to answer this question. I knew how they'd interpret the truth. "Not just yet," I said slowly.

"What's the holdup?"

"I don't know." I wished I had a better answer to give. All I had was Pete's reasoning.

"That's more of an official couple thing, don't you think?" he'd said when I asked him about it.

"I guess," had been my reply.

He must have noticed the look on my face, because then he added, "We'll get there. Soon."

I thought his idea of soon and my idea of soon were two totally different things.

"We won't try to steal him away from you," Lourdes said, bringing me back to the present. "And if he hits on one of us like that one boyfriend did with your friends, then he never deserved you in the first place. What else is there to be worried about?"

"You're right. How about lunch next weekend sometime?" I knew they were free the next day, but I wanted Pete all to myself once more.

"I'm free," Lourdes said.

"I can make myself available if need be," Gwenn added. "I'll have my assistant check my schedule."

·♥·♥·♥·♥·♥·

I was so nervous waiting for Pete to show up the next weekend at my house. Saturday, to be exact. A week from the last time I'd seen him, at our not-a-date lunch that turned into an evening of Pete showing me around the neighborhood he lived in. I didn't get to meet any of his neighbors, but that was okay.

I was already completely head over heels for him, though it was super important what Gwenn and Lourdes thought. And maybe once he met my besties, he'd be more open to meeting my family. Dominic was already beginning to not like Pete simply for the fact that Pete didn't seem to want invited to family dinners. I was quick to remind my brother that he didn't like the dinners either, but that didn't seem to help.

The front door opened and closed while I was in my bedroom closet digging out a math game I'd remembered I had that would be really fun for the summer school kids. I assumed it was Lourdes and Gwenn at the door until Pete's deep voice echoed down the hall.

"Luce?"

"In here," I replied. "My room."

His heavy footfalls came closer. When they stopped, I looked over to see him standing in my bedroom doorway. He hadn't actually been in my room before. It was also full of yellow, on the bed, the curtains, the shelves, and the plush rug. But at least the walls were white, and the floor was a light wood.

"Wow," he said, echoing his sentiments on seeing my living room for the first time.

I ignored his shock this time and gave him a bright smile. "Hi! They should be here soon." I motioned for us to go out to the living area.

Instead, Pete stepped into the room and walked over to sit on my bed. "You have the most throw pillows of anyone I've ever seen."

I eyed the messy pile of yellow and sage-green pillows, then moved my gaze back to Pete. On my bed. It took a lot to not fan myself. "What are you doing there?" I asked with a little wave of my hand over at him. My cheeks were red, I knew, without me even needing to see them.

"Are you thinking about all the things we could be doing on this bed?" Pete asked, leaning back onto his elbows. His T-shirt moved just enough to show off the tiniest bit of skin at the bottom.

Normally, I'd already have straddled him, but with our arrangement as it stood, I was apprehensive to even sit next to him. He patted the bed anyway. When I joined him, he turned onto his side, his whole body facing me. Then he placed his right hand on my knee, the other hand holding his head up.

"Why is this making you nervous?" Pete asked.

"Not nervous." I shook my head, my hair moving off my shoulders just a bit. "Filled with desire. That I can't act on."

A slow smile spread on his handsome face. "You could. You can. I'll let you." Then the smile began to fade. Pete cleared his throat and rolled up to sitting, removing his hand from my knee in the process. "Your friends should be here soon. They probably wouldn't want to walk in on something like that. We might want to leave this room."

He stood and held a hand out to me.

The room wasn't the problem. The desire to have Pete's body against mine was there no matter where we were. But I understood his point. I gave him my hand and let him pull me up. Then I heard two car doors shut nearby.

"Ready?" I asked with a grin. "They're here."

"Let's go spend the day with people who love you as—" He stopped a moment. "As, uh, as long as we're doing this, which obviously we are, what's one thing I need to know the most about this lunch?"

"Gwenn is allergic to apples," I told him, desperately wishing he'd finished his original train of thought. It had to have been something good, right? I was totally going to decipher every syllable of it later with my besties. "She doesn't eat pears, either, just in case."

"No apples. No pears. Got it." He beamed, and I leaned forward to lightly kiss his bearded cheek.

I motioned to the hall with my head. "Let's go."

·❤·❤·❤·❤·❤·

"Thank you so much for not grilling him," I said to Lourdes and Gwenn as we all relaxed in Gwenn's apartment later that night. "At least in front of me, anyway."

"Thank you for going to the ladies' room to give us time to ask Pete questions without you there," Lourdes said with a smile.

So I had done that, but Pete had to know it was coming. I wanted to see if maybe he changed his tune when I wasn't around. They'd even brought up that initial debacle with Charisma to him, and he never flinched. Lourdes said he showed genuine regret about the whole situation.

"Okay, so . . . thoughts?" I finally dared to ask.

Lourdes and Gwenn glanced at each other before looking back at me.

"We like him," Lourdes said with a grin.

Gwenn agreed. "So much so that I want him to meet Rhett. I think they might hit it off."

I gave a little squeal. "Really?"

Gwenn and Lourdes both nodded. They called him the sweetest, nicest, best kind of man they could have ever imagined for me.

"When those six months are up, you are going to have an amazing boyfriend. Until then, you have an amazing friend. We are so happy for you!"

Chapter 18

Pete

I'D NEVER CARED MUCH what the friends of my girlfriends—if you could even call them that—thought of me. It was different with Lucy, though. Everything was different with Lucy.

The next morning, she and I were at my house, cuddling on the living room floor, safe and dry away from the rainstorm outside that had ruined her plans of a picnic in the park. We'd started with the TV on, but paused it when we got onto the topic of Lourdes and Gwenn. I was honestly nervous about what they said to her after I went home.

"They loved you," Lucy gushed.

I let out a relieved sigh. While I'd suspected as much at lunch, there was something about the two of them that created doubt. What if they were the "nice to your face, then turn around and bitch about you when you're gone" kind of women? I couldn't be sure at first.

As we lay face-to-face next to each other, my arm around Lucy's middle, my hand at the small of her back, her phone beeped, indicating a new text. She picked it up, but instead of texting in return, she started a video call. I quickly glanced at the screen. It was her mom.

I pulled myself away, pretending to be thirsty. To keep up the ruse, and to stay out of view of the camera, I went into the kitchen.

Lucy still hadn't mentioned her parents' struggles to me, and as far as I could tell, the Larkins hadn't figured out the connection between me and their daughter's new friend. I couldn't be the one to bridge the gap.

When I noticed Lucy shifting as she talked with her mom, I turned my back and pretended to search the fridge for a bottle of soda I knew I didn't have.

"I'm still at Pete's right now," Lucy told Nadine. "With the rain as heavy as it is, I think I might hang out here longer than I thought I would. But I'm sure Pete's okay with that." Lucy laughed.

Gosh, I loved her laugh. I loved her smile. I loved holding her in my arms so much it almost hurt to move away. It was the first time we'd actually cuddled like that before. I couldn't wait to do it again.

"Hey, Mom, say hi to Pete." Lucy was suddenly closer to me than I'd expected. I was so busy thinking about the warm sensations of her body against mine that I hadn't noticed her walk into the kitchen.

I turned to find I was on camera with Lucy's mom.

"Pete!" Nadine exclaimed. "Oh my goodness!"

"Hey, Nadine." I gave a smile, but my stomach was dropping.

Lucy's face understandably scrunched up. She lowered the camera away from me. "How did you do that? I didn't tell you my mom's name."

Nadine, meanwhile, was calling to Kerrick. "Come see Lucy's new boyfriend! Our Pete is Lucy's Pete!"

I hadn't answered Lucy in the few seconds before her dad showed up on the screen. "Well hey, Pete!" He was so animated and so happy.

"Taking good care of our little girl?" Kerrick added. He didn't ask how or why this was happening. He simply accepted it as something that was good.

"Doing my best," I replied.

Neither Lucy nor I corrected her mom and dad about the "boyfriend" comment.

"Wow! I always knew you two would make such a cute couple," Nadine told us, pure happiness in her voice, as well as a tone that suggested she considered this all her doing.

I still hadn't answered Lucy's question. Her eyebrows remained furrowed. Finally, she lifted her phone up again and aimed the camera on herself. "We aren't an official couple yet, Mom. Just officially friends right now."

I couldn't help but grimace at the label, necessary as it was.

"So," Lucy continued, focusing on her parents, "how does my new friend know you?"

"Oh, Pete's on our mortgage account," Nadine said breezily.

There was nothing easy or breezy about it for Lucy and me. I could feel the temperature in the house drop at least ten degrees.

"Wait." Lucy shook her head. "How long have you known him?"

"Well, we've been with his bank for years. He's at Syracuse Financial. But we had our first meeting with him as the head of our account a few weeks ago."

"A few weeks?" Lucy screeched out.

"Around there," Kerrick added. "That was when we told you kids about the foreclosure."

Lucy gave me a death stare. "You knew about that before I did?"

I put my hands up. "I promise I would have said something to you if I could have. There are certain ethics to take into consideration."

"Does this mean there is no conflict of interest?" Nadine asked, clearly not listening to what Lucy and I were saying. "Ooh! Pete, you should come with Lucy to our next family dinner. We have at least one a week. Sometimes, it's the only way we can get all the kids together. Kenzie and Dominic would love to meet you."

"Kenzie's already met him, Mom," Lucy told her.

"So long as Lucy and I keep the official label of friends, we should be okay. The conflict of interest might not even apply. Before the day comes that that changes, I'll figure out what to do about the ramifications of someone in the department or even another customer finding out. I've already been researching as much as possible about how to keep everything with Lucy separate from my job with you two."

Lucy talked with her parents for a little while longer, moving on to other topics. But she didn't smile at me anymore. She barely looked at me.

Once she was off the phone, I burst out into the silence, "I'm so sorry, Luce. I couldn't tell you. To do so would have gone against my ethical code. I couldn't allow myself to be the one to disclose your father's health issues or your parents' financial woes to you if you didn't already know."

She nodded slightly, but didn't respond any other way.

I moved toward her and removed the phone from her hand, setting it down on the coffee table. Then I took her hands in mine. "Lucy, listen. Discretion is of the utmost importance, because my job and your parents' house could depend on it."

Chapter 19

Lucy

"WHAT ARE YOU SAYING? We can't ever date?" I watched and waited for Pete's reaction, hoping he wouldn't disappoint me already.

"We can. We can be friends before then, too. But there's no need to tell people about this connection between my friend and my clients. So long as we don't mention it, we should be safe."

"And what if someone who knows my parents recognizes the two of us while we're out? This is a problem, isn't it?"

"It's highly unlikely they'll also know I'm the one dealing with the mortgage. We just need to keep key people out of this conversation, like my boss and my coworkers. I can handle this, but I need your family's cooperation."

He eyed me. "What's going on?"

"It just feels like you lied to me."

Pete shook his head. "It was never a lie. Just an omission. I knew but couldn't tell you in order to protect all of us. But I'm so glad you know now, because I hated not being able to discuss this with you." He paused a moment. "You know, the first time I met your parents, your mom actually tried setting us up. She even showed me a stunning photo of you."

My eyes widened. "She did not."

"I about fell out of my chair."

We both laughed for a moment.

"If I could have told them, I would have. I would have said how much I already liked you. If I could have told you," Pete continued, "I would have. I need you to understand this."

"I do. Mostly."

He seemed to accept this. Then he said, "Can I ask why you didn't say anything to me about your dad?"

"I didn't know how. It's not easy to talk about. Dad means the world to me. And I didn't want the sympathy look from you. The one I get from everyone else." I rubbed my face for a second, then gave Pete a small smile. "I was afraid something that big might scare you away."

Pete's eyes flashed something I didn't quite understand. "Big things so early on can be scary."

"Yep. I never got to the point of telling anyone else I dated either. I just don't like the idea of the guy I'm into having to see me with that kind of intense, terrifying stress."

"If they ever felt for you what I do, they would have stuck around. I'm not the type of guy to run from that. I like you too much."

I couldn't help but lean in and kiss him on the tip of his nose. "Besides, Dad's alive. He's doing well right now. He's finally at a healthy weight and not so heavy due to the artery disease." Like he had been in the past, when his arteries were failing him, along with so many other terrible symptoms. "It was easier to focus on other things with you."

"I get that," Pete replied with a soft nod.

"I'm sorry for not telling you."

"I'm sorry for not being able to mention it to you," he said in return.

Then something I hadn't thought about yet hit me. "You can help them!"

But a shadow darkened Pete's expression. "Luce, I'm doing everything I can for your parents. Please don't ask me to do more." His tone said, *"Please don't ask me to break the rules for you."*

I knew he was right. I knew it. Yet I forged ahead with my thought anyway. "You are maybe the only one who can help them. Or at least the only one who cares to. You're the one in charge of the account."

"There are still rules of the bank and actual laws I have to follow. My job could potentially be on the line just from my connection to you if someone happens to be having a bad day that day. I cannot go out of my way to make this worse. It can't ever appear that I'm playing favorites or using my influence to help your parents specifically."

"No one would accuse you of favoritism," I said, doubting the words as soon as they were out of my mouth.

Pete grimaced. "You're asking me to jeopardize my job, when it's already potentially on the line just from me knowing you."

I ignored that last part for the moment. "Pete, I'm just asking you to help my family."

"Don't put that on me. It isn't fair."

"What isn't fair is that good, kind, honest people are going to lose their home, and no one at your company seems to care."

"*I* care," he snapped. "And people in my office care, and the man who used to be in charge of the account cared, too. Don't act like we're all heartless bastards. We're not." He took a moment to be silent. When he spoke again, his voice was softer. "Like I said, there are rules to this. I have to tread lightly and be as careful and discreet as possible. Pulling a miracle for your parents out of nowhere would raise a ton of red flags I can't afford raising."

"Okay. I understand," I whispered, a wave of disappointment washing over me despite knowing he was right.

I couldn't ask him to break his moral code. I certainly couldn't ask him to break any laws. I just hoped that there was enough in his power to try that could save my parents from losing everything.

My phone beeped with a new notification. One I specifically set for a particular fictional character.

Miss Havisham was back.

"What is that?" Pete asked as I sucked in a breath.

I hadn't wanted to tell him since it wasn't related to him in any way, but this time I let him see the message after I read it, and also the one that came before.

"'He's a liar. Don't trust him.' What does that mean? Don't trust who?" Pete asked, his eyes scrunched as he stared at my screen.

"Gwenn and I initially thought it was about the principal and the promises he's made about the potential annexation. But I've asked around, and there are no indications that he's going to backtrack on his promise to do what's best for our district."

Pete moved his eyes up to me. "So who else could it be about?"

I hadn't wanted to get into this part, mostly because I was afraid of the ramifications for all of us. "Well, there's Dominic, but Dom's a pretty honest guy."

Then it seemed to dawn on him. "You think it might be about me."

"I'm terrified it might be about you. That means someone found out about my connection to you and your work with my parents."

Pete muttered a curse word.

"Exactly. Someone might know that I know you, and now I'm being harassed about your job. I mean, you work with desperate people trying to save their homes."

"This is exactly what I was afraid of." Pete sighed, running a hand through his hair. "Some disgruntled customer or angry coworker—" He stopped.

"What? You know who it is?"

"Yeah, uh, you know . . ." He stumbled over his words. "There have been a couple customers recently who I haven't been able to help. They were in far too deep. But I try to give them as much encouragement as possible. Maybe they misconstrued that and took it to mean I'd help no matter what."

"But you can't do that," I whispered, his words about my parents' account fully hitting me.

"That's right." Pete gave a short nod. "But I promise I will take care of this."

· ♥ · ♥ · ♥ · ♥ · ♥ ·

"Sorry, Luce. I can't come over now," Kenzie told me later that afternoon. Her voice sounded a little far away.

"Are you in your car?"

"Yeah. I'm almost to Auburn now."

"Auburn?" I couldn't believe it. She was choosing Edin over me. Surprise, surprise.

"It isn't like that," Kenzie said. "Her bakery caught on fire."

"Whoa. Like *fire* fire?"

"I'm not sure how bad it is, but it's bad enough that she nearly hyperventilated when she called me a little while ago. I need to go see if she's okay."

From what I gathered in my conversations with my sister, Edin didn't really have anyone else who could help her and comfort her. Well, she had one person.

"Does Rhett know?"

"I'm not sure. Maybe." She got quiet for a moment. "I'll be at Edin's soon. I'll talk to you later, sis." And she was gone.

I was left feeling torn between my loyalty to Gwenn and my sympathy for Edin.

"Hello?" Gwenn said when she answered. "What's up, Luce?"

"Hey. I didn't want to text this."

"What's going on?" she immediately asked, her voice tight and unsteady.

"Has Rhett spoken to Edin?"

"I don't know. Why?" Gwenn's tone changed from worry to suspicion.

I needed to reassure her. "Kenzie just called me from Auburn. Edin's bakery caught on fire."

"Whoa. Is she okay?"

"I don't know. I think so. Physically, at least. I thought Rhett might want to know."

"Thank you. I'll let him know. And Luce? I know how you feel about her, but you did the right thing."

It was nice to hear someone say that to me. Everyone in my life as of late had been nothing but critical. It felt that way anyway.

Chapter 20

Pete

It was me.

I knew it.

Someone was coming after me. But who?

Miles came to mind. I wouldn't put it past him to mess with our heads and use that as a way to win the bet. But that meant Miles would have to know about the connection. He wasn't shy. There was no way he'd have that information and not loudly "whisper" it to me in the break room or my office or the lobby.

So Miles was out.

Maybe someone connected to Miles was doing it. Corkie could have figured it out even if her fiancé had no clue, which meant while Corkie was harmless, she could have inadvertently passed this information on to Drea.

Drea.

That was an idea.

I could easily ask Alec. If he'd ever figured it out, he never would have mentioned it to anyone. I hadn't told him, only Tess. Asking Alec was a far better idea than asking Drea, as much as my instinct was to shoot off a text to her asking her what the hell she thought she was doing. If it wasn't Drea, she'd definitely look into what I was accusing her of, and then a bigger mess would come out of it.

I decided to start with Tess.

> You haven't mentioned Lucy and her parents to anyone, right?

> I would never, and you know that.

> Why? What's wrong?

I reluctantly told her about the DMs.

> Not good, Pete. How can I help?

> No idea, but thanks.

Then it was Alec's turn, though I didn't want to tell him. Like Tess, he was often my moral guide. He was already in my ear often about breaking off the bet to save myself and Lucy. Adding a conflict of interest to that would only heighten his concern for me.

I ended my surprisingly long text with a question on what he thought might have happened, then waited for the aftermath. There was no way Alec was going to answer my question first.

> I assume you know the consequences if Shu-bin finds out.

> Yep. I'm keeping everything as discreet as possible in the meantime. Hopefully it stays that way.

> Except maybe it hasn't.

> Right. So do you know anything?

It took about a minute for him to reply.

> Sometimes the assistants talk. It's possible one of them heard something from Nella, but I doubt it, unless you pissed her off that day.

This had me wracking my brain, trying to pinpoint any moment that Nella seemed less than happy with me. I couldn't think of any. And honestly, doing something like this would have required Nella to be enraged, which isn't easy to hide. She often let me know when I was a jerk to her, garnering swift and sincere apologies. That hadn't happened in a long time.

> Are these messages worrisome enough to ask IT to look into it?

> Not yet. There's nothing concrete.

> Then keep an eye on it. I've read stories of assholes using bots to do stuff like this to extort money from people. They might start with you and move up in the bank's ranks.

Yet another thing for me to be afraid of.

Family dinner.

I often went to dinner with my own family, but never a girlfriend's. Ever.

Lucy wasn't even my official girlfriend yet.

But it was going to be all right. I liked Kerrick, Nadine, and Kenzie. I really, really liked Lucy. And I wasn't afraid of meeting her brother Dominic, no matter how many times Lucy mentioned that she thought he was an angry, bitter asshole.

Only, I couldn't shake the nervous feeling that crept up on me. It made breathing difficult as I rode with Lucy over to her parents' house Tuesday evening. It wasn't actually the next time they'd had family dinner. That was last night. I'd needed a day just to wrap my head around the idea. Unfortunately, I couldn't wait the several more I needed to feel comfortable with it.

"My parents actually live on the other side of town." She laughed. "Such as it is."

As she pulled up to the house, Lucy whispered a shocked, "Wow."

"What?" I swiveled my head around, trying to see whatever it was she saw. Was it a good wow or a bad one?

"Nothing, just that Dominic is here before me. That never happens."

I moved my eyes to her face again. Her soft skin looked a little pinker. She hadn't put the car in park yet, still holding her foot on the brake. "What does that mean?"

"If you want to bail now, I'll completely understand."

At her words, I scrubbed a hand through my beard for a moment. Bailing didn't sound like a bad idea. For about six milliseconds. But after that . . . man, I knew it was no good.

First, I needed a deep breath in. After slowly letting it out, I slid my hand over onto Lucy's—which rested on the steering wheel—and gave her the best relaxed smile I could muster. "Let's go in."

After exiting the car, we walked hand-in-hand up the steps of the front porch and through the open doorway. Apparently, they already knew we were there. I put my hand on Lucy's lower back after shutting the door behind us.

"Well, hey, Pete!" Kerrick's voice greeted me before I ever saw him.

"Hey, Kerrick," I replied as he came over and placed a friendly hand on my shoulder.

"Glad you could make it," Kerrick continued with a bright smile. It was the same one he wore when we were all on the video chat together.

"Pete!" Nadine came over and gave me a hug as well as Lucy. Then I noticed Lucy's brother, sister, and niece were also in the room, all offering their own versions of hello. Dominic's included a handshake, while Lucy's niece's was a shy little wave.

All throughout dinner, I noticed the main dynamic of Lucy's family was lively, if a bit loud. They liked to laugh and tease, but all in good fun. Well, Lucy and her siblings were a little harsh to each other, but her parents were amazingly kind. One thing stood out the most: love. This family loved each other fiercely.

They also accepted me as one of their own from the get-go. I was subjected to just as much playful mocking as the rest. No one mentioned my job or money or mortgages in any way, nor did they speak of Kerrick's health.

"You know, I'm a little surprised to see you here, Pete," Dominic said slowly after we'd all made our way to the living room. "Usually, Lucy's boyfriends ditch her well before this point."

Lucy scowled at him.

This didn't feel like the moment to remind everyone she wasn't technically my girlfriend, except Kenzie said it first.

Dominic chuckled. "That makes it even worse. You got corralled into this with no pay-off."

"Dominic." Nadine had only to use one word and that stern, motherly tone to make him stop.

"I do have to agree with Dom's first sentiment," Kerrick added. "I didn't think we'd see you here, Pete. Thought maybe you were too afraid of the potential risk to your job."

And there it was. My job. I hated that we hadn't made it all night without discussing it.

Lucy turned to me. "That never occurred to me, that you shouldn't even come here as my friend." Her eyes were wide, her complexion a bit pale at the thought.

I gave her the warmest smile I had. "It's okay, Luce. Don't worry about it." I didn't think I'd convinced her, though. Maybe my whole "we need to use discretion" speech was repeating in her head like it had been mine as we sat in the driveway. I thought it had been worth the risk to get to know the Larkins better. I supposed we both could have been wrong about that.

Based on Lucy's shift in attitude, becoming less animated and more withdrawn, I thought it a safe bet that it was all she could think about.

When we left at the end of the night, there were hugs all around. I was definitely included this time, even by Hayzel. Dominic was the only one who didn't hug me, but I was more than okay with that. It was already overwhelming how much I felt at home with these people.

I hadn't been consumed by the urge to ooze charm like usual. There was no need to be "on" the whole night, pretending to like these people the way I sometimes had to in my meetings with customers or even some of those in my department. Everything with the Larkins was easy and comforting. They were not the "be flashy to impress us" kind of people, and I loved them already for it. But that once again brought the whole conflict of interest dilemma to the forefront of my mind.

It might have been the result of different actions, but Lucy and I were completely freaking out over the same thing.

<h1 style="text-align:center">Chapter 22</h1>

Pete

THE AFTERMATH OF FAMILY dinner was usually just the strong desire to run an extra five miles or spend another hour at the gym to work off all the delicious but unhealthy food.

Not this time.

This time, I was floundering from the stress of having to hide my friendship with the Larkins and my growing desire for Lucy, in addition to already drowning in guilt about the bet. I hoped I wouldn't need to remind them all again about not mentioning our social gatherings to anyone until the whole mortgage mess was situated. Otherwise, any help I gave them or even led them to might be revoked or flagged.

I wondered what Tess would say. I hadn't told her in advance about dinner with Lucy's family. Miles still hadn't put two-and-two together, so I didn't have to worry about him keeping his big mouth shut, at least about the connection. He was still too freaking vocal about our wager.

"Can't be surprised she held off this long," he laughed to me Wednesday, after barging into my office uninvited.

It was beginning to feel like he was the predator and I was his prey.

"She'll probably put it off indefinitely if she can." Miles laughed again.

I wasn't laughing. I was fuming. And worried.

So much so that I showed up at Lucy's that night looking for reassurance. What kind of reassurance, I wasn't sure. I just needed her. Then once I was with her, I needed to be away from her. Everything felt too comfortable and too perfect.

"You okay?" she asked as I tried to nonchalantly avoid her welcoming embrace.

It wasn't that I didn't want her to touch me. I wanted her to touch me everywhere. But that wasn't the issue at the moment. It was more the fact that once Lucy and I were in each other's arms, I never wanted to let go. I wasn't sure of much else, but I did know that for certain.

Lucy moved toward me again when I didn't answer, her hands still on my biceps. Only when I didn't step away did she gently slide them around to my back. I did the same with my hands on her, closing the space between us enough to rest my forehead against hers.

"I'm okay now." I inhaled her scent. For a woman who loved the color yellow, she always seemed to smell like a flower I imagined to be pink. I didn't know for sure what it was.

"Want to talk about it?" Her breath was hot on my neck.

I shook my head no. "Just don't let go right now."

"I'll hold on as long as you'll let me."

I was drowning again. It was because of something far better than the guilt, but damn near as scary.

Chapter 23

Lucy

PETE SHOWED UP EARLY as promised tonight after an unexpected but totally welcome visit last night. I was still trying to finish the pear salad I promised to take to dinner. It was difficult to tell what he thought about another family dinner so soon, and he seemed unwilling to delve deeper than "I like your family."

I was more than happy that Pete felt comfortable enough to simply walk into my house when he arrived. That had to be enough for the moment. I wore my very best and brightest white tank top and silky-soft golden shorts with a tie belt. Didn't want to give Pete any doubts that I was dressed to impress him, no matter where we were going.

After greeting him with a chaste kiss on the cheek, I returned to the half-open bag of already roasted pecans—the salad's finishing touch—as Pete popped a few store-bought croutons into his mouth. He made a soft "mm" sound and grabbed a few more from the bag. I wanted to ask him how his day was, but that could've easily been misconstrued and taken as a question of whether or not he'd helped my parents that day.

I'd avoided talk of his job ever since I found out Pete was working with Mom and Dad. I had zero desire to make Pete think that's all that was important anymore, and I knew he was already feeling enough pressure.

Finally, I settled on, "How's life?"

Pete gave a soft smile. "Life's good. So are these." He ate a couple more.

"Stop." I laughed. "You have to save some of them for the salad."

The timer on my phone beeped to let me know it was time to go. "You ready?" I asked Pete, waiting to see if maybe he'd changed his mind.

His grin held. "Yep. Let's go."

"There's a rumor in town that Rhett's ex-fiancée is opening a second bakery here," Mom said to Kenzie as we all sat around the fire pit in my parents' backyard.

My sister watched me for my reaction. I knew she thought I'd say something bitchy, but I wasn't feeling it. Ever since she called me on the way to help Edin that day, my feelings about her had been shifting.

"Nothing's set in stone yet," Kenzie said to Mom. "Her bakery in Auburn just burned down. Electrical fire. She doesn't know what to do right now. She's been checking out a few locations, but really, she just wants her bakery rebuilt. They're saying that might not be possible."

"That's just terrible," Mom said.

Their conversation continued along that vein.

Meanwhile, Dominic and Pete were discussing the options Pete's neighbor had in adding a roof to his backyard porch and the costs related to each. In listening to Pete talk about his neighbor George—someone he'd told me about but I had yet to meet—I immediately picked up on how much Pete cared about him, just as I did the first time I'd heard about him. I hoped Pete talked about me the same way.

Well, in a much *different* way, of course.

Dinner ended without a hitch. My family opted for hugs with Pete again, except for Dom, but that was no surprise. What was surprising and also comforting was how well and how quickly Pete seemed to acclimate into this new part of our relationship. Dinner and hugs with my family no longer appeared to send a panic through him like it had before.

This was so much better than a little baby step forward. It gave me hope for our upcoming official status as boyfriend and girlfriend. If my family loved him—my family, who almost never got to meet the men I dated despite my knack for having lots of boyfriends—then we were far ahead of where I'd been with anyone else and would only keep going.

Chapter 24

WHILE CHECKING THE MAIL, I pulled out an envelope with an address in what I immediately recognized as Pete's handwriting. It had been eight days since we last saw each other in person. It was already August now. I shoved the rest of the mail between my arm and my side and ripped open Pete's envelope. It was a printout of Shakespeare's "Sonnet 18," which Pete recited to me the day we met.

At the very bottom, in his perfect scrawl, Pete wrote, *Always thinking of you. Miss you.*

He didn't write *Love you* at the bottom, but I knew he wanted to. It was so obvious. Clearly, he was as in love with me as I was with him.

I rushed into the house, tossed the mail onto my wood side table by the door, and quickly pulled my phone out of my pocket, sending a quick message to Pete.

> Checked the mail.

> You want to tell me all about your credit card bill?

Not funny, and no.

Water bill?

On second thought, maybe this letter is from my *other* cute non-boyfriend.

Also not funny.

Normally, I would have replied with *You know you love me*, but I couldn't do that this time.

Miss you, too.

I looked down at the poem again. He'd even highlighted certain phrases or lines that reminded him of me.

Pete didn't text in return, but he didn't need to. I knew how he felt about me. It was literally right there in front of me in black and white. He loved me. No matter what, everything with us would always be this fantastic because I was more than just a friend to him. We were in love.

Chapter 25

Pete

I COULDN'T GET THE bet out of my mind. Even when focused on other tasks, even when thinking about or talking to Lucy, it was consistently there. Miles didn't help this any. He clearly took a lot of pleasure in my discomfort, but then again, he took pleasure in all the things we competed in against each other. Wagers were no exception.

And I could help the Larkins with one thousand dollars. It seemed like chump change considering their debt, but an influx of cash like that might ease a little of their pain.

Except I had zero desire to win.

Lucy wasn't an object to "score" with. She wasn't a plaything or a hooker or a prize. She was the woman who made my heart thump and my insides constrict at the very thought of her. She had me wanting to whisk her back to the lake, spending all our time cuddled up beside the tree, watching the waves like we did that first day.

I couldn't help but mail her that poem, but then I wondered if maybe my motivations had been as pure as I originally told myself. Lucy loved her mail so much, I'd planned on mailing her a different classic every week. Miles would have considered this as a way for me to seduce her. The more I thought about it, the more I thought maybe he was right—or would have been if he'd known.

"I can't believe you're letting Miles screw with you," Alec said as we took turns practicing hitting at the baseball field in the park near his apartment today, the same day Lucy got her letter. "Just tell him enough is enough. No reason, no excuses. Just get the hell out of it."

"You know how he is. Remember when he harassed Ferguson for months when he backed out of a bet on whether Miles's sister would go out with him?"

"Yeah. Ferguson was crazy about her but never asked her out because of that."

"Exactly. Miles won, anyway. He always does, no matter what we do. This way, at least it's a fair shake, so to speak, and I won't have to be bullied about not following through."

Alec crashed his bat into what would be another double based on where it fell. "Can I ask why you get into these bets with Miles all the time?"

"It was never torture before. I used to enjoy things like this with him."

"Yeah, but he's an asshole. Doing these bets that you do, it makes you an asshole, too."

"Thanks, *friend*," I said in a pointed tone, removing the last ball we had from the bucket to hit.

He stood with his bat on the field, leaning his weight on it. "I am your friend. That's why I know I can say this. Tell Miles to go screw himself. You'll thank me later."

I considered this, saying nothing.

"You want crap from Miles, or crap from Lucy?"

"I'm going to get both no matter what at this point."

"Let me rephrase that. The way I see it, only one of them is going to forgive you. Because whatever you may think, that woman is crazy about you. It hasn't been that long. Cut out of the bet, beg Lucy for forgiveness, and move on together. Forget Miles."

He had a point. I knew he did.

But the next night, while watching the game at my house with all my coworker friends in attendance, I couldn't help but notice how easily Alec's voice was drowned out by Miles, and also Drea. They were the two loudest people in my life, and no matter how many times guilt consumed me when thinking of Lucy's sweet face, I knew I was stuck with things as they were.

Chapter 26

Lucy

"WHAT'S IN THE CAR?" Kenzie asked.

"My stuff," I told her.

We were at my parents' house today, the second exceptionally blistering Friday evening in August, prepping for our yard sale taking place tomorrow.

"The stuff you're selling?"

"Yes," I said slowly, wondering how she didn't get that. "I need help pricing it."

"You haven't priced anything yet?" Her voice was almost a shriek. "Didn't you read that article I sent you?"

"Of course I did."

"No, you didn't, because if you had, you'd know you have to price all the items before the morning of the sale."

"Kenz, this is before the morning of the sale," I replied in a tone as snarky as hers. I hadn't meant to do that.

Mom came out from the garage and joined us in the driveway.

Kenzie turned toward her. "Mom, where are the signs? I'd like to put them out now. We should have done that earlier this week." She sent me a side-eyed glance, knowing I was supposed to make the signs.

Except I hadn't. I forgot.

"You know what? Why don't we just work on getting things set up the way we want them, and I'll hang the flyers later," I said.

"You made flyers, too?" Mom asked.

Oops.

Nope. I had not.

There was no way I'd be able to make both so quickly. As it was, I needed to come up with an excuse to leave so I could run to the store and put some sort of sign together in a short amount of time.

"I meant signs," I corrected myself. "I'll put the signs up later."

"I really want to do them now," Kenzie told me.

"It can wait. Right, Kenzie?" I didn't wait for her to reply. "The most important thing is to get it all set up."

Kenzie relented. She looked to Mom again. "At least tell me where the balloons are so I can hang them at the end of the drive." Then Kenzie instantly looked at me and took in my expression. "Don't tell me you were in charge of those, too."

I hadn't wanted my parents spending their money on anything that wasn't essential, so I'd volunteered to get everything without cluing Kenzie in. I did actually buy the balloons, but hadn't remembered to bring them with me since I stupidly removed that bag from my car before loading it up with everything I wanted to sell.

"Things have been hectic at school," I began.

"I don't want to hear it," Kenzie snapped. "Things are hectic for all of us. Every single person has something in their life that takes up too much energy or time or brain capacity, but they still take care of their responsibilities."

She dug into her pocket and pulled out her keys, while tears began to burn my eyes. I blinked back as much moisture as I could.

"Where are you going?" I asked my sister.

"To fix what you didn't do."

"That's right, Kenz. Loser Lucy screws up again. Good thing I've got you to save the day."

She'd already started walking away before I finished speaking.

"I'll help you with your stuff," Mom told me with a sympathetic smile. It was the same one she always gave me when Kenzie had the upper hand.

Mom and I set to work unloading my car and putting sticky tags on everything. Pricing wasn't as hard as I thought it was going to be. Aunt Maria even stopped by for an hour to help, since she was the secondhand sales expert in our family. She knew the best bargains anywhere in the region, even as far as Pennsylvania, Vermont, and Connecticut. She also helped us rearrange some of the sale areas I thought I'd sorted really well.

By the time my aunt left, our hodge-podge sale looked more like designer displays in furniture or department stores. Similar items were mostly grouped together except for those that were being used as accents in the "vignettes" of Mom and Dad's for-sale furniture. Jade let us borrow display racks for clothes and jewelry from her store and had her brother Trevor deliver them to us.

However, even with all the help, organizing my classroom from scratch had been easier than this. I was glad to be done. Mom and I covered everything with tarps in case of rain or dew before the sale's start time. We didn't need to worry about people stealing any of our little stuff, and the rest was hard to move without making too much noise and drawing attention to the situation. Besides, no one ever robbed or burgled anyone else in Syracuse Falls. We pretty much had the lowest crime rate in the entire region, if not the state.

Mom and I sat down at the island for a cheese and cracker snack, wondering when Kenzie was coming back. Dad and Hayzel had already returned from her soccer practice. I was not about to text my sister. Mom did, but she only received a reply from Kenz saying she'd be back as soon as she could.

"Why don't you go home?" Mom suggested. "Kenzie and I can finish up here."

"You mean she won't come back if I'm still here." I knew I should go because I still had yard sale stuff I needed to finish—or start—whether or not my sister was going to do any of it. But then I didn't want Kenzie to win, and as ridiculous as this sounded in my head, it was exactly how I felt.

"I know your sister is a little hard on you sometimes."

"Just because I'm the youngest doesn't mean I'm incapable. There are a lot of other things I didn't forget to do. We've already gotten several bids on the items I listed online, as well as a few sales. At least four that I remember. I collected any bag or box that I could. And Kenzie's going to say, 'Well, I posted on social media and in groups and all the local papers.' By the way, I posted on social, too."

"I know you did," Mom told me, but I wasn't really listening to her. I wasn't intentionally ignoring her, either. I was just caught up in my frustration about my sister.

"No matter what I do, it's never as good as what Kenzie does." The sting of tears silenced me from saying more.

"Lucy, sweetheart, I understand. She needs to give you some grace. I do wish you'd do the same for her."

"I've given her more than enough."

We heard a car door close outside. Kenzie walked into the kitchen a minute or so later.

"I made and hung half a dozen signs. I also made and printed flyers and put them up in the diner, the grocery store, the pharmacy, the community center, and a few other places people will see them tonight or tomorrow morning. Jade's boutique and the nail and hair salons were already closed, so I'll try those first thing and hope someone's there." She avoided eye contact with me as she spoke.

I rapidly blinked my damp eyes since she wasn't looking. "Well, good night. I'll be back first thing in the morning."

"Bye." That was all Kenzie said, still looking anywhere but at me.

"Good night, sweetheart." Mom stood up and walked over to hug me.

I called goodbye to Dad and Hayzel and headed for the side door. I knew Mom and Kenzie were going to talk about me as soon as I left, but there wasn't anything I could do about it. All I could do was not cry in front of my stupid sister. At least maybe Mom could persuade her to understand that I was doing a lot more for the sale than Kenzie gave me credit for.

I texted both Lourdes and Gwenn once I was in my car.

Lourdes

You know your sister loves you, but she has a crappy way of showing it sometimes.

Gwenn

I have a couple showings, but I'll try to swing by and help in any way I can, and I'm totally available on Sunday.

I wasn't sure if I wanted help so much as a way for one of them to keep my sister away from my parents' house the entire weekend.

·♥·♥·♥·♥·♥·

When I arrived at Mom and Dad's this morning, I saw that, though I was by no means late, the yard sale was fully set up, including the money table and chairs and more stuff of my sister's I hadn't realized she was going to sell. Kenzie immediately gave me a roll of her eyes. I smiled in return, though I didn't want to.

Just as Aunt Maria instructed, there were no items down on the ground apart from furniture, floor lamps, and some exercise equipment. Before any customers showed, it was decided that Mom and Kenzie would handle the money and I would pack the items for the customers and also help with any "miscellaneous" duties. We didn't exactly vote on this. Kenzie pretended she'd just come up with this idea, and Mom went along with her because she didn't see any reason not to.

"Don't focus on your sister," Lourdes whispered to me while volunteering her help a little while later.

I acknowledged this, but wasn't sure I could take it to heart. My beloved sister was also the bane of my existence at this point. When I noticed a potential customer waving to get my attention, I walked over to see how I could be of assistance.

"Does this work?" she asked about a textured ceramic lamp I had put into the sale.

It was actually my favorite lamp I'd had in my living room, a dark chartreuse and teal beauty with a shell-like fabric shade. "It does," I replied with a kind smile.

"Can I see it?"

See it? Oh. I took hold of the cord and looked for a place to plug it in. Then I realized that we hadn't been able to dig out extension cords like Aunt Maria instructed us to. We'd decided to get them after everything was set up, but forgot.

"We don't actually have the extension cords out at the moment, but I promise you, it works."

"But how will I know what it looks like if I can't see it?"

"I'm sure you have an amazing imagination."

The older woman scoffed at me, clearly affronted.

"Here, Mrs. Lipowitz," Kenzie said, calmly hurrying over to us with Dad's orange extension cord. Kenzie plugged the lamp in for her, and of course the light lit right up.

"Oh, it's beautiful. Thank you, Kenzie! I'll take it," Mrs. Lipowitz said to her.

"Perfect! I can help you over here." My sister guided her to the table with the money box and extra packaging. Neither of them acknowledged me.

I moved the cord to an inconspicuous area where there was no danger of anyone tripping on it then returned to Lourdes. "Don't say it," I told her when she opened her mouth to speak. "I am trying to not let her get to me. I am going to be the bigger person and not dwell on her having just completely and unnecessarily taken over while cutting me out."

Lourdes patted my hand before helping me refold a few stacks of clothes that had been raked through. Gwenn sidled up next to us to help, greeting both of us. Another customer moved over to check out what kinds of goodies she could find in the pile. Her name was Mrs. Silver, a thin woman around my parents' age—someone I'd known since I was little.

I stepped away to help someone with the stupid extension cord again.

Then I heard Mrs. Silver say, "If the sale doesn't work, I'd love to buy the house."

Oof. That hurt. Never had I expected anyone from town to sound so giddy about owning my parents' property. I couldn't force myself to turn around and look at her, for fear I'd cry before getting a chance to say anything back.

Mrs. Silver must have been talking to Gwenn, because I heard Gwenn tell her, "I'm not sure if they're at that point yet."

"But you'd be the one listing it, correct?" Mrs. Silver asked her.

Gwenn reluctantly agreed that she would be. Though this surprised me at first, I assumed my parents must have already had this conversation with her in the past.

I finally turned to the both of them, keeping my eyes on Mrs. Silver for the moment. "I guess you'll just have to wait. We aren't giving any tours today." I practically breathed fire at her.

Gwenn calmly led Mrs. Silver over to a hanging rack of more sweaters and dresses, then returned to me and apologized.

"No need." I waved a hand in her direction. "She's callous and rude. You didn't do anything wrong."

"It doesn't make this any easier on you."

"No." I shook my head slowly. "It doesn't."

By the end of the weekend, far more was still on my parents' lawn than I'd expected. *Far* more. With all of our stuff together—including Dominic's, who came through and added to the sale even though he was still doubtful of it—we'd only sold a tiny fraction.

The total? Two hundred fifty-seven dollars. That was it.

I'd never been so disappointed about people not spending money.

All that work and nothing to show for it. That amount of money wouldn't put even a tiny little ding in my parents' debt, let alone any significant dent.

The more I thought about it, though, the more I realized I was wrong. That was over two hundred dollars more than we had before. Something was better than nothing. And perhaps a lot of little somethings could add up to a greater thing that might actually be able to do some good. But this was for me to ruminate on for a while and not bother anyone else with.

When my brother showed up later, I instantly put my hand up to stop him. "Don't say a word."

"Wasn't going to," he replied with a small shake of his head, but his jaw was tense, like it was taking a lot of effort to stay quiet and not rub it in my face that he was right and I was wrong about how well the sale was going to do.

We'd arranged for a charity truck to come pick up some of the items none of us wanted back, but I had an idea brewing for some of my stuff I still had at home.

Chapter 27

Lucy

Monday evening, I was all ready for community garden volunteer work, dressed in navy-blue leggings that were comfy but a little ratty and an oversize saffron-yellow T-shirt. I was just about to put on my gardening shoes when I received a new text.

Gwenn

Sorry Luce . . . I'm a little too tired to work in the garden today.

Oh no . . . what's wrong?

Idk. It started this weekend.

You were okay at the yard sale.

I was still feeling it then, but tried to ignore something that just can't be ignored anymore.

. . .

Maybe it's this gorgeous ROCK I have to carry around on my hand . . .

I immediately received a photo of Gwenn's left hand, and sure enough, there was a beautiful engagement ring on a certain meaningful finger.

You're getting married!

I'm getting married!!!!!

We have to celebrate!!!

Rhett

Hey, Luce. You can celebrate tomorrow. Tonight, she's all mine.

Rhett actually sent me a winking emoji along with his message. He rarely used emojis, so I knew how serious he was. I was so proud of him and so happy for them both. I replied to them together in one text.

Tomorrow it is! Love you guys!

I drove over to the garden anyway, finding my mom and Lourdes's mom already there. Lourdes showed up a little bit later. We chatted about Gwenn's engagement, but then needed to get to work. The most recent monthly dinner the garden volunteers held, made up mostly of fresh produce from the garden itself as well as other local ingredients, had been a hit, but Lourdes and our moms were already focused on the next one. Since I wasn't as good with the veggies as I was the flowers, I went over to the bed of pink coneflowers to weed and water.

My mom was nearby in the milkweeds.

"What do you think?" I asked her.

"Looks good," she said.

"You think everyone's going to complain if we keep the dinners on Friday now instead of Saturday? I heard a lot of grumbling the other night."

Mom wiped her forehead with a clean part of the back of her hand. "I wish I could say it'll be fine, but honestly, it doesn't look so good."

I knew what else didn't look so good. The bills. The mortgage. The debt. It was a lot to tackle at once. I chose to block out the negative thoughts I could, not that this worked in any way. Those Negative Nelly voices just nagged and nagged.

The next night, though, was all about bestie time, no stress allowed.

Gwenn, Lourdes, and I sat in Gwenn's apartment drinking her fave wine and listening to her tell the story of Rhett's proposal. Lourdes had apparently known ahead of time, only because Rhett needed her help to make everything the way he wanted it, including the fresh flowers she provided. I was okay with that, because my happiness for Gwenn and Rhett did not hinge on knowing ahead of time.

And though I was so amazed by the story and delighted at this turn of events in my bestie's life, I couldn't help but think of my own relationship—or future relationship—with Pete. I could see this happening for us clear as day.

Yes, I'd asked to be friends first. And yes, I wanted to be wooed. Pete was doing exactly that. I had no choice but to fall even harder for him, day after day. He was the most incredible man, the very best I'd ever met. It felt like destiny. I mentioned this about Rhett and Gwenn as well.

"It might be destiny," Lourdes said in reply, "but they still have to work at it. Fate has no control over real-life situations."

"Are you saying I need to remember this, too?" I asked.

"I think it wouldn't hurt to remind yourself of it once in a while. I don't believe in it, but let's say I do. If you and Pete are meant to be, just as you believe Gwenn and Rhett are, don't assume things will be peachy all the rest of your lives. Minimal effort results in minimal payoff. Even in relationships."

Gwenn, Rhett, and I settled into a booth at the diner a couple days later for a quick dinner. We'd all just finished up with work, or were putting it aside for the moment, in both my case and Gwenn's. I waved to my sister, letting her know we were here. Kenzie nodded back, then started taking her customers' orders. Dottie came to our table with a paper pad and a pencil, though I'm pretty sure she didn't need them. Rarely did Dottie ever have to write down the orders of her regulars, which included the three of us.

"Coffee?" she asked.

"Yes, please," I told her. Gwenn and Rhett said the same.

"Ready to order?"

"A few minutes, please," Gwenn said. "We're waiting on Lourdes."

"I'll get those coffees," Dottie said with a smile.

She didn't need to ask how we liked them. They would be perfect anyway.

Dottie walked away to the coffee carafes, and the three of us began to peruse the menus. The bell on the door rang. I looked up to see our friend rushing in.

"Sorry I'm late," Lourdes said as she hurried over to our booth, her nearly black hair bouncing with the movement.

I scooted to let her sit on my side. Dottie returned with four cups of coffee instead of three and began placing them on the table. We thanked her, and she walked away again to give us a little more time.

"Have you started on the guest list?" Lourdes asked Gwenn.

Gwenn and Rhett looked at each other, then Gwenn said, "Not yet."

"But . . ." I said, leaving room for her to finish my sentence.

Neither Gwenn nor her fiancé said anything.

"What's going on?" Lourdes pressed.

"Nothing," Gwenn finally told us.

"What was that look between you two?" I prodded. "Something's going on."

The bell on the door rang again, indicating more customers had come in. Kenzie appeared at the end of the table by Rhett and Lourdes.

"Dottie had to take a phone call," my sister told us. "She asked me to get your order."

I still hadn't made up my mind. Neither had my companions. We quickly settled on four burgers and two baskets of chili cheese fries to share. I added a chocolate-strawberry milkshake.

Kenzie was still at our table when Rhett said slowly in his Southern drawl, "It really is nothin'. I just thought maybe we should invite Edin to the wedding."

Lourdes and I gasped.

"Why?" Lourdes asked in a sharp tone.

"You can't do that!" I exclaimed at the same time.

Gwenn calmly sipped her coffee.

Rhett's phone beeped. "I gotta take this," he said, then he slid out of the booth and stepped away.

"You can't let him do that," I said to Gwenn as soon as Rhett was out of earshot.

"I don't see what the big deal is," Kenzie told us.

"You wouldn't," I retorted. "Edin's your new bestie."

"Maybe she learned her lesson," Kenzie replied in the tone she used to convey the fact that she thought since she was older, she was automatically wiser than me.

I rolled my eyes. "It wasn't that long ago that she was just awful to both of them," I told my sister in a tone that matched her self-righteous attitude.

Kenzie ignored me and focused on Gwenn. "Do you think she'd show up in a white dress?"

Gwenn took a moment, then replied, "No."

"Would she stand up and object?"

"She's your friend. Shouldn't you know these things about her?" I asked Kenzie.

"Not the time, Luce," she said. She didn't exactly snap at me, but her tone was unkind. She focused on Gwenn again. "Would Edin make a hate speech about you at the reception? Jump on or tackle Rhett to keep him from saying 'I do'? Lock you away in a bathroom? Cause a scene in any way?"

Gwenn gave a head shake. "No, I don't think she would."

"Then what does it hurt to invite her?"

"Kenzie!" Dottie called.

My sister walked away without saying any more to us.

"You can't listen to her," I told Gwenn. "Lourdes knows I'm right."

"Well—" Lourdes began.

I didn't give her time to finish. "Kenzie could be wrong," I insisted.

Then I saw Rhett making his way back to the table. "When will you have to decide?" I asked Gwenn.

"Within a week," she answered.

Rhett returned and sat next to his fiancée again. We quickly and smoothly moved on to other topics, but I still had a knot in my stomach. I knew this had to be Edin's doing. Why did that truly awful woman think she was entitled to anything else from my bestie's fiancé? Why couldn't she just go away?

Why couldn't all the awful women go away?

Chapter 28

Lucy

"WHAT. IS. THAT?" I nearly shouted. I was hanging out with Lourdes at the house she grew up in early Saturday morning. It was a rare occurrence to be in this house ever since she moved back home after her grandmother fell ill and moved in with Lourdes's mom as well. Her mom and Great Uncle Sal had taken her grandma out for the morning, but were expected home in the early afternoon for a family picnic that Lourdes's Gam-Gam asked for.

"What?" Lourdes came around the kitchen island to the side I stood on and looked over at my phone.

"Miss Havisham" apparently hadn't been happy just DMing me vague references to some man. I'd suspected it was about my principal and/or the annexation, or maybe even about my sometimes asshole of a brother. Now Havisham had gone public, but in a way that took me abso-freaking-lutely by surprise. And dang.

There was Pete's picture on a social media app. The caption read: *Don't trust this man!!!*

"Holy crap!" Lourdes said. "I mean, I know people probably get mad at him during the course of his job sometimes, but to go public like this is crap."

"Do things like this ever happen to you?"

"I get really nasty reviews occasionally. Usually from anonymous people."

"Pete said there are bots that do that, too."

"I believe that."

"Do you think that's what this is?"

"I think if they are targeting Pete but sending it to you, someone might be stalking him. You should have a chat with him about that. Figure out options of where to go from here."

After several deep, cleansing breaths—well, what I hoped would be cleansing breaths, though the panic hung around—I called Pete.

"Yeah, I already saw it." His voice was tight and a little flat. It was like he was shutting out any emotion attached to this issue. "I don't want to talk about it right now, but I will do everything I can to get it taken down."

"You okay?" I asked. This couldn't be easy for him.

"Don't worry," he said.

I noticed this wasn't an answer to my question. "How can you get it taken down? Does it violate any of their rules?" This was a promising thought. Maybe that horrible post would be gone by the end of the day.

"I'll look into it," he reassured me.

"If you want me to help, let me know." But I knew I'd look into it, too, with or without Pete knowing.

"What are you doing later today?" he asked.

"I'm with Lourdes now, and I was just going to hang around at home later when she has a family thing."

There were a few silent beats before Pete spoke again. "Maybe I can hang out with you at home?"

I smiled before I answered. "Love that."

Pete found me in my backyard a few hours later, sitting on my swing, reading *Jane Eyre* and drinking some ice-cold strawberry lemonade. He greeted me with a kiss on the side of my head, then eyed my book.

"In the mood for a little romance today," I responded to his questioning look.

"Is it romantic, though? Or is it just as bad as *Gatsby*?"

"You stop!" I laughed, though I knew he was serious, and kissed his cheek.

Then Pete noticed something in my yard I'd been ignoring. Focusing on it previously would have required me to ask my dad for help, and he wasn't able to. Or I would have to ask my brother, who would be unwilling. At the very least, if Dom did help, he wouldn't stop grumbling about what a pain the whole situation was. I didn't want to listen to that.

My neighbors were willing to help, too, but I hadn't asked them and also hadn't allowed them to volunteer. Part of me thought I could just take care of it myself, except I actually couldn't.

"How long has that tree been down? All its leaves look like they've been eaten off."

"The deer liked their new snack. It fell in that super windy thunderstorm."

"Luce, that was weeks ago."

I shrugged, hoping it was believable. "I don't mind it."

"You don't mind having what is essentially now a log take up half your yard?"

Okay, so I did mind.

"Who has a chainsaw around here?" Pete asked, his eyes focused on mine.

I told him the next-door neighbors to the east were the best choice. "I think they own three different chainsaws, but it's really not a big deal. It doesn't actually need done."

Pete nodded his head in a nonchalant way. "Okay." He breathed in and let it out as he kissed my temple, then he lingered for a moment before stepping back. "Do you have any more of that lemonade left? It smells delicious."

I set my book and drink down on the small glass table next to me. "I have half a pitcher left. Would you like me to get you some?"

"Sure," Pete replied with an easy smile.

I went through the back door into my tiny kitchen. After a quick wash of my hands, I grabbed a clean glass from the cabinet and the pitcher of lemonade from the fridge. Once the glass was full of a little ice, a few slices of strawberry, and a lot of lemonade, I returned to the yard. Pete wasn't there.

Still holding onto the glass, I spun around and searched with my eyes. Pete wouldn't just leave, would he? It didn't help that I was in the backyard and unable to see the road from my vantage point.

Then Pete came walking back through the gate with a chainsaw I recognized as my neighbor's.

"You were serious."

He nodded. "Yep. Your grass is too long, and this thing is a hazard." He motioned to the dead tree.

I watched in awe as Pete started up the chainsaw and began trimming off the branches. Then he moved on to the bigger limbs before tackling the trunk. Not much time had passed when I noticed just how sweaty this work was making him, especially in this oppressive heat. No matter how much my brain told me to get back to my book, my eyes wouldn't look away.

By the time Pete made it to the trunk, he was shirtless and drenched. I was literally drooling. I was also pissed when my phone let out the sound of my sister's ringtone.

"What's up?" I answered.

Unfortunately, I had no idea what she responded. Pete was wiping his forehead with his muscular arm, each curve and ripple begging for a wipe down from yours truly.

"Hello? You still there?" Kenzie's voice called out.

"Yeah. Yep. Sorry."

"What's going on? Why do I hear a chainsaw so close?"

I told her what my non-boyfriend was up to.

"Have you considered just jumping him already to get it out of your system?"

Every. Single. Day. But that was the point of the experiment. To see if we could develop feelings beyond the physical or the immediate. "Trust me, I can hold as much desire as he stirs in me. The time for jumping him, as you put it, will come. Until then, I'm more than happy to touch with my eyes only."

Pete turned off the motorized saw again and stepped near me for another drink of his still-cold lemonade—only because I'd added extra ice cubes for him. He caught my gaze and grinned.

"Maybe not 'more than happy,'" I said to my sister slowly as I gaped at Pete.

"He's distracting you, isn't he?" she asked.

I was quiet, watching his muscles ripple and flex as he returned to the downed tree. Maybe I needed to rethink a few things. But I couldn't admit this out loud.

As if able to read my mind, my sister said, "You are not a quitter for giving in before the six months are up. Having seen that man, I'd say you've earned a medal for holding out this long."

I couldn't agree more.

"Look, Charisma said a mutual friend of theirs showed her this awful social media post about Pete."

"It's nothing," I was quick to reply.

Pete started revving the chainsaw when he caught me staring at him, his muscles rippling more than they were before he noticed. And if I wasn't certain of being caught, his smirk told me everything.

I laughed. My skin immediately flushed. "Can't talk now, sis."

Kenzie laughed, too. "Okay, ogle your sexy non-boyfriend. And don't be afraid to get a little hands-on."

Chapter 29

Pete

"Mr. Shubin would like to see you in his office, please, Pete," my boss's secretary told me early Monday morning.

This was not good. There were any number of things he could have to speak to me about—my bet with Miles, my ties to the Larkins, and those damn viral social media posts. I mean, why the hell did tens of thousands of people care that I was an asshole? I wasn't the only guy to be a jerk sometimes, and it wasn't even like I'd done anything that bad. Choosing to sleep around when free to do so didn't feel like the kind of thing that should garner worldwide condemnation.

Shubin said nothing when I entered his office. He only turned his computer screen my way, giving me a full view yet again of one of the posts and the attached comments.

"This looks bad. I know," I began, before my boss put a hand up to silence me.

"I've never seen this kind of attack happen to someone I know personally," Shubin told me. "I don't know how it feels for you. I don't care to know. That's your business." He motioned around his office. "This is my business. These posts have the ability to greatly damage the bank's reputation. People are smart, and even if they aren't, it isn't difficult to tap on the keys a few times and dig up whatever one wants to know about someone else, including where they work."

I nodded but didn't speak.

"Any public photos of you relating to this job won't be too difficult to find, whether from our charity events or our customer service picnics. It's out there for anyone to see. Just because your name isn't attached to the viral posts doesn't mean it can't be uncovered by someone. Just look at the comments. I'm shocked not one of these women called you out by name yet."

So was I, to be honest.

Shubin sat higher in his chair. "Get your private life back to being private again, Amundsen. The sooner, the better. We need people to trust us. It's of the utmost importance when we are asking them to trust us with their finances and their home and automobile loans. You screw with this company's good image—especially after the recent merger—and you're gone."

I couldn't help but let a breath out. It was by no means over yet, but at least I wasn't fired on the spot. I thanked my boss, for what I wasn't entirely sure, and made a beeline to Alec's office. He wasn't there. After asking his secretary, I found him trapped in Miles's office. Well, trapped in the sense that Miles wouldn't shut up about whatever it was that Alec clearly didn't want to listen to.

"Pete!" Miles boomed when he saw me. He barked out a laugh. "We were just talking about you."

"What for?" I asked in a weary tone. I could already tell I wouldn't like the answer.

"It's freaking hilarious," Miles said by way of a reply.

"As I tried to explain to him, Shubin has every right to worry about the company's image, and you have every right to worry about your own," Alec said to me, clearly attempting to avoid giving Miles some pretty heavy side-eye at his guffaws. "Tess is worried, too."

The assistants must have been talking again for them to know all of this.

"It's bull is what it is," I told them. "I think I just narrowly missed getting fired."

"So you need those thousand bucks even more, huh?"

"Is that all you think about?" Alec turned to Miles. "The bet?"

It was sometimes all I thought about, but for a very different reason.

Miles relaxed his laughing a bit. "Come on, bro," he said to Alec. "It's all in good fun. And if Pete wants to win, you know it's going to be some *real good* fun."

I hated my friend. That was the point I'd reached. I hated what was happening to me online, I hated feeling like I had to keep a wedge between me and Lucy, and I hated the man who once was my best friend. Well, my best "have fun and forget everything else" friend, because honestly, that's all Miles had ever been good for.

"I'm going to start with the social platform first and see if there's anything they can do to remove those posts. I'll move on from there." I gave Miles a quick nod and turned to leave.

Alec followed with me and shut Miles's door behind him. "What have you told Lucy about this?"

"Nothing. I mentioned it could be bots doing this for blackmail or extortion."

"While that definitely happens, you think maybe you should fess up and tell her you know a lot of those women in the comments section? That they're telling the truth?"

"No way. I'm not adding to the damaging evidence that's already against me. She might forgive me for one or a few of those things, but I highly doubt she'd be willing to forgive me for all of it." I paused, feeling like a dark, ugly shadow was passing over me. "I told her I didn't want to discuss it, but Lucy still mentioned her suspicion that someone might be stalking me. That it may be the reason for the anonymous messages to her before things went public."

"I can't tell you that she'll forgive you, but not admitting the truth now will not help you in the future."

When I found Tess later in the day, she told me the same thing.

"Maybe I should hire an investigator. Find out who's doing this shit."

Tess was already shaking her head before I finished the second sentence.

"Why not?" I asked, scowling.

"Could it be a stalker? Maybe. But chances are high that an ex knows someone who knows someone else who knows Lucy. You've dated a *lot* of women, Pete. And I'm sure those disgruntled exes will only double down if you try to go at them legally. Besides, the investigator is going to find a lot of history on you in the process. Do you really want to relive your more asshole-ish days?"

She had a point. A trip down memory lane most certainly did not appeal to me. "I can't just sit on my hands and allow those women to destroy me."

"I agree, but maybe hold off on hiring a PI right now. If it gets to a point where either you or Lucy feel unsafe, then bring in the pros."

"You think I can ask Kevin in IT to help?"

She gave a laugh of obvious disbelief. "You seriously want to add another conflict of interest into this mess?"

No. No, I didn't. Tess pulled out her phone. "I'm texting you the number of a friend who might be able to help. He has a degree in computer science. Start with him, and go from there."

I gave her a side hug of thanks, and rushed back to my office, anxious to get those posts removed ASAP.

Chapter 30

Lucy

I HAD A PLAN, and I was sticking to the plan. I got six hundred bucks for one of my rolling carts at the end of August and a hundred for my coffee table earlier this month. If I was savvy enough, I thought perhaps I could get five hundred out of my vintage bed frame before September ended. I only paid one hundred seventy-five for it, but I'd cleaned it up and refinished it. It had to be worth at least five. I couldn't care less about my box spring and mattress ending up on the floor.

Pete wasn't suspicious of my "it's in storage" reply for the things he noticed missing. I hoped it would be the same for the frame. However, Gwenn and Lourdes were going to notice its absence for sure. They knew the yard sale was a bust. I needed to figure out a way to explain that selling my stuff was the only other thing I could do to help Mom and Dad.

I couldn't exactly get loans to help them. I was still in debt from college. Couldn't sell my car, either. I was literally out of other options.

Then I started to get that familiar swell of anger. It wasn't Pete's fault. My brain knew that. But damn it, why wasn't he doing more?

If he was falling in love with me as much as I knew he was, surely that love had to extend to my family. How could he just abandon family?

My phone beeped in a "new message" tone. It was from Miss Havisham. "She" sent screenshots of a post from social media—three different platforms. This time, it was a picture of Pete with his faced crossed out like a "no U-turn" sign. The text on the pic said, "Stay away! He's a liar!"

The original post had several likes and comments, but my stomach churned at the thought of reading what the comments said. Probably the same mixture as always. Some agreeing with the post, some saying that wasn't the right way to go about it, and some just there for fun.

While I still had my phone in my hand, and because I desperately needed a distraction, I checked the calendar. It told me that my seashell chandelier auction was over. The gorgeous, creamy-white light fixture sold for ninety-two dollars. I opened the app I was using to keep track of sales. Including the abysmal yard sale, I'd made over a thousand dollars. I was well on my way to my goal.

If I could just raise ten thousand on my own, surely the mortgage underwriter would see that our family really was doing our best and give us a break. We'd been through so much already. My parents had been through too much. My dad struggled for years and years, hiding his pain and discomfort and dizzy spells from us, not wanting to scar our childhood, as he once put it.

My eyes and throat burned at the thought of him being so desperately ill and still being the happy-go-lucky dad we'd always known, wearing a smile through it all. He took all our whines and complaints and bitch fests with such grace. Grace that I, for one, didn't think I'd deserved.

Never had I complained so much as when we didn't go to the cabin. I was a brat, and I hated having to live with those memories.

My parents didn't tell the three of us about Dad's condition until the year I'd turned twenty. That meant he hid his cardiac issues for almost eight years.

Whenever I thought back to that time, I pictured my dad all alone in a hospital room because Mom had to be home with me—since Kenzie and Dom were older by that point—pretending everything was okay. I was certain Mom was a nervous wreck those days, but Dad must have been absolutely terrified.

He was never one to shy away from expressing his emotions. Dad cried freely when needed. He named his feelings out loud. He told all three of us kids to never be ashamed of feeling something other than happiness. So the thought of him in the hospital by himself, crying out all the tears of pain and fear, gave me my own chest pains of a different kind. Dad did not deserve to lose his home because of his heart. Despite its physical ailments, my dad had the best heart of anyone I knew.

How could my friends be shocked at me for wanting to do all I could to help this amazing man keep the home they'd lived in for over thirty years?

I hadn't told my family about selling my stuff yet. The time wasn't right. Mom and I had already begged Kenzie not to give up her diamond necklace. The yard sale was just full of unneeded items, a few of which I had sold online. Most ended up being donated. Selling things I used every day was going to require a good spin, and I was fresh out of stories at the moment. I needed more time.

It was easy enough keeping Dom away. He almost never visited my house anyway because we saw each other so often at Mom and Dad's, and sometimes Kenzie's. I'd told my parents and Kenzie that I was still organizing all my back-to-school stuff and wanted visitors to wait until I was all done to come over. They'd grumbled a bit about this, though, and I wasn't sure how long the ruse would last. I couldn't stay in "back-to-school" mode forever. Kenzie didn't seem to mind as much. She was still pissed at me for the whole yard sale thing. It didn't matter how many times I apologized.

Pete

Did you see it?

The new post.

Yep. Hard not to when Havisham DMs screenshots of them to me.

She still at that?

I answered in the affirmative. Then I just couldn't hold back any longer.

I don't want to kick you when you're down . . .

But . . . ?

But there has to be something you can do that's within your limits. I'm not asking for anything illegal.

There was a *long* pause before Pete replied. So much so that I wasn't sure I'd even get a response.

I'm doing all I can, which isn't much of anything. I'm not allowed to do more. And I'm so sorry about this, Luce. I'm sorry for what you and your family are going through over this.

> I don't want you to feel sorry for me. I want you to help me.

> But I can't. That's my point.

I knew it was true. He'd asked me not to discuss this with him for a reason because he knew it would only break my heart. Pete was right, and I hated myself for begging him to do something when he had no power over it.

> Still want to talk?

> I never want to stop talking with you.

> Good

He even added a smiley face, which was new. Pete wasn't one for emojis. This brought a smile to my own face. We spent the rest of the evening on the phone, first texting, then on a three-hour phone call. Neither of us mentioned the social posts or the mortgage fiasco. It was four solid hours of absolute bliss.

Chapter 31

Pete

"WHAT WOULD YOU SAY to a camping trip with me and my friends?" I asked Lucy on Tuesday afternoon.

Alec and I were about to take our annual beginning of October trip—the last weekend the park was open for the season—even though this year was a little chillier than usual. Alec's brother and a few of our other mutual friends often came along, but Miles and Drea were both off the guest list. It was the perfect chance to spend more time with Lucy.

"Or is that even allowable as my friend and not my girlfriend?"

"I don't have a tent," Lucy replied.

I'd hoped she would have picked up on the flirty tone, or maybe she just ignored it. "How do you feel about sharing mine?"

I waited for her to respond.

"Tempted."

This made me smile to myself. "Would you like me to bring a tent for you to use?"

Of course, this wasn't the kind of talk that would get me the thousand dollars for her parents. I should have been smoother. It wasn't like I didn't know how. Then I started to doubt the whole thing. Maybe I should have just told her we'd go a different time. I wasn't sure. It was feeling too much like a con on my part, and I hated that.

"We can share a tent," she said, breaking through my thoughts. "It's okay."

I was happy, but unsure whether I actually should be.

"I'll meet you at your place," Lucy continued. "Follow you from there."

"What makes you think you won't drive over with me?"

"Won't you have your friends with you? I don't want to inconvenience anyone."

"Neither do I, but I also don't want to miss the opportunity to spend more alone time with you."

"How can I refuse that?" I loved hearing the smile in her voice.

Then we got to the park Friday morning, and all hints of Lucy's smile were gone. We found that Miles, Corkie, and Drea had all crashed our weekend. Drea was the one to cause this reaction in Lucy, but both Drea and Miles had me on edge. All I could do was focus on Lucy as much as possible and ignore those other two.

Once we had the tent set up, Lucy commented on its small size. I was glad Miles wasn't within earshot. Otherwise, he would have said something immature like, "You better hope that's the only thing she thinks is small."

But even without him around, he was still in my brain, playing tricks on me.

"I'm sorry I can't afford to buy my own tent right now," Lucy added.

She easily could have borrowed one. I could have borrowed one for her, too. We both seemed determined to tempt ourselves. I was torn about us doing this. I was also torn about only having one sleeping bag to share with her.

"Don't worry about it," I told her. "We'll be okay like this."

I was not making a single move on her without her starting it first, that was for sure. I didn't want it to come off as me taking advantage of her.

But it was still going to be me taking advantage of her even if she made the first move, all because of that bet.

This line of thinking hung around in my brain. So much so that every time Lucy tried to be near me, with her hand on my arm or her leg touching mine, I found myself moving away. Not because it was unwanted—quite the opposite. I wanted everything she offered to me, including those gorgeous smiles. I just couldn't handle the guilt. It gnawed unceasingly.

With every lame excuse and every rebuff of her cute flirting, Lucy's smile dropped a little further down. Not as much on her mouth, but definitely in her eyes. I hoped she would think it was because I was trying to respect our six-month rule. Honestly, though, I knew better. I saw it on her face. She had no idea what was going on, and I had no way of telling her, as much as I desperately wanted to.

After a campfire lunch of burgers and roasted potatoes, Lucy walked over to the car. I was afraid maybe she was mad, but she quickly returned with a paper bag. From inside, she removed a bag of marshmallows, a few bars of chocolate, and two kinds of graham crackers.

I thought it brilliant she'd brought all that along, since my friends and I often wanted s'mores but never bothered buying the stuff to make them.

"Oh, how quaint," Drea commented, her syrupy tone dripping with acidic sarcasm. "S'mores for adults. And nothing decadent or sophisticated in sight. My dream."

"S'mores are a great idea," I said, giving Lucy a bright smile. Then I moved a little closer to her and kissed the side of her head.

Lucy smiled at me, but it was clear she understood Drea's intentions.

"We should totally have s'mores," Drea added, her tone now light after a dirty look from both me and Alec. "I haven't had them since I was a teenager."

"What about that time I ate marshmallow cream and chocolate syrup off you?" Miles asked her.

Lucy was understandably shocked. Her eyebrows jumped five inches, and she turned to me with wide eyes, silent.

From the corner of my eye, I could see that Corkie's head dropped a bit as she ignored her friend and her fiancé. Leave it to Miles to destroy people with no thought as to the repercussions.

"Oh, I forgot," Drea said with a laugh, as if it was a totally normal conversation and not uncomfortable at all.

Corkie stood up. "I'm going for a walk by myself." She turned to but didn't look at Miles. "We don't talk about exes, remember?" Then she was off.

Lucy's phone beeped. I looked her way when she ignored it. She never ignored messages.

"What's up?" I asked in a whisper.

She shook her head. "Just Charisma. Apparently found another link to those posts and thought we should know."

"Why does it matter to her?" My voice was barely more than a grumble. Then I reminded myself that Charisma was Lucy's friend.

Lucy kept her voice low, too. "She doesn't want us to get hurt. She and I grew up together. This isn't an easy thing to deal with." Lucy motioned to her phone, which I understood to mean the smear campaign against me.

Lucy and I didn't talk any more about it. We all made the s'mores, anyway even though none of us still seemed in the mood. Lucy roasted the marshmallows over the fire with a stick I found and sharpened. No one else wanted that task. Honestly, we all either felt or looked like we wanted to get the heck away from the campsite and everyone else.

Well, I still wanted to be around Lucy, only she kept putting her soft, smooth hand on my arm again. I could just barely feel the heat of it coming through my sweatshirt sleeve, and if it hadn't been chilly, I would have shoved my sleeves up all the way so we could have skin-on-skin contact.

After s'mores clean-up, Miles and I had a moment alone. He turned to me with his goofy, up-to-something grin. "This is it, bro. I've been watching your girl. You're about to get a grand from me, and I'm not even mad about it." Then he laughed.

He might not have been mad, but I was. Actually, I was more than mad. I was livid. How had it gotten this far? I was about to destroy Lucy's trust in me. I probably already had, only she didn't know it yet. George's words still rang in my ears. *"You'll find the right solution."*

And so I did. Without being able to remove myself from the wager, there was only one honorable thing to do, or as honorable as it could get. I wouldn't sleep with Lucy. Even if she begged me. I seriously hoped she wouldn't end up begging me because the hurt and confusion on her face just might kill me.

We just had to make it through one night of camping in the same tent, then I could make up an excuse as to why we needed to leave. But that was hours and hours away.

Corkie hadn't returned by the time we decided to walk down to the volleyball area. I'd hoped with her around, maybe Lucy would have another new friend to talk to. That maybe Corkie could drown out the bitchiness of Drea. Granted, this was made more difficult without Tess. Tess was good at shutting Miles and Drea down when necessary.

As it was, Lucy only had me and Alec on her side, though she didn't know Alec all that well.

At some point—having already played three games of volley-ball—Lucy lost interest in being a spectator. "I'm just going down to the beach," she came over and told me as I was about to start my second set, this time with Drea as my partner.

Alec and Miles were on the other side.

"Maybe I'll find Corkie and see if she's okay," Lucy added in a whisper.

"That's a good idea," I replied. Lucy wasn't the only one worried about Corkie, though the two who should have cared the most didn't seem to.

After playing a while, Drea spiked the ball so far out of the court that Alec had to run and get it. Miles pulled out his phone, but based on his smirk, I doubted he was texting Corkie. Drea sidled up to me in their absence.

"We're doing great, partner," she said with a smile.

"What?"

Drea motioned to the net. "The game. We're doing great."

"Oh. Yeah, I guess."

She stepped closer and reached out to my face. Her hand barely brushed against my chin before I could move out of the way. This didn't faze her. "I'm surprised you're hiding your sexy face behind all that hair."

I gave no answer. Instead, I searched in the area Lucy went, hoping to catch sight of her. Alec wasn't back yet, either, the ball having rolled toward a group of people he seemed to know one of. He couldn't come back fast enough. I silently willed him to head our way, but he didn't budge.

"It's for Lucy, isn't it?" Drea pushed.

"What?" I asked again.

She rolled her eyes playfully. "The beard. I can't believe she'd want you to keep that. You're far too sexy without it. You'd think she'd know that."

Again, I gave no reply.

Then Drea pushed even harder. "It's like you two are married. She gets what she wants—with no sex, of course—and you get . . . what exactly?"

Damn. That one got under my skin.

"You are way off-base."

"Off-base about what?" Miles asked, finally cognizant of the fact that Drea and I were still around.

"They're practically married." Drea said this to him with a laugh Miles was familiar with. He laughed about things in the same derogatory way. "She's making him keep his beard, though I've seen lots of photos of him without one. She's hardly said anything to us, his friends. And she won't have sex with him."

"If sex is off the table, Corkie can forget the wedding," Miles said with an easy tone, like their engagement was a joke.

I ignored him, too.

After staring in Alec's direction and catching his gaze, I waved him over. He brought a couple people from the group with him, and we played a few more games before heading over to the beach for a break. We found Lucy and Corkie there, the latter having gotten over what her dense fiancé said earlier that afternoon.

Finally, it was late enough and we were tired enough for bed. But this brought back a reminder of the other problem. Lucy and I had to share a sleeping bag.

We lay in our shared bed with Lucy's back against my chest and my arms wrapped snugly around her.

"That was an interesting conversation Miles started," Lucy said.

"Yeah. He doesn't always follow Corkie's rule of no discussing exes."

"I hadn't realized they had that kind of history."

"Corkie and Drea were friends before either of them slept with Miles. I think Corkie liked Miles longer, but Drea is one of those gets-what-she-wants types."

"Gee, I hadn't noticed." Lucy's tone took on the same sharp sarcasm that Drea's had earlier that day. "Well, she at least tries hard. I hope she won't get *everything* she wants."

I nuzzled closer to my beautiful non-platonic friend, giving her body a squeeze. The warmth of Lucy had me sweaty for quite a few different reasons. I had to shift our bodies so as to avoid a certain suddenly urgent one. "She won't. I promise."

"What about you?" Lucy asked, not bothering to stay where I moved her. She'd scooted all the way back to lie against me again.

My muscles stiffened. "What about me?"

"Your exes. I've told you how often I used to fall in love and how many men I've dated. You never mention your past."

This was not the conversation I wanted to have with her. I heaved a sigh. "I've never had any STIs. I've never been married or lived with a girlfriend. I'm not sure I ever considered anyone my girlfriend. I don't have any kids. I have never abused anyone nor will I ever."

"I know all that, or figured it out." She turned her head enough to look in my eyes expectantly.

"Why do you need more?" I asked. But I wasn't asking because she didn't deserve the truth. I asked because I was ashamed of the rest of my story. Those social media posts didn't exist for no reason. I'd moved on from hoping it was a bot or a plan for blackmail. Nope. It was good, old-fashioned, unadulterated—and well-deserved—hate for yours truly.

"I guess numbers don't matter," Lucy eventually replied.

She rolled to face me completely, my arms still around her. That was a skill I thoroughly enjoyed watching and feeling.

"Why is this so hard?" I asked, kissing her forehead.

She gave me a sly smile. "We both know why."

I chuckled. "Not that. Why is it so hard to think if you as only my friend?"

"I hope we both have the same reason for that, too."

At this, I nodded, my eyes catching the gaze of Lucy's light brown ones.

She leaned in and kissed the bottom of my bearded chin. Then she said softly, "I don't think we should do more overnights."

Reluctantly, I agreed. It was such a strong temptation. Almost too strong.

As it was, gratitude filled me over the fact that Lucy didn't kiss me on the lips. If she had, I couldn't say that we'd finish out these six months of celibacy. I could actually guarantee that we wouldn't, based on the heady glow on Lucy's face and the sparkle in her eyes. Also based on the fact that her hand was sliding up and down my chest. My T-shirt was the only barrier between us up top, and as she played with the hem of it, I knew she had the same thought.

"We should probably sleep," I said. It took a lot of self-control to get those words out. They were a little raspy.

Lucy agreed and rolled back over. I fell asleep holding the woman I never, ever wanted to let go of. That terrified me to no end.

Chapter 32

Pete

"I wish I could help more," I told Nadine and Kerrick as they sat in my office Wednesday morning, two weeks after the camping trip. I was five days out from having shaved off my beard. I didn't leave a single hair behind. I even kept it smooth after the initial shave. Based on the way she stared at me, Nadine clearly cared, but I wondered if it was a sign that Lucy might hate it, too, since Nadine would probably know something like this. I hadn't seen Lucy to know for sure.

"Well, there is the wait list for the state assistance," Kerrick added.

"There is that. However, you were already granted mortgage modifications and refinancing. You were granted forbearance twice. You also received referrals to state and national agencies who help homeowners keep their homes. I believe those housing counselors have done all they can for you."

I would have canceled the Larkins' debt if I had the power. I would have eliminated the requirement for the remaining mortgage balance to be paid. I would have done anything and everything to help these people if I could. They'd already had to fend off judicial foreclosure due to their mortgage delinquency and did so by the skin of their teeth. But it just wasn't in my power to do more. All I had was one more extension, and it was almost up.

"So there isn't anything else you can do?" Nadine asked.

All I could manage was a shake of my head.

My meeting with the Larkins ended with me passing on the phone number of a mortgage counselor I'd recommended to many customers. She was kind and helpful, but I had a feeling she'd tell the Larkins exactly what I did. They had reached a point where no more help could be found.

Then I wondered what would happen if the Larkins did lose their home, or at least their cabin. Since I was in charge of their account, would they blame me, or would Nadine, at least? Worse, would Lucy?

She'd begged me to do something before, and I refused. My moral code apparently only went so far, considering what immoral things I was doing in the meantime, like a certain bet to get her to sleep with me. Lucy had enough ammo to hate me forever. I didn't want to add to that list. I strolled down to Tess's office. Her assistant was away, so Tess called me in after I announced myself with a knock.

"I have to help the Larkins. I refuse to sit by and let this happen. That involves contacting people Shubin will also have contact with. I can't screw this up."

Tess waited after I finished my speech. Finally, she said, "They've heard all the sob stories, Pete. There isn't anything you can do. Except maybe keep them from having to fend off judicial foreclosure again."

"How can I do that?"

"I'm assuming they still have their attorneys."

I nodded.

"Let me write down some notes." Tess grinned.

Chapter 33

Lucy

FOLLOWING ONE EXTREMELY LONG day at school on the first Friday of November, I strolled through our town grocery store, in need of bread, cheese, and fruit for the rest of the week. Someone behind me called my name. I turned and saw Jenni Jo Holley coming down the aisle toward me, her basket a bit fuller than mine.

"Hey, Jenni Jo," I said with a wide but exhausted smile.

Jenni Jo used to babysit me when I was little. She also ran the Apple Lane apartment complex. She started working there in her early thirties, and it didn't take long for her to earn a top management position. I respected Jenni Jo as someone fair and firm. She never had a problem with anyone unless they were late on their rent, and even then, she tried to give the residents a break if possible.

"How are you?" I asked.

She told me about the disastrous date she had the night before and also about how quickly all the empty apartments were getting snatched up. "Vacancies don't last long anymore. We even expanded our wait list. Our town is growing again, faster than some of us expected."

I wasn't sure how I felt about this. I liked my little town being *little.*

"How are things with your boyfriend?" she asked, wiggling her eyebrows with a grin.

"He's not my boyfriend, he's my—"

"Non-platonic friend," Jenni Jo said, finishing my sentence for me. "I know." She laughed.

"Did Gwenn tell you?" As a real estate broker who often worked with renters, it made sense that my bestie could have had a conversation about this with Jenni Jo. Gwenn and Rhett were also moving into the Apple Lane apartments, since Rhett had stealthily put himself on the wait list long before he ever proposed. Gwenn didn't have far to go from Syracuse, and Rhett didn't regret the longer move from Auburn if it meant Gwenn being able to get home from work in only a few minutes.

"The whole town's talking about it, though your bestie and her very cute fiancé might have also mentioned it in passing. So what's going on there?"

"If the whole town is talking about it, you already know what I'm going to say."

"Friends first."

I nodded and motioned for her to walk along with me, since I was getting zero shopping done and still had many more tasks to come once I left the store. We turned the corner into the bread/cracker/rice/pasta aisle.

"No one thinks me capable of it," I said, letting out a sigh.

"I think you're capable of doing whatever you put your mind to. It isn't like you don't know how to be friends with a man."

"True. But my attraction is trying to get in the way."

"That's the beauty of the 'not platonic' part, though. You don't have to pretend to not feel more for him. You can show him your feelings without physically acting on them."

When we were done chatting and paying for our groceries, Jenni Jo and I gave each other a friendly wave and walked to our respective cars. I spent the rest of the evening grading and planning after the school board suddenly decided our curriculum—that they'd already approved—was "too easy" and needed to be overhauled. The whole mess honestly reeked of the annexation battle.

Finally, I crawled into bed, exhaustion having filled every nook and crevice inside me. I heard the phone ring with a faint shrill, a ring that, though I couldn't remember the last time I was this tired, I knew at once I had to answer.

"Hey, gorgeous," Pete's soothing voice cooed. "Did I wake you?"

"No," I replied softly, my eyes struggling to stay open. I had already clicked off my light, and the darkness tried calling me to sleepy land. Fighting to remain awake, I asked him to tell me about his day. Readily, he obliged. He told me about work, about some of the silly people there that filled up his day, and about a fast-approaching deadline for a report he had to finish.

In all of this, I somehow began to drowse. Despite my best efforts, Pete's calm intonations relaxed me more than I could resist.

"Luce?" he whispered, obviously aware that I might not have heard everything.

"I'm here," I whispered back, attempting to prop myself up on my pillows. "It's just been a busy day."

"You sound like you're already asleep."

"I'm never asleep this early," I whispered. Well, it felt like I mumbled it.

"I think tonight might be a first," Pete said softly.

"Me too," I whispered in return. My eyelids were too heavy to keep them open any longer.

"That's all right. I'll let you go. We'll see each other tomorrow, okay?"

There was a muffled sound, then silence.

Then Pete said, "Wait. Not tomorrow." He made a frustrated groan, almost like a growl. "I'm not free again until the day after the financial expo."

"That's two weeks from now."

"Yes."

"Two weeks without seeing each other."

"In person, yes. But we can do video calls."

That he was somehow never available for.

I was too tired to argue. "Okay. I miss you, Pete."

"I miss you. Always. It's just—" He paused, something I noticed but couldn't react to as I felt myself drift off. There was no fighting sleep this time.

There was also no fighting the urge to call him as soon as I woke up the next morning, only to end up hearing his voicemail prompt right away.

"Sorry I conked out last night," I began. "Needed sleep more than I thought. Call me."

As it was Saturday, it was also my first of a two-day break from the kiddos. Gwenn and Rhett were doing wedding stuff, and Lourdes had family things that needed taking care of.

It wasn't too early to text Charisma, since she was usually up early on the weekends even though that was supposed to be our time to sleep in. She didn't get back to me. Then I remembered that she had plans to attend a football game with Dominic and some other friends. I'd declined the invite, expecting alone time with Pete.

I got alone time all right. Just not the kind to make me happy. I wished I'd gone to the game.

When Charisma texted me back almost two hours later, I was deep in freshening up my secondhand wooden rolling cart I used to store some of my teaching supplies. When I told Charisma what I was up to, she called me.

"Why is it so quiet? I thought you were at the game."

"I am," she replied. "Just wanted to see how you are. So how are you?"

I sometimes hated that, since my friend was also my sister's bestie and even my brother's bestie, she was privy to all the drama I could sometimes hide from others if I wanted to.

"I'm fine," I told Charisma. "This cart is looking really great. I mixed my leftover sunshine yellow with my leftover marigold in one of the paint pots, and it's going to look fantastic. Just need to finish the last bit of sanding before I can paint."

"No Pete today?"

"Nope. Not for two more weeks. Maybe I should crackle this. But I never like the way the crackle paint turns out."

"Have there been any new posts?"

"Not this week. Maybe all the Pete hate died down."

"Yeah. Could be." She was quiet for a moment. "All that Pete hate didn't make you question a few things?"

Well, of course it did, but I had a feeling what I'd worried about was not what she was asking. "Not really, no. I know Pete. Whoever started that smear campaign clearly doesn't."

There was a loud roar of shouting coming through the speaker. "You okay?" I asked her.

"That's just the people tailgating next to us. They accidentally broke their grill."

After some more noises, including Charisma calling to Dom, she told me she needed to go see if they could help their tailgating neighbors and that we could talk later if I still wanted to.

Not long after, once I was all done sanding and had moved on to painting, I heard Gwenn call, "Luce?"

From the sound of it, she was still near my unlocked door in my living room area.

"I'm in here," I called to her from the kitchen, two rooms away.

She walked in, eyed my open windows and painting task, then asked, "You okay?"

"Fine," I said, too breezily.

"Lourdes," Gwenn yelled at the sound of my front door closing. "She's in here."

"Lourdes is here, too?" I asked. "When did Charisma call you?"

Gwenn looked like she was trying to come up with a reasonable excuse instead of just admitting that they were here because all three of them were concerned about me.

"Hey," Lourdes said as she, too, cautiously entered the room. "How you doing, Luce?"

"Why does everyone keep asking me that?" I forced a laugh.

"Because you only repaint things when you're upset, and you just redid that cart five months ago."

"Your last breakup," Gwenn reminded me.

As if I couldn't remember. "I can paint something in my house and it not mean anything." I gave another laugh, but they didn't smile. I turned back to my work. "Thought you two were busy today."

"I needed a break," Lourdes said.

"Rhett and I finished early," Gwenn added. "What's going on with the house and cabin?"

"Nothing. Same as before," I told them without looking over.

"Which isn't nothing to you," Gwenn reminded me.

"And Pete?" Lourdes asked.

I tried to respond, but my voice caught. I cleared my throat. "It's fine. We're fine. Just not spending a lot of time together."

"Which can happen with friends," Lourdes said.

"I want to be more than friends with him, and you know that," I snapped.

"I know that." Her voice was calm and kind. "But maybe Pete doesn't. Or maybe he's comfortable in your friendship now, and he might not want more."

"Ouch." I drew out the word, making it sound like it had an extra five vowels in the middle.

"When was the last time you two discussed your six-month agreement?" she pushed.

"We don't need to. He flirts with me all the time. And so what if he pulled away from me on our camping trip? That doesn't mean he isn't falling in love with me. I think he's already in love, honestly. He just hasn't said so yet."

"As long as you're comfortable with your relationship as it is," Lourdes said with a shrug.

"There are married couples who go months without seeing each other and are still madly in love. Pete and I can handle a couple weeks."

"You and Pete won't see each other for the next two weeks?" Gwenn asked, her voice rising at the end. Her tone said, *"Oh, so that's it!"*

I let out a sigh and finally paused in my work. "Yes, and it sucks. This whole thing of waiting six months is messing with my head. I'm okay with it, then I'm not, then I am. I know I'm the one who did this. I caused all this chaos in my brain, and in Pete's, too."

We just had to ride it out. That was all. There weren't *that* many days until the six months were up. I could suck it up and not let my worry get in the way. I could spend time without Pete and not completely fall apart. I could do this.

Chapter 34

Lucy

"Surprise!" we all yelled as Lourdes led Gwenn into the flower shop the next evening. They were still bundled in their coats. It was a chilly Sunday night, just about five weeks before the wedding.

"What is all this?" Gwenn asked, her eyes wide and her face bright.

"It's simple," I said as I stepped forward from the group. "You need a party to celebrate you, but also need wedding decorations. And don't tell me yet again how they aren't necessary, because they are. Ergo, crafting bridal shower." I motioned to the part of the room behind me.

"Aw, Luce. Lourdes. This is great. Thank you."

"You don't really sound like you mean that," Lourdes whispered to her, still holding her own smile.

"No, I do. Really. It's so sweet of you guys to do this for me. I've just never had anything like this before."

Gwenn stepped over to hug me after giving Lourdes a quick hug. She said hello to Kenzie, Charisma, and Jade, then she greeted the other guests for the party, including Ruby, who grew up in the Falls and had recently returned to open the home base for her interior design business, and Florence, who worked as a pharmacist in our local drug store. I took Gwenn's and Lourdes's coats for them and tossed them onto one of Lourdes's smaller workbenches.

Her large work table, normally covered in floral supplies, was now covered with cute boxes of crafting supplies, though it didn't look all that different. There were scissors and hot-glue guns; ribbons in several shades of lavender, wisteria, hyacinth, and white; paper roses in similar colors; fake pearls to add to the roses; frosted white candle holders; and tinted glass vases that glistened like purple gems. We also set out glitter spray, but couldn't decide if Gwenn would want anything to sparkle or not. She was unpredictable as far as accessories went.

Gwenn had been careful to choose wedding colors that were in no way Christmas or holiday related, but I did have to admit the frosted white candle holders came from the seasonal aisle.

Lourdes and I decided the plain candle holders and vases needed ribbons. Per Kenzie's suggestion, we also agreed the pearls would be a nice addition to the vases' ribbons as well. We didn't need to do too many of each, as there were only going to be about twenty to twenty-five guests at the wedding, which didn't require too many tables.

We also had a few bottles of Gwenn's favorite Pinot Noir as well as carafes of both a purple-hued cocktail and a mocktail Lourdes and I made a bit earlier. Ruby had volunteered to bring trays of snack food and appetizers, and Kenzie and Charisma both brought cookies for dessert. I hoped beyond hope Kenzie's cookies weren't from Edin.

"You didn't have to do this," Gwenn said as we all moved toward the food and beverage table.

"We wanted to," I replied. "Kenzie, Lourdes, and I figured that with Lourdes's fresh-flower centerpieces on the tables, we could have small LED candles as well for added ambiance. Maybe some paper garlands hanging on the sweetheart table for you and Rhett, as well as on the cake table, gift table, and the buffet table. Maybe some along the walls. With the twinkle lights, that should spruce up the hall a lot."

"Wow," Gwenn said with a slight laugh. "You all have really put a lot of thought into this. Much more than I have."

Everyone else was done filling their plates and had sat down to eat, so the three of us did as well. We all snacked and worked at the same time. Lourdes had already completed two candle holders and two vases as examples for the rest of us to follow. Though Gwenn nixed the glitter idea, the decorations still began to have a sparkly brilliance.

Half of us trimmed the vases with ribbon and pearl strands, and the other half decorated the candle holders with ribbon and pearl clusters. I surreptitiously snatched a larger pearl from the container and held it up against my ring finger. It wasn't a diamond or even a rhinestone, but it gave me an idea of what to look forward to.

"What are you doing?" Charisma leaned over and asked in a hushed voice.

Startled, I tossed the fake pearl back onto the table. "Nothing," I replied.

"Are you seriously thinking about marrying him?" Then she softened her face and her tone. "I mean, you two aren't official yet. Have you changed your mind about that?"

"I think I have. Pete's been so great. I don't want to make him wait any longer. He's had enough time to make me believe he won't hurt me."

"What about those messages and social media posts about him? They seem pretty damning to me. How can you look past that?"

I was so sick of answering this question. My reply was automatic, the same I'd given over and over. "Maybe I wouldn't if I believed them. If I saw any hint of that Pete in the man I love, I'd say forget it. Probably. But I just don't see it."

"So if I said that maybe you're the one who finally tamed the flirt?" Her eyes flashed at me, clearly watching me for a reaction.

"I think maybe the same could be said about me, too. You see? Pete and I are perfect for each other in so many ways."

Charisma didn't reply. She only gave me a small smile. But after a few moments of working on a candle holder, she said, "I'm sure you're right. He's ready for a relationship this time."

I grinned at her, making it as convincing as I could. "I know I am, and I know he is."

I returned to my work, but not for long. Lourdes started peeling off the pearls she'd put on the two vases in front of her.

"What are you doing?" I asked her.

"Trying something," she told me as she pulled off the residual hot glue.

Kenzie stopped in the middle of gluing pearls onto the vase in her hand. "Are we doing it wrong?" she asked.

Lourdes shook her head no while digging through the pile of ribbon spools near her. She pulled out a wide grosgrain in a deep wisteria color. After trimming the ribbon to the circumference of the vase and gluing it on, Lourdes added the pearls once again.

"Oh! So pretty," Florence exclaimed.

We all agreed the darker ribbon was so much better. Then I groaned. Kenzie had been on the last vase we needed. But Lourdes was in charge of the fresh flowers, and therefore got to decide what the vases looked like.

"Anyone else want a drink refill before we get started?" Kenzie asked.

Just about all of us said yes. Kenzie laughed and began refilling cups. I offered to help, but the mom in her—or maybe just the stubbornness in her—waved me off and carried on by herself.

"How are things going with Pete?" Ruby asked me.

I was in the middle of shortening a length of ribbon I'd cut.

"He wants to date, but she doesn't," Kenzie replied before I had a chance to.

"It isn't exactly like that," I said.

"It's more serious than you think," Charisma added to my sister.

I jerked my head up and silently pleaded for her to not tell Kenz about me imagining an engagement ring on my hand. But who was I kidding? Kenzie was Charisma's bestie, not me. She was going to find out anyway. Just hopefully not today.

Since the candle holders were just about done, I helped revamp the vases along with Lourdes, Gwenn, and Kenzie. Eventually, it was time to move on to the paper flower garlands.

But then Lourdes scooted back from the table and stood up. "We need a break," she announced. "Time for presents."

"Presents?" Gwenn asked in surprise.

"Of course. This is still a shower," I told her.

Lourdes and I brought out the gifts from their hiding spot in the storage room. We all oohed and ahhed over Gwenn's new kitchen gadgets and super-fluffy linens. Then came the few naughty presents Lourdes called a surprise joke.

"Joke's on you." Gwenn laughed. "I love strawberry flavors, edible panties or not."

"Those are not for you," I told her.

"I'd pass around the negligee, because it's even softer than the towels, but I don't think anyone wants to feel up my sex clothes," she told us.

"That one's not a joke," Lourdes said to Gwenn. "You'll never want to take it off. Or wear anything else."

I reached over to feel this amazing negligee. "Wowza," I couldn't help but say.

If I had the money, I knew I would have bought one for my six-month-ending celebration with Pete.

"Lourdes is right," I added. "I'd wear that under everything, or instead of it. Take this on your honeymoon and nothing else. Just wear your coat, and you'll feel like a million bucks all day."

"I don't think she's going to have any problems with how she feels on her honeymoon." Kenzie laughed. She'd used that tone again.

"You don't need to tell me that. I've had way more—" I began, but I stopped myself before I really snapped.

Kenzie ignored me.

"Oh! Here, ladies. Gifts for all of you," Lourdes said as she pulled out the large bag from behind her chair. Then she stood and walked around the group to distribute all the goody bags full of lavender essential oil body cream, luxury chocolates, and aloe-infused eye masks.

Some of the guests dove into their chocolates. Charisma started rubbing a small dab of body cream onto her arm.

"Is it true that Rhett's ex is opening a bakery here?" Jade asked Gwenn.

"Why don't you ask Kenzie? Edin's her new bestie," I said.

"There's no reason to be snarky," Kenzie told me. "You act like she doesn't deserve friends."

"You act like she isn't the enemy," I replied.

"She isn't my enemy." My sister glared at me.

"Mine either," Gwenn added.

"She's really nice," Charisma—Kenzie's actual bestie—said to us all.

What in the world was happening with everyone?

"I told Edin she might want to look at the abandoned storefront on Main," Kenzie replied to Jade.

"You what?" I screeched.

"Her bakery burned to a crisp. What do you expect her to do?" my sister said.

"Go anywhere but here," I snapped.

"Do you not want a bakery in this town again?" Kenzie asked. "Because I'm sure others would like to have one."

I was shaking my head before my sister even finished speaking. "We don't need one. We have Button's and Capelli's. And way to be loyal to Gwenn. Nice job." My last words dripped with sarcastic venom.

No one else dared to speak.

Kenzie narrowed her eyes at me. "I love the diner. You know that. But neither the diner nor Capelli's has a full bakery at its disposal. We make a few pies and chocolate chip cookies and two kinds of cake. Capelli's pretty much only adds cheesecake to the mix. Doesn't this town deserve better than that?"

"Didn't she just win first prize in the contest at the Butterscotch Pie Festival a couple weeks ago?" Jade asked. "I heard hers was incredible."

"All her stuff is," Kenzie replied.

I couldn't care less about her food. Edin was the reason I had to skip the pie contest for the first time in ages. "Is it not bad enough that Rhett invited her to the wedding? You didn't want to," I added to Gwenn.

"Lucy, we talked about this," Kenzie said in her big sister, *listen to me* tone.

I ignored her and looked back to Gwenn, who began to speak.

"I didn't, but Kenzie's right. I don't think Edin will cause any trouble."

She was wrong, but I didn't bother saying so. I was still fuming at Kenzie's scolding of me. Edin was not a person I trusted, nor would she ever be. She was also not someone I thought deserved a spot in my beloved hometown. I really wished she'd just stay where she was. Gwenn should have hated the idea of having her in our town as much as Lourdes and I did, even if my sister was too stubborn to see the truth about her new BFF.

As I readied myself to speak, Lourdes came over to me. "Help me find more ribbon, Luce. I have a lace one in mind that would be perfect for the trim on the table runners."

"What table runners?" I asked as I stood and followed her.

"Jade volunteered to embellish the ones I bought."

"What about the tablecloths?" I thought I'd picked out the prettiest white ones I could find. Was there something wrong with them?

"We still have them and will use them. They're perfect. But now we'll have pretty lavender runners on top of the white."

And yet again, I was being left out of a design change.

A part of me knew I couldn't blame Lourdes for being excited about Gwenn's wedding, but I felt like crap that we'd agreed to go fifty-fifty on the stuff Gwenn and Rhett couldn't afford to buy, only I couldn't hold up my end of the bargain with all the new stuff Lourdes was adding.

I mentioned this while she and I searched through her spools of ribbon. She waved it off.

"Please don't worry about it. You're trying to save two houses. Let me do this. I'm going to do everything I can to make this wedding special for our friends. A tiny budget shouldn't stop them from making it the best they deserve. Besides, you can't tell me you're not tapped out. You've sold just about everything you own." She re-rolled a spool that wasn't wrapped quite right.

"Yesterday, a pair of diamond earrings an ex-boyfriend gave me a few years ago sold in an online auction. I only got a hundred bucks for them, but it went straight into the fund."

"Have you told your family about that fund yet?"

I shook my head. I also hadn't told them how often I contemplated selling the rest of my valuable belongings, or at least ninety-nine percent of them, at a pawn shop. Hadn't told Lourdes and Gwenn, either, so I brushed that thought away.

"Luce, it's okay to let the cabin go. You still have the memories that came with spending your summers there. More importantly, you still have your family."

"I'm the only one in my family who hasn't given up hope. I won't."

"Okay." Lourdes relented, giving up on this topic and choosing to move on to how well I thought Gwenn's shower was going. The spool in Lourdes's hand was the exact gray she'd described when we were looking for supplies for the shower creations but couldn't find. "By the way, please stop picking fights with your sister."

"She pushed me into it, and you know that."

"I know Kenzie pushes your buttons, and I know how much you hate Edin. But this is neither the time nor the place." She moved to walk away.

"Wait." I stopped her. "Have you figured out what to do about the flower shortage yet?"

A few weeks prior, Lourdes had tearfully mentioned that the flowers she wanted to use for Gwenn's surprise bridal bouquet were unavailable.

"I will offer as many favors and trade-offs as possible to get what I want," Lourdes told me with a serious expression.

I raised my eyebrows at her.

She laughed and playfully smacked my arm, which made me laugh, too. "Not like that."

"When's the last time you did something like *that*?" I asked. She hadn't mentioned any new dates in a while, and Lourdes was not one to get herself into a relationship. In fact, because we grew up in the same town, I knew for a fact, even before our acquaintance grew to friendship, that Lourdes had only ever had one boyfriend.

"That's also a conversation for another time." Her eyes told me it was too sad to think about at the moment.

Lourdes and I returned to the party. I went to Gwenn to make sure she stayed distracted while Lourdes surreptitiously handed the ribbon and table runners to Jade.

By the end of the night, we'd finished all the wedding crafts and even got to see a picture of the shoes Gwenn bought for the wedding. We all pitched in with wrapping the vases in bubble wrap and placing them in a few medium-sized boxes, along with the garlands so I could take it all to my house for safekeeping.

Once everyone left—Gwenn only departing at our insistence—Lourdes and I cleaned up the remaining supplies and trash.

"Have you finished the mock-up of the bouquets yet?" I asked.

"Not yet. I have a design in my head, but I keep tweaking it," Lourdes answered.

"Maybe you'll tweak it back to the original."

She chuckled. "Probably. Gwenn will like any version, I know. I just want it perfect for her."

I gave her arm a squeeze. "It will be."

We loaded the boxes into my car and said good night. I decided I wanted to immediately unload them as soon as I arrived home. The best place I could think of for them was at the bottom of my closet, but I had to move a few things out of the way first.

My phone rang when I was carrying the second-to-last box in. Once the box was safe in its new home, I checked the phone, hoping it wasn't bad news.

It was Pete.

I called him back. "Hey. How are you?" I asked after he answered.

"I'm good. How was the party?" Pete asked me.

"It was great. We totally surprised Gwenn. My sister was a little bitchy to me, but that's no surprise. She always does that when we're around other people. She thinks she knows better than I do."

"You sound a little worked up."

"I guess I am. Wedding stress, sister stress, mortgage stress, work stress."

This was usually the moment Pete would offer to help take all my stress away. He didn't.

"Maybe you could come over and make me unwind," I said. I wasn't sure how he'd take it, or even exactly how I meant it, but my body temperature had risen already at the thought.

"I can't. I'm working late."

"On a Sunday?"

"Yeah. Lots to catch up on. Just wanted to check in with you."

"Oh." My voice was flat. I didn't bother hiding my disappointment. "Okay."

We were nearing the all-important six-month mark, only Pete wasn't making much of an effort to show me he was ready for the next step. I didn't care that he said he didn't have the next two weeks free. I wanted a sign from him. I *needed* one.

I swallowed and smiled, though he couldn't see me. It was a tactic I'd learned from teaching. A smile on the face could contribute to a smile in the voice. "That's okay," I said, my voice much more chipper than before. "If you want to come over later, you can."

Someone was talking in the background. Whoever it was sounded angry.

"You have to go, don't you?"

"Yeah. This new system wasn't installed correctly, and it corrupted some files. Well, a lot of files."

I hoped that if my parents' file was corrupted by the glitch, maybe that meant they would be granted more time until it was fixed. And that it might never get fixed. Then I remembered that would be a nightmare for Pete and wished everything to work out for everyone.

Pete and I quickly hung up.

Once I was finally in bed, I kept my mind on my non-platonic friend. Maybe he needed me to help him unwind, not vice versa.

Less than four weeks. That's all we had to make it through. Maybe I'd get my own negligee in that supple fabric. I'd have to find another piece of jewelry I could sacrifice in order to buy it, but for Pete, I'd do just about anything.

In the morning, I woke up to a text from him I'd slept through.

> Sorry about last night. I moved some things around. Dinner?

I didn't care how he managed to suddenly be free when it was supposed to be two more weeks before we could see each other. I needed him in front of me, around me, near me in any way possible.

> Family dinner tonight.

> Am I not invited?

> Do you want to be?

If we were going to be official at the end of these four weeks, Pete needed to be able to see my parents socially despite being in charge of their mortgage account. I wasn't sure what he wanted or how scared he was of that dynamic. He'd only done dinner with the whole family a couple times, and though it went well, he never asked to be invited again. He also couldn't make it every time I extended an invitation after that.

> It is part of being a boyfriend.

Everything in me fluttered. My cheeks grew warm. Heck, they were burning hot. All of me was. I fanned my face before replying.

Dinner's at six.

I'll be at your house at 5:15.

I didn't know how he would pull off getting out of work so early, and I didn't care. We'd get over half an hour alone before needing to leave. Oh, the things I knew we could do in that time.

Four more weeks. Four more weeks. Four more weeks.

I repeated it to myself like a mantra. Approximately thirty days. I could wait. I could resist the temptation to leap into Pete's arms and tell him I loved him a million times before pulling him into my bed. We'd already made it this far. I had to keep reminding myself of this.

Four. More. Weeks.

Pete arrived at his promised time. I nearly tackled him when I jumped into his arms, against all my promises to myself throughout the day that I'd keep my hands and body off of him. He held me tight, his arms around my back, his face nuzzled into my neck. But wait.

Something was different.

Something was missing.

I pulled back. "What did you do to your beard?" I hadn't meant this to come out as a screech. "How long has it been since I saw you?"

His cheeks pinked up. "I thought I'd try something different. You don't like it." This wasn't a question.

I shook my head. "It isn't that. I love getting to see your whole face." Slowly, I rubbed my hands on his soft, now-smooth cheeks. "But I really liked the beard."

Pete pulled me into him again, lifting my legs up and helping me wrap them around his middle. "I've been keeping it away, but I'll grow it back. I promise." He buried his face into my neck again.

"I'm not worried about the beard. I just missed you. I'm so glad we didn't have to wait two weeks for this," I whispered into his ear. I'd actually wanted to nibble the part of his neck just under his ear but refrained.

"Me too," he whispered back. Then he pulled away just enough to kiss the side of my head, above my left ear.

I dropped my feet back down, and Pete walked with me hand-in-hand over to my sofa. He sat down, and I straddled my legs over him, making sure I didn't move too close into his body. Pete smelled way too good for me to trust myself in that moment. Then he took his hands and scooted me closer, anyway.

"Is this okay?" he asked.

I nodded. "More than okay. I like being close to you."

"What are we going to do about this?" he asked, his voice breathy and uneven as he kissed a line across my jaw.

"Same thing we do every day, Pete. We try to control ourselves and wait."

Pete pulled his head and torso away just enough to look me in the eye. "We can do this?" Not sure if he meant it that way, but it came out like a question.

"We can do this. Four more weeks. That's my new mantra. Or at least the thing I repeat to myself a quadrillion times a day. Eventually, we will be able to use our alone time for more than just cuddles and kisses."

He gave me a sweet grin. "I like the cuddles and kisses."

I finally leaned in and nibbled the spot on his neck, happily receiving an aroused moan in return. "Me too."

"Four more weeks?"

"Yep."

"When it feels as good then as all this other stuff does now, I'll have to start coming over here earlier. Forty-five minutes won't be nearly enough."

With a burst of laughter, I heartily agreed. Then we returned to our clothes-on, hands—mostly—off kissing before having to leave to make it to dinner on time. Well, twelve minutes late, but I blamed Pete for that. I couldn't help how weak his thumb strokes on my left hip bone made me. I also couldn't help having removed his shirt because of it, nor could I help ogling all the slightly less tanned than in the summer, rippling mountain of muscle that made up Pete's sexy torso.

I needed a few moments with my eyes squeezed shut, inhaling the deepest of breaths, before I was able to remove myself from the straddle and stand.

Four freaking more weeks.

Chapter 35

Pete

WHEN I FINALLY GOT home that night, after a pleasant dinner with the Larkins and what felt like a forever-long drive away from Lucy, I tossed my wallet and keys on the table by the door, pulled off my shoes, and made a beeline for bed. If I hurried, she might still be awake.

Dressed only in my boxers under my sheet, I clicked on Lucy's name in my contacts list and gave her a call. Her voice was sleepy when she answered. I was too late.

"Hey," I said softly. Not quite a whisper, but gentle enough to not startle her.

"Hi."

Her eyes were closed, of this I was certain without being able to see her. She was probably snuggled up with her favorite white-and-yellow fleece blanket covered in a sunflower pattern. Lucy liked that blanket so much, she even kept her house cold enough in the summer to be able to still use it.

"Miss me?" she asked in a hushed tone.

My reply was immediate. "Always."

Lucy didn't respond.

I kept my voice soft. "Had a good time at dinner. Your family knows how to make me laugh, that's for sure. But I had an even better time alone with you."

Still no response.

"Luce?"

She didn't speak or make a noise in any way. I couldn't stop what was coming next. It washed over me and consumed me, and I had to let it out. With Lucy asleep on the other end, it also felt like the perfect time.

"I love you, Luce."

Then I waited. For a reaction, maybe. For those words to wake her up. I was nervous that they might. But she remained silent on the other end.

I softly said good night then ended the call.

Chapter 36

Lucy

WEDNESDAY EVENING—THE DAY BEFORE Thanksgiving and just over two weeks before the wedding—Kenzie and I sat together on my living room floor. It was empty apart from all the wedding decorations we'd all gathered for Gwenn. Lourdes had given us the stuff she bought as well. Kenzie had a plan for it all and was showing me her ideas, grouping items together as she went along.

I was glad Kenzie had been brave enough to offer input. I was even happier I'd been forced to swallow my pride and accept her help. There were a lot of things I sometimes couldn't stand about my sister, but no matter what, she was brilliant when it came to design.

With the wedding decisions out of the way, we relaxed and enjoyed the delicious pie Kenzie had brought from the diner.

"So, is Lourdes giving the toast or are you?" my sister asked.

"I'm giving a speech, then Lourdes is doing the toast. She doesn't want to, though."

Kenzie raised her brows. "Really? I thought Lourdes would do anything for Gwenn."

"She would. She just doesn't see how she can stand up there in front of a group of people and talk about true love."

"She doesn't have to talk about love. Just Gwenn's love with Rhett."

"That's what we told her."

"Lourdes still hung up on her ex?"

I nodded. Words weren't necessary. Kenzie understood. I knew this for sure with her next words.

"Have you ever missed someone so much it hurts and takes your breath away, only to discover they aren't thinking about you at all?"

My heart ached for my sister. I didn't know what it was like to have a husband up and leave. But though I didn't know that exact kind of pain, I knew what it felt like to be abandoned by a guy I loved. Unfortunately, I didn't have any insights or anything else I could say to make it better for her.

Kenzie gave a soft sigh. "Cal's in town."

I jerked my head up, ignoring the centerpiece I'd been looking at. "When did you see him?"

"I didn't. I found out from someone at the diner who saw him. He hasn't called. He won't call."

"Are you sure?"

She nodded. "This isn't the first time he's done this."

Time seemed to slow down a little. "Wait. Every time he's come back, you said he dropped off money to you. I know now that he never gave you money, but he never contacted you either?"

The tears in her eyes had me leaning over to squeeze her hand a moment.

"He's just here to visit family and some friends."

"That doesn't include you and Hayzel?"

"Guess his former wife and daughter aren't important enough, apparently."

She grew silent, and I let it go, even though my blood was boiling at this point. I'd liked my former brother-in-law to an extent, but when Kenzie unexpectedly got pregnant, he changed into a shell of himself, at least as far as loving husband was concerned. He still played the part, but she told me later—in hindsight—that in their alone moments, he wasn't so much cold as distant, like he wanted out way before he left.

"Are you writing about Gwenn and Rhett or you and Pete?" she asked.

"Am I not allowed to put my feelings into my speech?"

"Of course you are, but—" She put her fork down and rubbed her forehead. "It's stupid, Luce. It's so stupid."

"What are you talking about?"

"You're being stupid right now."

"Sugarcoat it for me, why don't you?" I said tersely. "What is it this time, anyway?"

I mean, I hadn't done anything about the social media posts and "Miss Havisham," but both had pretty much gone away on their own. I didn't know what happened with Miss H, but I assumed bashing Pete online had only been fun for a limited time before those harpies moved on to their next victims.

"Making Pete wait six months."

"Not entirely six months. Closer to five."

"Does it matter. You've wanted each other since June. Why not go for it?"

"Kenz, you know my reasoning for this."

"I do, but it doesn't matter. Again I say, you're stupid. You have him. He's right freaking there in front of you. Wanting you. *Loving* you. It's obvious. So just give in to him instead of pushing him away."

"I haven't pushed him away. I've given us time to reach this point. I doubt we would have without that. Would we have slept together? Absolutely. Would we still be in love? Doubtful."

"You seriously believe that? Luce, knowing someone better doesn't make it hurt any less if they decide they don't want you anymore. All it does is make it feel like a personal attack as opposed to a change of mind."

"What is your problem?"

"Nothing. It's nothing." Kenzie stood up and carried her mostly full plate to the kitchen. She returned empty-handed. "I'm going home. Hayzel's with Mom and Dad helping them prep for tomorrow, and I'd like some time to myself before I need to go get her."

·❤·❤·❤·❤·❤·

Kenzie's words still nagged at me as I lay in Pete's arms on his sofa Friday night, after I didn't see him on the holiday. Pete and I already had dinner out and decided to watch a movie at his place. As his soft breath caressed the back of my shoulder, I sighed.

"What's wrong?" he asked, pausing the movie.

"She's right. My sister's right. I'm so stupid."

Pete gently turned me toward him, his eyes on mine. "Hey, don't say that. What's this about?"

I opened my mouth to speak, then shut it. We'd danced around the word for so long, but I knew we both felt it. It was time. It was probably well beyond time.

"I love you," I whispered.

Pete's confused face brightened, but quickly returned to its scrunched state. "I love you, too, Luce. Do you think loving me makes you stupid?"

I immediately shook my head. "Not at all. But I think making you wait this long is stupid. We love each other. We should be able to express that in more *physical* ways."

Pete's beautiful eyes grew wide. "Does this mean—"

I kissed his jawline, where his beard had slowly begun to grow back in, though there were only tiny prickles. "I want you to make love to me. Right now."

NEVER, *NEVER* DID I think I'd hear Lucy say that twice before the six months were up. Well, I thought I might hear her say it, but I also feared she would. She was on my sofa—which might as well have been a bed—in my arms, begging me to sleep with her again and I had to say no again.

I wrapped my arms tighter around her, pressing my hands into her bare back. She'd wanted us both to be comfortable after our dinner, so once we got back to my place, Lucy removed my shirt for me then changed into a sports bra with plenty of cleavage and tight black leggings that showed off all her gorgeous curves. Those curves called to me now.

I decided to speak before kissing her, afraid that if our lips locked, she'd never let me move far enough away to say anything. If I couldn't say what I knew I needed to, then we'd be in trouble. Well, *I* would. "Lucy, I love you more than I think I could even put into words."

She continued kissing my jaw, then moved down to my neck. I couldn't hold in the moan that arose from that. It wasn't the only thing I was having a hard time controlling.

"You came up with a plan for us, and it has worked. It's worked, right?" I moved back so we could look into each other's eyes.

Lucy nodded, though her eyelids were still a little closed, I noticed, as she let the heady sensations wash over her.

"Six months. We've done most of it already. We can make it one more week."

She jerked back, eyes fully open now and full of fire. "Are you serious?"

I would never just take her, and I also couldn't let her give herself to me yet. Our lovemaking could not—*would not*—have any damn thing to do with Miles. I wasn't going to let that happen.

"Seven days. We can spend as many moments together like this as we want." I bent down a bit to tenderly kiss her lips, which she happily leaned into. "But let's wait. Let's go by our original plan."

She shook her head again, blonde hair falling farther down on her neck. "It sounds so unromantic now. Scheduling sex? You don't think it's dumb?"

"We're not scheduling it. We're anticipating it. And we can tease until then, as little or as much as we want."

Now a grin slowly grew across her mouth. "I much prefer *much*."

"Me too."

Our lips connected again, soft at first. Lucy deepened the kiss this time, and it took twice as much energy to control myself and not rip the rest of our clothes off right then. I kept her pressed firmly against me, our combined, increasing body heat keeping us warm enough that we tossed the blanket off to the floor.

After we slowly ended the kiss, I moved my mouth over to her ear and whispered all the things I couldn't wait to do to her. I gave her as much dirty talk as I knew she could handle and then some. We spent hours that way, first kissing then dirty talking, until Lucy reluctantly had to go home. We did much the same Saturday night after spending the day away from each other. But Sunday . . .

Oh, Sunday.

Lucy and I had the whole day together. I couldn't let us stay in again. It was torture, all that teasing. I loved and hated it, especially knowing that if it weren't for Miles and my stupid pride, I could have already shown her just how much I adored her. I could have done all those things I'd whispered in her ear since June.

I talked her into brunch, even though all the good places were filled to the brim. After finishing our meal, we went over to the zoo. I knew she would have loved the antique shops better, but it wouldn't have been fair to take her shopping when she didn't have money to spend on it.

We weren't hungry for lunch, but since we were still out and about, we drove to my favorite steakhouse for dinner. But it was Sunday night. So many other things to do were closed or closing. Lucy clearly didn't want to go home. That left my house.

Where we could remove a few items of clothing, snuggle up, and have as much sexy time as we wanted. The sparkle in her eyes told me that was exactly what Lucy was thinking. Before leaving the restaurant, I excused myself to the bathroom. While in there, I quickly sent off a text to Alec begging him to be available so I didn't have to be alone with Lucy.

> What could possibly be bad about that?

I contemplated lying or coming up with an excuse. I just couldn't think of one. And I knew Alec would understand my dilemma.

> She wants to make out.

> Again I ask, what could possibly be bad about that?

One more week.

It's killing me.

Why don't you guys come over? I'll have something going on here.

I owe you one.

I'm gonna hold you to it.

Wait, no I'm not, because we both know Miles would.

That right there was exactly what best friends were for. It was nice to remember I did actually have goodhearted, reasonable, "I won't hold this over your head" kind of friends.

"Alec just texted me asking if we wanted to come over," I told Lucy when I returned to the table.

"Oh. Okay," she said, sounding a little deflated. "Is that what you want to do?"

I took her hand in mine, then brought it to my lips. "I want to be with you, wherever we go. But it would be nice to hang out with him for a while. You like Alec, right?"

"Of course I do. He's a great guy. If you want to go to his place, then let's go." She gave me a bright smile that made it all the way to her eyes. That told me she wasn't lying.

Alec was true to his word. He had a game on, as well as music on standby for commercial breaks. He'd also invited his brother, his brother's girlfriend, and a few other friends so he wouldn't feel like the fifth wheel. His most recent date obviously hadn't earned girlfriend status.

Then there was all the food Alec had somehow managed to gather. Altogether, it looked like a well thought out, not spontaneous in any way party. I was amazed, and Lucy was none the wiser. It was another lie, but this time, it genuinely was for her own good.

Hours later, when it was time to go, Lucy gave Alec one of her amazing smiles and thanked him for a good night. I thanked him as well, sending off a look that said, *I owe you one.* Alec waved me off, letting me know we were good.

I feared the drive back to my house would be awkward, but Lucy's body language told me I had nothing to worry about. She sat relaxed in her seat, turned slightly in my direction. She grinned at me, then yawned.

"Bored already?"

"Not at all. I had a good time. His brother's girlfriend invited me to a paint-and-drink event a few weeks from now. I think I'm going to go with her."

I loved this. I loved that Lucy got along so well with Alec and that Alec stepped up for me when I needed him. I always tried to do the same for him. If only all our friends could be like that.

·♥·♥·♥·♥·♥·

"Hey, hey," Miles said as he strode up to me in the lobby of our building Monday morning.

It was too early for dealing with him, but I greeted him in turn anyway. No sense in being as big of an ass as he often was, even if in a different way. We walked together to the elevator, which would take us to our offices.

"You're running out of time with that chick, bro," Miles said, not even bothering to lower his voice.

I wanted to say, *"Her name is Lucy,"* but Miles didn't care, and I was tired of correcting him.

"End of the week, dude," he continued as I pushed the button for our floor. The doors thankfully closed before Miles opened his mouth again. "How do you not have her wrapped around you yet?" He wiggled his eyebrows like I'd be amused or something.

I wasn't.

"Don't you think this has gotten a little out of control?" I asked, trying to manage the sharpness in my tone.

"Dude, this is the best wager we've ever done!" He laughed.

My right hand clenched into a fist. I had to shake it to make it let go and relax. There wasn't anything else I wanted to say to him. Miles had clearly discarded our friendship months before. Or maybe we hadn't had a true one.

How could he be so giddy about me conspiring against Lucy and lying to her about it? I could not handle the thought of tricking her to get her into bed. No matter how I looked at it, it was wrong, and I was wrong for having let my pride get to me.

"Hey, aren't you going to a wedding with her soon? I heard the assistants and Tess saying something like that the other day."

So maybe I didn't like how much the secretaries talked. I needed to remind my assistant to not discuss my personal life with anyone in the office. I also needed to ask Tess to stop gossiping, too. She knew it was hard enough having Miles around.

"Yeah, Lucy's best friend is getting married next month."

"You are so lucky," Miles told me, emphasizing every word.

"Why's that?" I couldn't help but ask, knowing I'd probably regret it. Just like every conversation I had with this guy.

"Bro, women go wild at weddings." He raised his eyebrows as high as they could go, grinning wide. "You know this. You've always cashed in on it."

"I don't think Lucy's the 'go wild' at weddings type."

"But she'll be a *single bridesmaid*. They can't help themselves." He laughed. "And if not her, there's always more. Don't waste the opportunity." He nudged me with his elbow.

I stopped listening to him after that. I hadn't even wanted to listen to him before that. Miles was no longer my friend. In looking at the differences between Alec and Miles, I knew Miles had never been my friend to begin with. Not really. We'd liked to one-up each other and be each other's wingman, and I couldn't forget about those "epic" wagers we'd often get into. I hated him and me and all of it now.

Despite my apprehension, I knew I couldn't spend the rest of the week avoiding Lucy. But every time I heard her voice or saw her face, I was reminded that if the truth ever came out, in her eyes I would be equal to Miles. Her disgust for me would be the same as her disgust for him. Actually, it would be worse against me, because I promised her that she could trust me, even with those social media posts telling her not to. It didn't matter that it had been at least a month since any new ones showed up. They were still out there.

Lying about it probably being a bot or someone looking for ransom money—while entirely possible but highly unlikely—made me even more of an ass. No matter how I looked at our relationship, it was glaringly obvious. She deserved better.

<h1 style="text-align:center">Chapter 38</h1>

Pete

I WAS IN SHUBIN'S office—for what reason this time, I was far too scared to guess. I hated getting called in to talk to him. He never asked us to join him so he could tell us all the wonderful ways we'd been excelling at work, that was for sure. We were almost at the end of a long workday. It was Friday, my first official date with Lucy less than twenty-four hours away.

I silently squirmed in the chair across from my boss, waiting for him to speak first. That was the way things worked with him.

"What's this I hear about a wager between you and Piven?"

"It's over now," I began. This needed to be clear from the get-go.

"I was told it possibly involved customers of ours," he added, leaning back in his chair, making it clear he had all the power in this conversation.

There was no way for me to not know this. I was ready to grovel on my hands and knees to keep this job if need be. I hoped it wasn't going to be necessary. "It did not."

"Not in any way?" He raised an eyebrow at me, but other than that one small movement, his face remained expressionless.

I shook my head. "No."

This wasn't a direct lie. The bet was about Lucy, before I met her parents. And Lucy didn't use this bank.

"I've not known you to make such a questionable decision before," Shubin said.

"And I won't ever again. I admit I stupidly fell into it. I can't speak for Miles," I told him. I said it knowing damn well Miles would never wise up and become a decent guy. "I promise to not mess up anymore."

"If the rumors of this get out—"

"They won't. The bet had nothing to do with this company or our customers."

Shubin took a few moments before speaking. "You've already attracted quite a bit of negative public attention."

"I have, I know, but—"

Shubin's expression hardened. "Let me finish."

* ❤ * ❤ * ❤ * ❤ * ❤ *

"Do you have any idea how lucky you are?" Tess whisper-hissed at me after nearly tackling me in the hallway.

I'd just left Shubin's office, feeling so lucky and so grateful to still be employed.

"Only your excellent track record at this company saved your ass," she added with a pointed look.

"Tess, I'm thanking my lucky stars already. I don't need reminded of that."

She continued to follow me down the corridor. "Are you finally done with Miles?"

"Yep. After I go give him his freaking money." My voice was gruff.

"Losing the money hurts that bad?"

"I don't give a shit about the money. Never did. Paying Miles off won't erase what happened. What I did. I should have known better. I did know better, but got sucked in anyway. This will forever hang over me. Lucy will never understand my side of this. I can't ever let her find out."

"Pete, you might not be able to control that."

"I can do my best." Though more and more, it was becoming glaringly obvious that my best was never going to be good enough. My "best" was absolute shit. We walked right past my secretary's desk. I didn't make a move to head to my office.

"Where are you going?" Tess asked.

"It ends now. I can't stand one more minute of this not being over."

Except Nella snatched my attention because I'd forgotten an important meeting. That led to two more. I was antsy to finish things with my former friend in a way I couldn't put into words, but too many other people and other things needed my attention. All I could do was wait it out and practice the breathing technique Lucy once told me about from her yoga class.

"Six months, Petey Boy," Miles said with a happy grin as I finally entered his office.

I didn't need to dig in my wallet. I'd taken care of that in my own office before coming down here. Reaching into my front right pocket, I pulled out the thousand dollars in cash and threw it at Miles's desk. He sat behind it with wide eyes.

Before he could even ask what the hell was happening, I snapped, "Don't ever speak to me again."

He scoffed. "What the hell, bro?"

"Don't 'bro' me. We aren't friends anymore. Not sure we ever were."

"What are you talking about?"

"I'm going to lose my girlfriend and my job because of you!" I exploded at him.

Miles chuckled. That damn bastard *chuckled*. "I mean, bro, you didn't have to go along with me, though it was the most epic bet."

"Yeah, you said that already. And what choice did I have? What choice did you leave me with, 'bro'?"

He put his hands up for a moment. "Hey, don't come at me with that shit. Did I force anything on you? No I did not."

"Yeah, you did, Miles. And you know what? You aren't worth this. You aren't worth my time."

Narrowing his eyes at me, Miles said, "Your precious Lucy deserves better if you're just going to wimp out all the time."

Sure, *now* he learned her name. I wanted to tell Miles that Corkie sure as hell deserved better than him, but it didn't matter. I was done. I said as much, to which he laughed again.

"Whatever you say, Petey Boy."

"Don't ever call me that again, you hear me, Piven?"

Miles got to his feet. "Back off, Amundsen. We had a deal. We stuck by it. Far as I can tell, it all worked out just fine."

I stormed out of his office before we came to blows. It had taken a lot of energy to contain myself. I'd never felt the urge to punch someone before, but Miles had my brain flipped upside down.

I stalked down the wide corridor to my office, but got stopped by Alec.

"What's going on, man?" he asked.

I told him about my blowup with Miles.

"That's rough, man. At least it's over now."

"Except it isn't, is it? It'll never be over."

As I slumped in my desk chair, I got a new text.

Lucy

Miss you. Love you. One more day.

She'd added little hearts in between each phrase and several more at the end. I tried to text back, but my hands began to shake. Miles's laughter still taunted me without the jackass even being around.

I couldn't believe what I'd put Lucy through for these six months. June to December. She had no idea what a jerk I was. There was no way I could calmly or rationally respond to her. Not right away. Everything I thought to say made me feel like a fraud.

Chapter 39

Lucy

PETE LEFT ME WITH hints of our first official date, and he showed up at my place right on time. It was a Saturday, and though it was December, we knew our park was open. However, I didn't know what to expect. For me, the lake was mostly only a summer getaway. Through all those years, I'd never seen it in December.

"What if it's all dead and brown and gray?" I asked. "I don't like the idea of it looking so sad."

"There's the evergreens to give it enough life," Pete reminded me. "Sometimes, even the brown is a lot more beautiful than you'd think."

I scoffed without meaning to.

"It's something very special up there right now, what with all that early snow we got," Pete explained calmly, a wistfulness in his eye, "and I want to share it with you."

How could I say no to that?

We drove up to the lake in Pete's car. The parking lot was mostly plowed but empty, which surprised me. Pete and I bundled up with our gloves, scarves, and hats. He grabbed the small cooler we'd brought. I scooped up the stack of folded blankets into my arms—for what reason we had them, I wasn't entirely sure. I wasn't sure what was in the cooler, either.

We walked down a tiny, shoveled path. Just ahead of us, toward the lake, there was a pristine whiteness everywhere, as if no one, human or otherwise, dared disturb the perfect snowdrifts.

With his gloved hands, Pete dug a bench out from the sparkling powder, covering it with a few of the blankets I held in my arms. We sat down, covering up with the remaining blankets. He opened the cooler, which did not contain ice. It was lined with foil and towels, and had what looked like those long socks full of rice or beans that my dad sometimes used to warm and put on his neck when it was sore.

Pete handed me a thermos of what I quickly discovered was hot cocoa.

"The whipped cream melted," he said in a disappointed tone after removing the cap.

I knew a few other things that would melt whipped cream—much better than cocoa—but it wasn't time for that yet. I slowly took a few sips from my warm drink, cuddling as close to my boyfriend as I could.

Boyfriend.

He was finally more than just my friend, after all that time.

I had chills thinking of it, and I knew those chills had nothing to do with the wind. It was all from the man who'd wrapped his free arm around me. I looked over to admire the man I loved. Pete had stopped shaving off his daily stubble, and the beard was in the beginning stages of finally taking shape again.

Though facial hair honestly didn't make any difference in how I felt about Pete, knowing he cared enough about my opinion to grow it back sent a tingle all through me.

Once we finished our cocoa, snuggled in our cocoon of each other and the blankets, we packed up and headed back to the car. After a few minutes, I realized exactly where Pete was headed.

"The cabin?" I asked.

He grinned. "Kenzie gave me her key."

I let out a soft laugh. "You planned this well."

"I did. We deserve it." His smile was so big, it crinkled around his eyes.

Pete had instructed me to pack an overnight bag, but for some reason, I hadn't expected this. He eyed my facial expression at a stoplight.

"I know you've never taken a guy there before, so if you want to go somewhere else, we can."

At his words, I immediately shook my head. "I can't think of a more perfect place to spend this time with you."

My boyfriend reached over and squeezed my hand before returning his to the steering wheel. He took all the roads I would have taken, even though there was a second way to the cabin that was a few minutes faster but not as pretty.

Once we removed our outerwear and set our bags next to my bedroom door, Pete stuck a hand out to grab me by the waist, pulling me close to him. Our legs and stomachs touched as he wrapped his arms around to my back, fully embracing me in a tight but glorious hug. Then he let out a deep sigh.

"You okay?" I asked, hoping the sigh wasn't a sign of him changing his mind.

"Perfect," he said in admittedly a soft, dreamy tone.

I splayed my hands wide, slowly rubbing my palms up and down his back, first on top of his cream crew-neck sweater, then ever so slowly under it. Pete's skin was not only hot, but scorching against mine. It burned in the best way, telling me that this was finally going to happen. No more waiting. No more stopping ourselves in the middle of kissing. No more mantras.

This was it.

I lifted up onto my tiptoes, making sure to press my hands into Pete's back in order to steady myself. I was already feeling lightheaded and a little out of breath from the sensations taking over my brain.

Pete slid both hands under my sweater, resting them on either hip. He had to slip down into my leggings in order to maintain that intoxicating skin-on-skin contact. Slowly, he slid his thumbs back and forth as he moved his mouth forward to meet mine. I watched him until the last second before our anxious lips made contact, reveling in the desire spread across his face.

We moved with each other, deepening the kiss and stretching it out until we both groaned. Then Pete slid his feet backward, his body beckoning me to come with him to the bed. Within moments, our sweaters were gone, as were his jeans and my leggings. I felt another chill, but again, it had nothing to do with the cold and everything to do with the man who had me beyond ready for this next step in our *finally* official relationship.

We lost track of time as we lost ourselves to each other. Six months of pent-up everything came out in a whirlwind of explosive satisfaction and comfort. Lying in bed later, nothing in between us, Pete held my hands in his, with his arms wrapped around my body. I was facing away from him, sharing the pillow. All this skin-on-skin was absolutely electrifying.

"I love you, Luce," Pete said into my hair. He tilted his chin up and used it to nuzzle the hair off my neck, exposing even more skin. Then he kissed the spot he just exposed.

"I love you, too. Probably since the moment we met. But it's so much better now." I turned my head and body enough for Pete to see my smile. Also to kiss his lips for what I'd planned on being only a minute or two.

Only we didn't stop kissing, which led to round two.

We showered and went out for a late lunch. Then we returned to the cabin for rounds three and four. I forced us to take a little break and do something else, desperate for a breather so I wouldn't hyperventilate. Pete and I decided on Monopoly in the nude. Never did I think I'd play my family's board game naked, but it was seriously the best being able to do what felt like such a risqué thing with Pete.

I wasn't sure what time it was, but when we were suddenly famished and in need of sustenance, we ordered pizza delivery. Of course, if Pete had his way, we would have been deep in the middle of round five when the food arrived. It was a good thing I stopped him from letting me win the game just to end it sooner.

In the morning, bleary-eyed and satisfied in a way I'd never known before, Pete and I shared a slow breakfast of coffee before packing up and returning to his house, where my car waited for me.

"I can't believe I won't see you for a week," I said with a sigh, still hating our busy schedules.

Pete nodded. "The wedding."

It took all I had to not let thoughts of our potential future wedding take up residence in my mind. "Gwenn will be happy you're there."

"What about you?"

"I'm happy whenever I'm with you, no matter where we are, but it means so much to me that you're going with me."

He smiled, but his eyes didn't light up the way I'd expected them to. "Wouldn't miss it for the world."

Chapter 40

Pete

Big day today.

Yeah, for people I barely know.

BUT THIS FELT LIKE a lie. If it was the truth, it was my fault and only mine. I'd already started getting ready. I was carefully trimming my beard, mindful to not nick anything and have to shave it off again. Lucy was not going to be happy if I did. I hated remembering the look of disappointment in her eyes when she saw it was gone because of Drea, though I obviously hadn't mentioned Drea's part in that.

I'm not Miles. You can admit to me that they became your friends. It's usually a good idea to try to like your girlfriend's friends. But remember: *platonic*.

> You know, the opposite of what you and Lucy did.

> And you also know the only bridesmaid you're supposed to hook up with tonight is the one who invited you, in case you forget.

Okay, that one was uncalled for. I'd never do that to Lucy. I tossed the phone onto the bed as I entered my bedroom to select a suit. Lucy said "smart and dressy" but not too fancy, and I had an entire closet full of that at my disposal. But my mind kept wandering back to Tess's words.

I walked back to my bed and picked up my phone again.

> You think Lucy thinks I've done that before?

> . . .

> Have you done that before???

I started typing an immediate no, but then stopped.

I usually went to weddings only when I was single. That cliché about drunk and/or lonely bridesmaids looking to hook up with random hot guys proved true in just about every case, and it was often too good to pass up. But there was the possibility I'd been someone's date and left with someone else. I hated myself for not being able to remember.

> Radio silence means yes?

There was no way I could answer her. Tess was good enough to let it go and not text again.

I changed into my dark gray suit pants and black dress socks. As I sat on the bed after adjusting the second sock, I stared at my phone's dark screen. Lucy would be calling or texting soon. She'd already texted earlier to say good morning. I'd slept in and missed seeing it right away. By the time I saw it, a simple "good morning" in return sounded stupid. But though I wanted to say a million more things than good morning, I couldn't bring myself to type those words either.

I'd gone radio silent on Lucy, too. Again.

That stupid wager was over, but it was always going to hang over me.

Lucy deserves better.

Those words were coming at me from so many sides. Miles, those psycho harpies on social media. Even Rhett had said once that Lucy deserved more than someone just half-assing it in their relationship, though he didn't say it was about me specifically. And though I promised Lucy I wouldn't miss the wedding, I had so many thoughts about not wanting to go, thoughts there was no way in hell I could ever say out loud.

I promised her I wouldn't miss this wedding for the world. She was counting on me to come through for her. Yet the doubts just kept coming. My white dress shirt was finally on, but I couldn't make myself button it. The socks itched, so I took them off and started pacing the room barefoot.

Women go nuts at weddings, Miles had said before I blew up at him over that damn bet. He'd also told me that I usually did, too.

The last time we were in the break room together, after I was determined to not speak to him and he was determined to act like we were still friends, he said it yet again. He'd also added, "Maybe you can get lucky with another bridesmaid, but honestly, either way, it's a big freaking deal going. You're a brave man to attend a wedding with a woman you didn't even like enough to sleep with for six months."

"Don't listen to him," Alec had said under his breath when Miles began to walk out of the room. Tess had agreed.

"It is a big deal though," Alec added as an afterthought.

"Don't freak him out," Tess told him. She turned to me. "It's going to be okay, Pete. Just because you've never had a real relationship doesn't mean you can't do this. You like Lucy. Remember that."

I was still remembering that three days later.

When my phone beeped, I practically jumped.

Alec

> Game and a beer tomorrow? Or will you have plans?

Since she was a bridesmaid, I assumed Lucy had a lot of things to do on Sunday. However, I didn't recall ever sticking around someone's wedding weekend long enough to know what went on the next day. None of my close friends or family members my age were married, so I didn't have that to draw from, either.

Lucy would want to see me, though. No matter what, that was a constant. She always wanted to see me and spend time with me.

> I'll have to let you know.

> You're not proposing to Lucy at this wedding today, are you? You know how sentimental some women get . . .

> That's not even funny.

But was he right?

Sure, Lucy and I just started officially dating, but we'd been getting to know each other as friends for the past six months. We already said those loaded three little words to each other. Was a proposal so wholly unexpected? Or would Lucy think so at least?

Chapter 41

I SMOOTHED DOWN A stray hair of Gwenn's that she'd caught on her engagement ring, secured it with a bobby pin, and spritzed the hair with a bit more extra-strong hairspray. Lourdes helped Gwenn choose which shade of eyeshadow she wanted out of the palette.

"The gold is too *gold*," Gwenn kept saying. "I like the base of the super-light tone of gold, but that other one is awful."

"But you hate the lavender," Lourdes reminded her. "And all the other purples."

"Why did I have to choose purple as a winter wedding color?" Gwenn lamented. "It doesn't even make sense!"

"Of course it does," Lourdes soothed her. "You created an amazing color scheme. Purples, white, and metallics. It's fabulous."

"Absolutely," I added with a nod.

Gwenn eyed the last remaining eyeshadow choice, a deep plum. "Luce, what do you think?"

I hated to rush her into a decision. It was also rare for Gwenn to be so indecisive. However, I knew I needed to be firm and kind and helpful. "The plum would be fantastic with your eyes."

When Gwenn smiled, Lourdes and I both blew out our breaths in relief. The three of us were in Gwenn and Rhett's apartment, getting the gorgeous bride ready for her ceremony in only a couple hours.

Syracuse Springs Inn's tearoom was prepped and ready thanks to Susie and the wonderful staff she employed there. Kenzie was doing the event room at the community center in Syracuse Falls. I couldn't let my rivalry or whatever was going on between my sister and me come into play when it came to Gwenn's wedding. Kenzie was the perfect person to decorate the reception room.

She and I had yet another talk about it the night before.

Kenzie had begun the conversation with, "I don't want to step on any toes." It was the third time she'd said that to me.

While she said "any" toes, I knew she meant mine. Lourdes never had an issue with my sister helping out.

After a few moments, I replied, "Weddings are about bringing people together. You have a gift for organization that Gwenn respects, as well as an eye for design. And I can't say no to you just because you and I aren't getting along at the moment."

Kenzie's eyes got a little watery. "You mean that?"

I reached over and hugged her shoulders. "Of course. I think you have the wrong job."

As I refocused on the present, I sat with the fact that I hadn't heard from Pete all morning.

Lourdes told me not to worry. Pete knew I was busy doing bridesmaid things. And that was true. But it was also true that my new boyfriend had spent the last week avoiding me, or that was how it felt, at least. He wasn't answering calls or texts. He'd promised to attend the wedding, but we hadn't really spoken since that Sunday morning when we left the cabin.

It felt like I had plenty to worry about.

Archer, the wedding photographer—a super nice guy who graduated with my sister in Syracuse Falls—took several different portraits of Gwenn as Lourdes and I applied the finishing touches of her brand-new shoes and short veil. I didn't have time to check my phone again until we were already at the inn, waiting for Lennox to give us the signal to begin.

I surreptitiously checked my screen, but there wasn't anything new. Lourdes turned to me as I heaved a sigh.

"Whatever's going on with you and Pete, please let it go right now, okay? We are here for our best friend and the love of her life."

I didn't ask her how she knew it was about Pete. I didn't think I needed—or really wanted—to.

"He's supposed to be here," I managed to reply without choking up.

"We can't delay the ceremony just for him."

I sucked in a sharp breath. "I didn't say we should."

But, well . . .

"Would it be so bad to give him five more minutes?" I asked in a whisper.

Lourdes's eyes grew wide before she scrunched her face ever so slightly. "Luce, sweetie, I know you love him and want him here for this. I get it. There's someone I'd like to be here with me, too. But today is not about us. Make that your mantra if need be, but please let that sink in."

I didn't say anything.

"You can figure out where Pete is later, okay? Because today, whatever Gwenn wants, she gets. Whatever you want will have to come after all of Gwenn's wishes. And while you and I both know she'll understand you wanting to wait and would probably agree to it, you shouldn't ask her to."

Lourdes was right. I had to admit that.

She and I both smoothed out our amethyst-hued bridesmaid dresses and joined our bestie before her walk down the small aisle to her true love.

An hour and a half later, after the ceremony and the pictures, Lourdes and I met up with Kenzie at the community center, giving Gwenn and Rhett some alone time before they needed to arrive at the reception. There hadn't been a dry eye in the space after Rhett choked up during his vows. All this time later, I was the only one who was still a little weepy.

Looking around the reception, I knew for certain that my sister was wasting her talents at the diner. If I didn't know better, I never would have guessed this was the same community room from before. Kenzie even managed to get rid of the funky smell, though I didn't want to ask her how or even what it was.

Edin never did show up to the ceremony.

"You think maybe you think too much about things or see too much into them to see the whole of a situation?" Kenzie asked as we stood in the doorway to the reception room and admired her amazing work. However, her words were not said in a rude or harsh tone. They were the gentlest words my sister had said to me in a really long time.

"I guess I was wrong about her. This time," I replied cautiously.

We both chose to leave it at that.

Rhett and Gwenn were due any minute, and all the guests had arrived and were mingling in this cozy space. All except Pete.

He still hadn't called or texted. I didn't know what to do. I'd never expected this to become a habit of his. I also couldn't bear the idea of having to spend the whole of the evening without the man who only a week before told me over and over how madly in love he was with me. It was too much. This felt like the one time I depended on Pete's presence the most, and he wasn't there for me.

Chapter 42

"I won't go on and on about love quotes from classic literature, though we all know I could."

I heard Lucy's voice before I could see her.

She laughed, as did everyone else in the room, from the sound of it. After stepping through the open doorway, I moved a few feet off to the left, but Lucy didn't see me. She was holding a microphone and facing Gwenn and Rhett.

"I shipped you two from the start, not because I always do that, even though I do." She paused, and several others laughed along with her again.

The lump in my throat kept me quiet.

"The bond you two formed was something special, right from the start. Though there were some rather large obstacles on your path to this day, you have proven that true love is worth every bump." She sniffled and sucked in an uneven breath.

Lourdes stood and gently took the mic from Lucy, who wiped at her eyes, gave a smile to the room, and sat down at the table where she'd been standing.

I couldn't breathe.

Lucy's words affected her more than I'd expected them to. She never told me what she'd written for her speech. From watching her movements, I assumed she wasn't only thinking of her friends. She was thinking of me.

I wanted to go to her and wrap my arms around her and hold her close to my chest. I wanted to reassure her that I loved her just as much as she loved me, but my feet wouldn't budge.

Lourdes finished her speech, everyone toasted Gwenn and Rhett and cheered, then things moved on. But I kept my eyes on Lucy.

She finally happened to look in my direction and caught sight of me. Her pinked face brightened, and she waved. I managed to make my way over to her near the wall by her table. Lucy immediately wrapped her arms around my middle and buried her face into my chest.

I quickly wrapped my arms around her, too. "Hey. It's okay." I nuzzled close to her and breathed her in. She even smelled like lavender to match her dress. I was surprised she'd changed perfumes for this.

Then she pushed back. "Where have you been?"

What could I say? That I panicked? That I couldn't handle the pressure of being there for her in such a bold, "I am committed to you" way—even though I'd been committed to her from the start?

"I hadn't realized you needed me here," I lied. "Thought you'd be busy with wedding stuff."

"I was, but—" Lucy shook the thought away.

"Hey. I'm here now." I pulled her closer again.

After holding each other for a few moments, Lucy looked up and me and leaned her mouth nearer to mine. I moved closer, too, and slowly lowered until our lips touched, heat from both of us spreading to the other. We kept it chaste, though, as there were other people in the room.

Lucy gently broke the kiss and squeezed me again. "I have to get the cake ready to serve. See you soon."

I walked over to the little table that was being used as a bar. Non-alcoholic, I quickly saw. I was about to pour some good, old-fashioned punch into a cup when Kenzie stepped up to me.

"You know what Lucy was thinking of with her speech, don't you?"

I didn't reply right away. "Uh, yeah. I'm pretty sure I do."

She narrowed her eyes the littlest bit. "Please don't act like it doesn't mean anything."

"I didn't do that."

"But you do, though. You do it to her all the time. Just—" She took a breath. "She's a little fragile right now is what I'm saying." Then Kenzie softened her expression and walked off.

I poured my drink and chugged the first cup, desperately wishing it had alcohol in it. As if watching Lucy make that speech wasn't hard enough for me, I now had to talk about it? And why was it Kenzie's business? Being Lucy's sister did not grant her privileges like knowing the details of our relationship.

I was working on the second cup of punch when a woman I didn't know moved next to me and got a cup of her own. She chose to pour from a bottle of sparkling cider. When we happened to make eye contact, we both smiled.

"I'm Florence," she said.

"Pete," I replied.

Florence's face brightened. "Oh, you're Lucy's Pete!"

At being called Lucy's Pete, a burning heat spread through me, but I couldn't tell whether it was a good thing or not.

Florence didn't wait for an answer. "Your girlfriend did such a good job helping to pull this wedding together, don't you think? And her speech was just beautiful." She smiled, but I couldn't.

"She isn't my girlfriend," I replied automatically.

I immediately regretted this.

Florence scrunched her face. "Oh, I'm sorry. I thought you two just made it official."

I couldn't say yes, we did make it official and she was finally my girlfriend now. I couldn't say I'd just made a mistake. That I messed up.

I needed to get away and out of the room, just for a few minutes. "Excuse me." I tried to rush away as fast as I could, but I spilled my drink as I hastily set it back on the table. I didn't know what else to do with it.

As I turned to go, I saw Lucy watching us from only a couple feet away. She obviously heard everything. Her skin was red and her eyes wide.

"Luce," I began. But I didn't have anything else to add.

She turned and ran. I followed her out the door to the parking lot, but she had a head start on me, even in heels.

I couldn't believe myself. The one thing I'd been avoiding for six months finally happened. I hurt Lucy. I hated myself more than ever.

Chapter 43

Lucy

PETE'S QUICK, HEAVY FOOTSTEPS followed me out the door into the salted and plowed parking lot. When he finally caught up with me, I couldn't turn to face him. My body shuddered as I choked on my sobs.

She isn't my girlfriend.

Then what was I?

The biggest idiot in the world, that's who. Kenzie was right. It was so freaking stupid, but not for the reason she gave.

"Babe, please," he begged, his voice strained.

I whipped around with eyes full of fire.

Pete almost took a step back from me. "I didn't mean it. It was an accident."

"You sure say a lot of asshole-ish things by accident," I snapped.

"I've had to tell everyone you're not my girlfriend for so long that I just got in the habit of it. But I swear, I know I shouldn't have said that to her."

"You told me you love me," I cried, tears running down my face unabated.

"And I do," he said, coming toward me again, his arms open to embrace me.

I pushed myself away from him. "You need to leave."

"You can't be serious."

"You have to leave because I can't. I'm a wreck right now, and I can't be. This is my best friend's wedding. I have to be able to support her and be happy for her. You are done ruining this day for me."

Pete flinched at my last words. He looked like he was going to reach a hand out to me. It rose up a few inches into the air, but he dropped it back down. "Good night, Luce." Then he strode away to his car.

I hurried around the building to the back, never glancing over at the man I should have been slow dancing with. From the back door of the community center, I could get to the bathroom without anyone seeing me. I rushed to the nearest mirror, grateful at least for waterproof makeup. I ran a paper towel under the tap and used the dampness to cool off my neck and cheeks.

When the music changed, I knew it was time for Gwenn and Rhett's first dance.

I had to pull myself together and act like everything was picture perfect. Like Lourdes said, this was Gwenn's day, and what she wanted, she got. She wanted to share a dance with her new husband and not have to worry about her crying bestie. This was not high school prom. I practiced my smile in the mirror for a few moments. It was showtime.

"What's wrong?" Lourdes asked as soon as I stepped over to her in the reception room.

So much for that.

"I can't talk about it now."

Lourdes silently patted my arm, and then we watched our dear friend enjoy the happiest night of her life. And with me having to go home without Pete, it felt like my worst night.

Chapter 44

Lucy

My relationship had abruptly become less *Cinderella*, and more *Anna Karenina*. Obviously, I had no intention of throwing myself under a train, but I wasn't in a good place. There was something about Pete's freak-out at Gwenn and Rhett's wedding.

It was now weeks after the wedding, and he'd disappeared. Just dropped out of my life. My brain kept playing back those freaking words again. *She isn't my girlfriend.*

I heard nothing from Pete. No poems, no letters, no notes. No calls or texts. No dates. No contact of any kind. I called and texted him every day for the first two weeks like I normally would have. What he said hurt me, of course, but hadn't we promised just a week before to become a real couple? Real couples didn't break up after only one argument. They worked through it. He wasn't giving us a chance to work through the argument.

His silence was a constant bother to me. So much so, I had to block out everything else nagging at me, including Miss Havisham and all those women on social media. Miss H hadn't contacted me in a while and the online fervor had died down, but that didn't mean it was easily forgotten. How was it possible that Pete had shut out all that and also me?

Lourdes called me one Saturday, asking me for a ladies' night out. "You and I can go to the bar or dinner or a coffee house or wherever you want. Let's just go and not talk about men, please." Her voice was soft and a little sadder than I'd heard in her in a long while.

I hoped she was okay but knew she didn't want me to ask. "How about the coffee shop in Camillus? We haven't been there in forever."

"Sounds good. I'll be at your house soon."

·❤·❤·❤·❤·❤·

"My mom suggested a redesign of the front of the floral shop," Lourdes said as we sat at a small high-top table.

At her words, I flicked my eyes up from my coffee to look at her face. "I thought you didn't want to change anything Gam-Gam did."

Lourdes moved a little, as if she was thinking about changing her mind on this. "I know I did. I mean, the flowers and vases and stuff like that is different all the time. But my mom is suggesting shuffling everything to different areas. We don't have the money for any kind of renovation. Any changes would be purely superficial. Baskets, accessories, maybe some shelves."

"I know Momma Marjie means well. She wouldn't suggest changes if she didn't think they were necessary. How do you feel about moving your grandma's stuff around?"

Again, Lourdes took a few moments to consider my question. "I think if she was aware of it needing to be updated, she'd understand. As it is, I'm not sure bringing her to the shop after the redesign is a good idea. I'd hate for the changes to spark something in her brain that she finds upsetting. It's difficult to calm her down when that happens, especially since it's too often about stuff she remembers that doesn't exist anymore."

I nodded. Gam-Gam's dementia had deteriorated her mind far faster than anyone expected, though she was also still able to take care of herself longer than they'd expected as well, but that time was running out. Lourdes's family was doing the best they could to take care of her, but things were going steadily downhill.

"You know how people ask what you would change about the past? There might be a few things I'd change from before, but honestly, the only time I want different is now. I want her to be who she was before this took over her. I want her to know what's happening today and what we did yesterday, not look at me and think I'm my mom or wonder why things are falling apart in the house when, to her, they are supposed to be brand new."

She took a few moments to breathe.

"Maybe I want to change all three for her? Past, present, and future. Make things right in a way no one can do. No one can magically make this disease go away."

My heart broke for my bestie, as it did for all of her family. I couldn't imagine the pain they lived with. I had my own pain, but it was vastly different, even if it was as intense.

Lourdes steered the conversation back to the ideas her mom had for the shop and how it might all come together. We brainstormed ways of turning cheap items into beautiful displays while still keeping the basic flow the shop currently had.

There was no room for any more talk of our disappointments, which was fine by me. Tears had been flowing too steadily out of me as of late.

·♥·♥·♥·♥·♥·

Thursday, after hours of teaching and several more hours of grading, preparing, and just keeping busy to occupy my mind, I gave in and called Pete.

He didn't answer, of course.

"I don't know what happened that night. I really don't understand it, Pete. Did we not just have our first official date as a couple at the lake? Did we not just express our love verbally and physically? Wasn't that what we spent six months working toward?"

I quickly hung up, instantly regretting the call.

It was back to Plan A: distraction.

I called Gwenn. "How's newlywed life?"

She laughed. "Pretty much the same as engaged life, except with more paperwork."

"You're legally, officially Gwenn Rhys-Mason now?'

"I sure hope it's official, or I had all those business cards printed up for nothing." She paused. "Still haven't heard from Pete?"

"It shouldn't surprise me given his behavior at your wedding."

"But it does." This wasn't a question. "And of course it does. I know Lourdes and I tease you about how fast you fall in love with men, but I thought Pete would be the one to stick around. Everyone saw the sparks between you two for six months."

We'd had more than just sparks. Pete and I had a connection like I'd never experienced with anyone before.

"Why don't you ask Charisma what to do? She knew him before you did. She might have some insight."

"I doubt it. They only had a handful of dates. It isn't like they had a relationship."

"The only other thing I can suggest to you is move on."

"Not a chance. Pete and I are in love. Real love. You don't just give up on that."

Chapter 45

Pete

Lucy's face popped up on my screen when I received another new text from her. I read this one just like I read all the others, despite the tightness in my chest and the knot in my stomach.

I missed her more than I could ever begin to tell her. Only I didn't tell her anything. I couldn't make it better. I didn't deserve the chance to.

After forcing myself to breathe normally again with my eyes squeezed shut, I opened them to check my schedule for the day.

There it was. The appointment, in some ways, I'd tried to forget. The Larkins.

How was I supposed to face them? What could I possibly say to them that would encompass all the apologies and explanations they—and especially Lucy—deserved?

With her parents sitting across from me at my desk two hours later, I thought for sure I was going to lose my nerve.

"We are nearing the end of your final extension," I said slowly, cautiously including myself in this, letting them know I was not going to give up just because I was struggling with Lucy.

Nadine and Kerrick nodded but remained silent, eyes still on me. Damp, reddened eyes, like they'd already cried before our meeting.

Shit.

My eyes stung now, too, but I cleared my throat and continued. In a lower voice—even though I'd closed my office door in anticipation of this conversation—I said, "I've spoken with debt counselors and other mortgage experts on your behalf. I'm doing everything I can. I won't give up." My voice wobbled at the end, and I cleared my throat again.

"Do we have any options?" Kerrick asked.

I laid out the truth for them, the truth we'd all been avoiding. Without concessions from people in my company who I was sure wouldn't give in, there wasn't much I could do for the Larkins. The debt counselors were still working on their end, but I couldn't tell Kerrick and Nadine just yet. Technically, it was outside of my job description and could possibly get me fired for trying to reach beyond what was possible for me. But I meant what I said when I told them I wasn't giving up.

"Thank you," both Nadine and Kerrick said to me with small, sad smiles.

That nearly broke me, hearing Lucy's parents thank me. Seeing them so grateful to me and hopeful after everything that had gone down. I couldn't even avoid eye contact with them just to make it through the rest of the appointment. I had to face them and let them see the pain in my eyes. There was no hiding from it.

We all shook hands at the end of the meeting, and the Larkins were gone.

I slumped down in my chair and pulled my phone out. Then I pulled up the photos of Lucy and me together, slowly scrolling through each one. I thought perhaps I could pinpoint the moment I'd subconsciously decided to flake on her. Like maybe I could see it in my face. But all I saw and all I felt was the happiness of that time. Of having her close in my arms. Of pushing the limits of non-platonic friendship while falling in love.

"Pete?" my assistant said.

"Yeah?" I asked, my eyes still on Lucy's.

"I called to you three times. Your eleven o'clock is here."

I finally tore my gaze away from the photo of the woman I loved and put my phone back on my desk, its screen now black. "Right. Send them in."

·♥·♥·♥·♥·♥·

How to stop thinking of her?

I couldn't say I hadn't resorted to googling that to find an answer. I tried calling her several times, but each time I had my phone in my hand, I couldn't follow through. More than once, I started a text to her, only to delete it.

So it was back to wondering how to get her off my mind. But really, the better question was: How could I ever apologize for all I'd done?

The bet.

The reason why those women came after me on social media.

The truth of who I'd been for so long but didn't want to be anymore because of Lucy.

I wanted to deserve her, but was nowhere near deserving. Yeah, I managed to keep my job through it all, hard as it was, just so her parents' account didn't get handed off to one of my coworkers, because I knew none of them gave a damn. I was the one who cared the most about what happened to the Larkins. Even Alec admitted that he probably wouldn't have gone through as much trouble as I did just to help them.

And the thing was, it wasn't any trouble for me. I'd do that again in a heartbeat. I'd do it a million times over if it meant making up for just a little bit of what I'd done in my past and perhaps convincing Lucy to forgive me.

I got a new email notification from a contact I'd made in my endeavor to help the Larkins. The beginning of the message gave a jump-start to my heart.

You're definitely on the right track here. I spoke with Rose confidentially, and while the fund is indeed usually only for Pennsylvania teachers, there are no rules that exist saying funding cannot be used for teachers in other states. Let me know how you want to proceed.

The small non-profit I'd found—one that helped teachers with medical bills they couldn't afford to cover on their own—might actually be able to help the Larkins. It wasn't a perfect path to the result I wanted, including quite a few compromises that would need to be made. And it could never get back to anyone that I was the one who set this into motion—not the Larkins, not Shubin, not even Tess and Alec—because while the fund was absolutely available to Kerrick and Nadine, as the one in charge of their mortgage account, I could be fired if it was discovered I went so far out of my job description.

I immediately emailed my contact, asking for more info in order to set things into motion. Time was ticking.

Chapter 46

Lucy

"Hey, Luce. Can I talk to you?" Charisma's voice came through my phone.

"I'm on my way to the bookstore," I told her.

It was the beginning of February. Almost time to start planning for the end of the school year. In June. I'd already started dreading that month.

"Do you need something?" I added.

"Can I come over?"

"I'm closer to you now, so why don't I just come there?"

"Okay. How soon can you get here?" Her voice was a little off, not quite the way it normally sounded, but I couldn't figure out what exactly was different.

I detoured my car away from the direction of the bookstore and toward Charisma's apartment. It didn't take me long to get there. Once she let me in through the door, I could tell she'd been crying.

"Hey, what is it?" I had intended to sit on the sofa, but the look on her face kept me on my feet.

Charisma's lips quivered. She moved her mouth to speak but didn't. I'd never seen her so unsure before, and I'd known her practically my whole life.

"What's going on?" I pressed.

"I need to say something. About Pete. But first, let me ask you something. Did you two ever clarify if you were allowed to date others during those six months?"

My already sinking feeling turned into something like drowning. "I didn't think we needed to."

Charisma took a moment before replying. I couldn't decipher the look on her face, but whatever she felt, it clearly pained her. "Remember when you introduced us?"

"When he didn't remember you?"

She winced but continued. "Anything else about that day?"

"You two said that you used to date each other. But you both told me it was no big deal."

"We did, and it wasn't. Until it was."

"What do you mean?"

"We didn't date for very long. He wasn't what I was looking for. Really, neither of us wanted a relationship."

"Right. Well, I don't know about Pete, but you've never been one for commitment, anyway."

"Lucy, I didn't know he was still looking. And looking. Actively. You know what I mean."

I did, but it didn't matter. It didn't mean anything. They both said so.

She continued. "He turned out to be a real heartbreaker. I found out that, when our dates were over, he'd leave me and go straight to another woman's bed or car, or he'd leave another woman to come to me."

"But you weren't in a relationship."

"Does it matter? Hurtful is hurtful. Did he even wash the sex off of him?"

"Ew." I let out a sharp exhale, feeling the room spin a bit.

"Exactly. I hate that I've even had to wonder that." Charisma shuddered. "I found a few of his exes, and he did the same to them.

He's never been a one-woman man, even when he promised he would be."

I couldn't speak.

"What was it he promised you?"

I had no answer I could give verbally. Every part of me was in a painful knot.

"I've been pointing out those social media posts and DMs for a reason."

"Because you think he's an ass?" I finally found my voice.

"Because he is."

"You can't let something on the internet from some rando sway your thoughts and opinions."

"I know Pete, Lucy. Better than he thinks I do."

"How so?" My tone was sharper than I meant it to be.

"You know how many women want him?"

The only woman that mattered was me. Pete said so. Charisma's words were just to hurt me. She was more like my sister every day. "I can't judge him based on how others react to him."

"He wants them, too. Plenty of women catch his eye. Oh sure, he's friendly. He's also great at making excuses. I guarantee you that any woman who throws herself at him is getting a good time out of him without you ever being aware. He'll never tell you. But trust me, he's screwing any woman who unbuttons her top or hikes up her skirt or even licks her lips in his direction."

"I have enough issues with Pete right now. Why are you adding to that?"

Charisma's eyes became a little watery. "Because there's something I have to tell you."

"There's more?"

She nodded, closing her eyes for a second or two. When she looked at me again, they were so full of tears that a few drops began to spill out and roll down her cheeks. "It was me," she said hoarsely.

My throat was tight. "What was?"

"The posts," she whispered. "The messages. Miss Havisham. I did that."

"No." I stepped back a few feet. "You're my friend. We grew up together. You'd never do anything like try to ruin my happiness and a man's entire life."

She cried harder. "I'm so sorry. I never meant for it to become what it did."

"What did you think would happen?" I snapped. "How could it not have caused trouble?"

"I sent the DMs and made the first few posts. But the rest were made by others. Pete has hurt a lot of women. I started seeing posts that I knew I didn't make and had no idea who created them. It became an explosion of vitriol against Pete. So many times I asked people to take them down, and they all laughed at me."

My body began to shake. "He almost lost his job because of those posts. They almost ruined his life. How could you?" I screamed the last question at her.

"I'm sorry," she sobbed.

I was crying now, too. "You chose to be my friend. But you also chose to degrade and destroy the man I love. No matter how he made you feel or how he treated you, blasting him on social media was not the right way to deal with that."

"Maybe you're right, but I didn't know what else to do." Charisma wiped away some of her tears, but more fell. "He was going to hurt you, too. He could have already."

"You don't know that for sure. Even if he did, I'm a grown woman. I've handled my fair share of cheating boyfriends and nasty breakups. I would have been fine without your 'help.'" I put my fingers into air quotes.

"Luce, you haven't spoken to him in weeks. Are you fine now?"

Her question physically hurt. "You made your choice. Now I need to make mine."

"Which is what?"

I took a breath before answering her. "Whether I still want you in my life."

Charisma flinched, tears still streaming down her reddened cheeks.

I hurried to the door. I had to get out of her apartment.

"Lucy, wait," she called to me, following me to the foyer.

I swiveled around. "Fix it, Charisma. Tell Pete."

She stopped her feet before making it all the way over to me. "Are you crazy? I can't do that."

"You nearly destroyed his career. You have to fix it, or at least own up to it." I wiped away the hot tears on my face. "Maybe he'll forgive you. I doubt it, but I suppose it's possible. He must know you don't like him. I'm not sure about my forgiveness."

"You and I have been friends since we were kids."

"And yet you lied to me for months." I opened the door and walked out.

Chapter 47

Pete

MARCH MEETINGS ARRIVED. I'D been without Lucy for nearly three months. I still missed her more than I'd ever missed anyone before. I also still knew she was better off without me.

There was a knock on my door. I looked over from my computer screen when the door opened and saw Tess walk in.

"Got a minute?" she asked, closing the door behind her.

"Sure," I told her, though I actually didn't.

I was waiting to hear some news about Lucy's parents' properties. It had been weeks since I'd received an answer from anyone involved, and even longer since I'd heard anything definitive. I desperately needed good news to pass along to them. I was both lucky and thankful they hadn't asked for someone else to take over the account, removing me from their lives the way I removed myself from Lucy's.

"You look a little miserable," Tess commented. She had her arms wrapped around her torso as if she was cold, even though she wore a sweater.

"Thanks for that." My tone was sharp.

"I just mean you look sad. Still haven't talked to Lucy?"

I shook my head. "I don't know what to say to her." If I even thought it a good idea to contact her, which I didn't.

"It's been three months. If there was anything you could say, I think you would have figured it out already."

I didn't have an answer.

"Does this mean it's over between you two?" Tess's tone was soft.

"Yeah. It's over between us." I almost choked on my words because I knew they were the truth, though I wished they didn't have to be.

Tess didn't reply. She slowly walked over toward me. Instead of sitting on one of the chairs in front of my desk, she came around and pulled herself up on top of it, her legs brushing against me.

"It's a little warm, don't you think?" she asked.

As she removed her button-up sweater, the first thing I noticed was her cleavage. It was hard not to, considering there was a lot of skin suddenly inches away from my face. Her mostly sheer white shirt was unbuttoned to her stomach, and her bra was clearly missing.

"Tess . . ." I began. I had no freaking idea what to say next. I didn't feel a zing when our bodies touched. I didn't feel any of those physical sensations I'd expected to come about naturally.

She swung one extremely high-heeled foot to the other side of me and adjusted her bottom on my desk, hiking up her skirt in the process so the tops of her very open thighs were no longer covered by it. I could see the straps of the lacy black garter belt she wore underneath the skirt, barely holding up her lacy black thigh-highs. Damn. She was wearing sexy lingerie for me. At least I assumed so.

I didn't dare look any farther to see what other clothing items were missing, but I had a good guess about one of them.

"The door isn't locked," I said stupidly.

She was still way too close to me, wearing a perfume I'd never smelled on her before. It would have been heavenly—if it had been Lucy.

I scooted my chair back, taking the risk of seeing more—well, less—under her skirt. With steady breaths, I locked my eyes on Tess's and refused to look anywhere else.

"Do you care?" Tess laughed. "I know all the stories, Pete. We're work besties. You've never turned down office sex. The riskier, the better." Then she winked.

"Maybe before, but—"

"I'm offering you a chance to cash in on something you and I both know you want. We've flirted for a long time." She drew out the word *long*.

"Not lately," I was quick to respond.

"You've said quite a lot of naughty things to me, with an eager growl to match."

I didn't have a reply for that one. It was true. Before Lucy, I absolutely would have been up Tess's skirt already, wanting to see what wasn't showing and doing whatever she'd allow with it. While I'd never thought she and I would get together before, I never would have turned her down.

But I didn't move any closer. I didn't make any motion that would indicate my desire to touch Tess. I didn't have that desire in any way. I wanted to make her leave, not screw her.

I had to be careful, though. As Tess said, I'd had my fair share of dirty talk with her as friends. I was terrified she might take my rejection badly and claim harassment against me, friend or not. It was a no-win situation, but still, I had to get her the hell out of my office.

"I never should have led you on," I told her. "Lucy is the only woman I want."

Tess slowly closed her legs and slid down off the desk. "But you broke up. You haven't spoken to her in months. You just told me it was over."

"I did, and it is."

"But you don't want me, is that it?" Tess angrily pulled her skirt back down .to where it was when she first entered my office and started buttoning her top.

"Breaking up with Lucy hasn't changed how I feel about her."

Tess snatched her sweater off the desktop—sending a few papers flying into the air—and shoved her arms into the sleeves. She didn't bother buttoning it, but instead held it closed with her arms. "You're an asshole, Pete. I hope you're miserable about her forever."

She stalked out of my office and slammed the door before I had a chance to say more.

Chapter 48

Lucy

IF EVER THERE WAS a day that I most regretted checking my DMs, this was certainly it. I'd had a decent day up to this point, if feeling slightly less like I was drowning in misery from both Pete and Charisma was "decent." A full workday at school hadn't helped much in boosting my mood. Rumors were still swirling about the proposed annexation, and I couldn't tell whether I was more anxious or angry about it.

When I saw I had a new message request, my stomach clenched. What could it possibly be now? Miss Havisham—I mean *Charisma*—and her online cronies weren't enough?

Before looking at it, I texted Gwenn to ask her if she had heard any more about that cheaper rental. She quickly called me.

"Not yet," she told me, a crunching sound in my ears.

"Am I interrupting dinner?" I asked.

"Nope. I have a showing I need to leave for in a few minutes, and it'll be a long one. I'm actually taking them to two separate properties. I won't get a chance to eat for a few hours." She paused, which I assumed was because she needed to swallow or take a drink of something. "So, the house. There's no news yet. I think the owners want to fix up the bathroom tile first. They tossed that out the last time we were in contact. But that would only delay things by a few weeks. It shouldn't be too much longer before I can try to get you in."

I thanked her for working so diligently for me, and we hung up.

Then I was all alone, just me and my message request.

I could do this. I could handle it, whatever "it" was. I'd already seen the truth about my non-platonic friend slash boyfriend slash whatever the hell we were anymore. My heart had already been shattered into a billion tiny pieces. It wasn't possible for things to get any worse.

Who was Tess Macari?

There were several paragraphs before my eyes. Too much to take in right away. I saw snippets of words.

Pete.

Work.

Friend.

Lies.

Bet.

Bet? Like a wager?

Who *was* this woman?

I looked at Tess's profile page. There it was in the work and education section. Tess really did work with Pete. They had the same job title at the same bank, same location. Her friends list was private, but I assumed he was on it. I wasn't brave enough to look at his, even though we technically were still friends on there.

There were no public photos of Tess and Pete together and none of any with him that she'd tagged him in.

I went back to her message.

Hi, Lucy.

I'm Tess. I work with Pete. I consider myself good friends with him, and that's why I am asking you to please listen to me. Hear me out.

We have a friend. Miles. Miles is an ass, if you didn't notice the weekend you all went camping together. When you and Pete met,

Miles was shocked at you two not sleeping together. Honestly, we all were. That's just how Pete operates. He doesn't do "friends first" or relationships in any way. He is absolutely a "wham, bam, thank you, ma'am," get up and go kind of guy. Doesn't even lie about it to his friends, though he lies about things I'm sure would crush your soul.

You see, Miles took his surprise and turned it into something I never thought Pete would agree to. Miles bet Pete that he wouldn't be able to get you to have sex with him before the six months of your waiting period as friends was up.

Now, as his good friend, let me say first that Pete was initially horrified at Miles's suggestion. That much was clear by the expression on his face. But Miles being Miles, he pushed and pushed until Pete agreed. They made it a thousand-dollar wager on whether or not Pete could get you to screw him.

Not sure who decided on the price, but either way, Pete was a willing participant. And he knew he could do a whole lot with a grand in his pocket. There were many times I could see the gears turning in his head on how to go about this. I figured it would have been a piece of cake if it was only up to him. I knew he was more than capable of getting a woman to drop her panties for him. I think I'm the only one he's never gone for. Yet, anyway.

Looking back, I'm sure you can recall moments when Pete was actually trying to seduce you for the win. There has to be more than one occasion, because that's just how he is. He knows how to charm. It's his very best quality and—perhaps now—his biggest downfall.

Which leads me to Drea. I'm sure you remember her. She's hard to forget, including for Pete. Even when you two were an official couple, I'm sure she was still throwing herself at him. She always had, since they met. I don't know how often or if he ever turned her down. He even shaved his beard because of her. Sorry you had to find that out from me. I'm sorry you had to find all this out from me. I'm sorry it all happened in the first place, because you deserve better than this.

I don't expect you to message me back. If you've read this far, at least you know the truth. Do with it what you like.

Holy—*WHAT?!?!?!*

Pounding, terrifying waves of nausea crashed over me, mingling so effortlessly with rage. I was beyond incensed.

How *freaking dare he*?

Oh gosh.

I'd begged him to sleep with me because the teasing was too much. The teasing. Yep. Pete knew exactly what he was doing there. He knew what he was doing with all of it. The love letters. The whispering in my ear. The cuddles. The dirty talk.

More nausea came, and with it, a painful, burning flood of tears.

My phone rang out Lourdes's ringtone, making me jump. I answered but couldn't say hello.

"Lucy, what's wrong?" my bestie immediately asked over my audible sobs.

"He lied to me." I fumbled over every word and sucked in sharp breaths between each one.

"I'll be there in two minutes."

Before I knew it, Lourdes was next to me on my living room futon, holding me in her arms while I cried. Kenzie was on her way, and Gwenn was doing her best to finish up or reschedule her remaining work for the day.

I couldn't tell Lourdes the story. All I could do was hand her my phone and let her read for herself.

"That stupid prick," she said over and over. I couldn't read her expression, as my eyes were closed, swollen from all the crying. "Who the hell does he think he is?"

"He said he loved me," I cried, not bothering to address her questions.

"He also told Florence you weren't his girlfriend when you were," Lourdes said softly.

"Thanks for that," I retorted, the sobs causing my body to shudder with each inhale and exhale. Each word dripped with acid.

"Maybe the wager kept him with you, or maybe he used it as a way out. I don't know. But I do know that clearly he doesn't deserve any of these tears." She took in a breath, giving my shoulders a squeeze. "But you know I'd never tell you not to cry. Let out as much or as little as you need to."

I kept crying, but eventually the tears became small streams, no longer tsunamis.

"I assume you've already social media stalked this Tess woman," Lourdes said once I could breathe normally again.

"It was the first thing I did after glancing through the message. I think she's legit. She doesn't seem to have any reason to lie to me. Though I couldn't bring myself to check Pete's profile."

Lourdes gave me a look, then picked up my phone again. "Here she is," Lourdes told me in a whisper. "In his friends list."

I nodded in painful acknowledgement.

"Are you going to message her back?"

"How can I not? I don't think I can ask her all my questions, but I at least want to acknowledge that this is a big deal. For me, and probably for her, too."

"She said they're good friends. Why did you never meet her before?"

I lifted my shoulders for a moment. "The only women he ever mentioned to me apart from his family were Miles's fiancé Corkie and Drea, and both only because I met them on a camping trip. Two trips, actually. They were both there when Pete and I met." I swiped at more hot tears that had left my wet, cottony eyes. "He'd never let me look at his phone. Never mentioned anyone outside the realm of those forced into my acquaintance. I should have suspected something. I should have known Drea was a bitch to me for a reason. She had Pete, too, or she was trying to get him."

"I'd like to hazard a guess and say you never would have believed Tess if not for your conversation with Charisma."

"You'd be right." I gave a sardonic laugh. "Never thought I'd feel even a tiny smidgen of gratitude for Charisma's brutal way of honesty. Pete probably cheated the way Spence did to you."

Lourdes winced. "I'm sorry for you. For that. It sucks."

I could only nod in reply yet again.

My bestie didn't say anything for a while. She was still on my futon, down at the end. "What are you going to say to Tess? Or have you not thought about that yet? Because I wouldn't answer her without a plan."

"All my initial questions sound so stupid now. I don't have to ask how she knows or if this is even real. None of those things I had for Miss Havisham. No. There's only one question I have now."

I opened the app again and clicked on Tess's name. Then I accepted the message and began a reply.

> Why are you telling me this now? Why not before?

She answered much faster than I expected her to. I had a response in a matter of minutes.

> You deserve to know. Pete's an ass. I hate that he did that to you, and I hate that I was too afraid to tell you sooner. I think you should be careful, for your sake.

> Take back your heart.

If more frightening words existed, I didn't know it in this moment. Those last four were enough for me.

> Has he ever done anything like this before?

Guess there was another question lingering around that hadn't occurred to me before, but boy was it a crucial one. I squeezed my phone in anticipation—or dread.

> Unfortunately Pete and Miles make wagers all the time. It's highly possible his sex life has combined with their hobby in the past. Knowing them both as I do, I'm sure they probably laughed a lot about it, both then and now.

And that was it. That was all I needed to hear from her. There was nothing else she could say that mattered. I typed and sent the words "thank you," then hid our conversation and closed out the app.

"I'm here," my sister said as she opened the living room door and stepped in.

She immediately came to me for a hug, then Lourdes encouraged me to share my story all over again. It was brutal and agonizing, especially watching Kenzie's expressions change. I'd still have to do this one more time with Gwenn, I knew, but at least my sister would finally understand the hell Pete had put me through and why I found it so hard to let him go.

It was going to be so easy to let him go after this, though, right?

Chapter 49

Pete

IT WAS HARDER THAN I thought avoiding Tess all the rest of that day. She obviously never let on that anything had transpired between us, and I did my best to give off the same nonchalant energy. But I knew she had black lace lingerie on for me, and she knew I wanted absolutely nothing to do with it.

If I'd just called Lucy back or texted her or showed up at her house, maybe this debacle with Tess never would have happened. Maybe Lucy and I would be happy, and no other woman would think she had a chance with me. But I also knew that I'd screwed up so badly that I wasn't worthy of happiness with Lucy. I wasn't worthy of her looking at me the way she did. I might not have deserved to lose my best female friend because of it, but I certainly deserved Tess's wrath, and Lucy's, too.

At home later, with Tess's naked skin and pouty lips haunting me in the hours since it happened, I pulled out my phone from my pocket. No matter how many times Tess flashed in my mind, she was always immediately replaced with Lucy. I could see Lucy in that open, unbuttoned top. Lucy in that sexy garter belt, her legs open while perched on my desk. Lucy inching closer to me, undressing me in my unlocked office, the way I'd fantasized about her many, many times before. I wished with all I had that it could have been her.

There was only one thing I could do.

I'd obviously stopped sending Lucy letters with romantic poems that made me think of her. Those poems were just as heartfelt as if I'd written them for her myself. I'd loved her long before I could say I did. While I couldn't send her anything now, I could still pour out my feelings, even though she'd never know them.

While I could have done this in a text, I was afraid that she'd text me again or I'd hit the wrong thing and it would be deleted or missing. The only way I could guarantee not losing it was to compose a new email.

As I started typing, the words flowed a lot easier than I'd expected them to. Maybe someday, all these words would be enough to move forward.

·♥·♥·♥·♥·♥·

It was crazy awkward with Tess at the office.

There was no getting around that.

I didn't know how to make things right with her, either. Just another failing on my part when it came to women. I used to think I knew everything about how to get them on my side, but all I knew was how to make them lust after me. I drew a blank as far as any follow-through.

Tess wouldn't speak to me except for important work-related conversations, and she did her best to make sure those were all group discussions. She refused eye contact completely. All my texts to her went unanswered.

Shubin called me into his office one day in the middle of March.

Again.

This was getting old *fast*.

I had never worked so hard in my life to keep my job. First those social media posts, then Miles, and now whatever this was. It wasn't even done in a nice way.

He just walked past my door with, "Amundsen. My office."

Shubin hadn't added "now," but there was no choice about it.

"You have a meeting today," he said once we were both seated.

"I have several, sir."

"You have one in particular. Kerrick and Nadine Larkin."

Oh, right. They'd postponed our last meeting that was scheduled a few weeks ago. I was still doing every single thing I could think of to try and help the Larkins save their home.

I couldn't speak. All I could do was nod.

"My secretary tells me there might be a reason you'd want to transfer their account to someone else."

I quickly shook my head no. "Not at all."

"You know, Amundsen, there's a reason Lewis chose you to take over this account. You are more than just good at the actual tasks at hand. You understand?"

I did. Everyone else in the office had suggested in one way or another that they'd have already given up on helping the Larkins by this point.

"Good. I know there have been some shadows over you these past six months." He gave me a pointed look. "But I'm confident you won't have any more of those in the future." There was that look again, this time as a warning.

"No, I won't, sir." I paused a moment. "Speaking of the Larkins, I came up with a plan I think will work. It involves a big compromise on both our parts—ours and theirs—but I think if I can guarantee them one particular thing, we can finally break through and reach a satisfying solution."

I paused again. My contact within that Pennsylvania nonprofit said everything was all set for the funding for Nadine and Kerrick.

However, I felt I needed to be honest with my boss, even if it meant that he might fire me. The Larkins were worth it. *All* of them.

"There's something else as well. A nonprofit for teachers and former teachers can help them with some of their debt. Not all of it, but a fair amount, which would ease their burden and make it easier for them to focus on repaying the mortgage their main mortgage."

"They contacted this nonprofit?"

I took in a breath but kept it as steady as possible. I also kept the rest of me steady and calm though I was anything but on the inside. "No. I did."

Shubin didn't react for a few moments. This was typical of him, though. I waited it out and didn't give in to worry. I was promising the very thing he wanted for this account: money returned to the bank.

Then he leaned back in his chair. "Tell me more."

Chapter 50

Lucy

"Luce?" my brother's voice called from the other side of the house. It was Friday evening, when he and I were both done with work for the day.

I rushed out of my bedroom and down the hall in order to try and cut him off before he made it farther into the living room, but it was too late. He was in full view of the fact that my sofa, tables, and fancy bamboo chairs were gone. Only a cheap futon and equally cheap, scratched-up coffee table sat in the room.

"I figured it was bad, but not this bad. What the hell's going on?" Dominic asked in a hard tone. He stood by the still-open door with his hands on his hips, scowling eyes glaring at me.

"What do you mean?" I asked, but in no way was it believable that I didn't understand him.

"Don't do that," he snapped. "Where is all your stuff?"

I rubbed my forehead with my fingertips before even attempting an answer.

"Seriously. What did you do? And what's all this bullshit I hear about you putting your things in storage? Because you and I both know you can't afford that. So talk."

Wow. The town gossips must have been too busy with my break-up to get around to my stuff being gone if Dom was just now hearing this.

"What do you want me to say?"

"Damn it. Stop stalling, and tell me what you did."

Even though he and I had pretty much only seen each other at family dinners as of late, my brother still knew me better than most people. I decided to go about it a different way, since lying wouldn't work and I couldn't think of anything he'd be interested in enough to divert away from our current conversation.

"You always told me that I had too much stuff. Well, my style is now minimalist, so thanks, bro. It looks good, don't you think?" I gave Dom a smile, but his mouth remained tight and angry.

"What's this I hear about you giving up this house?"

I again feigned ignorance and stepped aside to refold the sofa throw that was perfectly fine before.

"Are you really going to give up stability, comfort, and sanity to save twenty dollars a month?"

There was no way to stop my mouth from falling open in shock. "How do you know?"

"I ran into Jenni Jo the other day. She said you were checking out apartments, but none are available at the moment. Then she said you were wanting a new rental to save some money. After I heard about you going over to the house on Elm with Gwenn, I put two and two together."

Since I was trying to keep my eyes from filling with tears, I avoided both eye contact and replying to my brother.

"Don't be stupid," he added. "Don't give up this house you love. That house isn't anywhere near as nice as this one, and it's in a part of town that you hate. Besides, twenty bucks a month isn't going to erase anyone's debts in this family, and you'll just end up more miserable than you already are."

With all the other things I'd cut back on, I figured twenty dollars a month could do more than Dom realized, but remained silent. I was clearly not going to win this argument.

Dominic's ringer went off.

"That's Charisma's ringtone," I said in shock.

"Yeah. So?" my brother said, checking his phone. It looked like he was texting her in reply.

"You still talk to her?"

"So does Kenz."

"I can't believe you people!" I shouted.

Dom quickly raised his eyes at me. "What are you talking about? Charisma's our friend."

"And I'm your sister. How can you possibly still talk to her after what she did?"

"Pete deserved everything he got from that—and worse—and you know it."

"Charisma nearly destroyed his life."

Dom shook his head. "I can't believe you, Luce. Pete's life was never going to be destroyed. So he might have lost his job. So what? He's intelligent and educated. He'd have easily found something else."

"I cannot understand how you don't see the ruthlessness of her actions."

"Ruthless? Seriously? Charisma did what she did because she was in pain. Like the pain Pete caused you. I'll say it again. Pete deserved what he got, and he sure as hell doesn't deserve what he lost."

That was probably the nicest thing my brother had ever said about me, but then, he just as easily could have meant Charisma instead. "But Dom—"

"Luce, I don't care what you think the root of all this is. You can tell me that I don't understand all you want, but I actually do."

I couldn't reply, but Dominic eyed me like he expected me to.

"What about Charisma?" he asked. "What about you? What about all those other women he hurt? Do none of you matter?"

"We matter," I whispered.

"But . . ." Dom said, clearly expecting more.

"But so does Pete."

"Mom and Dad are losing their home, and you're losing your damn mind!" Dominic yelled at me.

"I don't need this right now," I replied, doing my best to keep my voice steady.

"Why are you being such a blockhead?"

"Stop talking to me like that."

"Somebody has to. Let's just forget about Petey Boy for a moment. Selling a few tables and chairs and sofas isn't going to raise hundreds of thousands of dollars. All you're doing is sticking your head in the sand."

"No, I'm not. And I've sold a lot more than just those three things."

"Why do you care about that damn cabin so much?"

"Because—" This required me to really think about the way I wanted to say it without getting too emotional. My brother wouldn't react well if I left it with only "because" as the answer. "I want to preserve our family vacation home. We made so many memories there, Dom. I want to be able to take my kids there like Mom and Dad took us."

"If your kids like going on vacation, they won't care if it happens to be the same run-down cabin you vacationed at. That's only important to you."

"You're right, Dom. It *is* important to me. We spent a lot of time with Dad there. And before you say Dad spent a lot of time with us at home, too, I know that. But it was different at the cabin. He was relaxed. He didn't have to worry. There were no papers to grade and no lesson plans that needed attention. Nothing but our family relaxing in pure bliss."

"Except it wasn't bliss, Luce. Don't you remember the time we lost power because of the hurricane? How we couldn't come home because so many of the trees got knocked down and the roads were flooded?"

I didn't.

"Or the time Mom accidentally set the deck on fire when we were roasting marshmallows?"

"She didn't set the deck on fire. It was just a chair."

"No, it was the deck. Why do you think they sent us down to the Merwins' house?"

"I didn't realize."

"No, you didn't, because you never stop to think about anyone else and their feelings or their memories."

"Yes, I do."

"Not when it comes to that place. Complications happen no matter where you are. It's absolutely shitty what Dad is going through, but that doesn't mean we should cling to the past. Dad is still here. Let's focus on him. Let's focus on helping him and Mom. Let the rest go."

Chapter 51

Lucy

I HADN'T BEEN FACE-TO-FACE with Pete in months. The feeling that once gnawed at me was now devouring me.

"Do something," it demanded. *"Do something!"*

But what could I do? He'd stopped all contact with me. And that wager . . . it was so much. Perhaps too much. But I still was desperate for his side of the story.

I texted him, despite assuming it wouldn't do any good.

> Where did you go?

> If you wanted out, you should have just told me.

> I'll be fine. I'm not going to die without you. But I at least deserve honesty.

After I sent the texts, I dropped down onto my used, uncomfortable, but cheap futon. I started scrolling through our old messages. Nothing like tormenting myself with memories. I was only missing sad music and alcohol. I already had the burning eyes and tear-streaked face.

My phone rang, and Kenzie's picture popped up on the screen.

"What do you think of going to Mom and Dad's tonight for dinner?"

"Why? Is it a special occasion?" I tried to muffle my sniffle.

"Since when do we need a special occasion for family dinner?"

"We don't." Except I didn't want to go without it being one.

"Anyway, I think Mom and Dad have news."

"Good or bad? Because I'm not sure I can take any more bad news right now."

"Don't know. Mom was being very cryptic. Meet you there in an hour? That'll make it seven. And you can't use work as an excuse to get out of this. It's Saturday."

"See you then," I replied, letting out a sigh, of course.

Dominic just yelled at me yesterday. Dinner wasn't going to be easy.

I washed my face, only reapplying my moisturizer. What good had it done, crying the way I had over a man I meant nothing to? I'd done this way too many times in the past. I was heartbroken and miserable because of Pete, and instead of picking myself up and putting myself back together, I chose to wallow.

My eyes were red, my skin was red, my clothes were blue, and my heart had finally had enough. No more memory lane.

When I was getting out of my car at my parents' house, Kenzie was pulling into the driveway. Dom was already there. My sister, niece, and I walked in together, only Hayzel talking, telling us a story about puppies someone's dog had and how much she wanted one. I assumed Kenzie had already told her no several times, but that hadn't deterred Hayzel.

Once in the house, we all took turns greeting each other with hugs and smiles. After the usual chitchat, Hayzel turned to my parents and said, "So, is it good news or bad news? Aunt Lucy doesn't want any bad news."

"Come sit down." Mom motioned for all of us to go to the living room.

"What's going on?" Dominic asked without moving.

"Well—" Dad started, before stopping and looking at Mom. They gave each other a look I didn't understand.

"We heard from Mr. Shubin today. The house is safe!"

I immediately jumped and clapped my hands. Kenzie and Hayzel squealed in joy. Dom went over and shook Dad's hand then hugged him. We all came together for another round of happy hugs.

"How? What happened? How is this possible?" I asked.

Then I looked closer at Dad.

"Oh. You still have to sell the cabin."

"Yes," he said with a slow nod. "Part of my medical debt is being taken care of thanks to a nonprofit that helps teachers. Someone contacted them on our behalf. The bank took that as a good sign, and made us a deal. If we agree to sell the cabin, they have agreed to cancel out most of the mortgage debt. We only owe thousands, not hundreds of thousands. It came from well above Pete's head, but it wouldn't surprise me if it was his idea. It wouldn't surprise me if this deal with the tiny nonprofit in Pennsylvania was his idea, too." Dad looked in my direction.

The cabin was going away.

This had been a long time coming.

I knew it. I'd tried to stop it, but it was inevitable. "It's time to let go of the past," I said to all of us, myself included, even with my heart pounding at the thought of Pete doing the thing I'd begged of him months ago and saving my parents' house.

Then I looked at Mom and Dad. "Sell it. Please. You've struggled enough. There's no reason a vacation house you don't use should cause you to lose your home or your ability to buy food or pay bills or live." I moved my eyes Dad's way. "We should all just let it go."

"You were the one holding on to it," my brother said, then Mom shushed him while wiping at the burgeoning flood of tears in her eyes.

"Your sister has made tremendous progress, Dominic. Be happy for her."

"I am," he said, his voice soft. "I'm happy for all of us."

That was the nicest thing I was going to get from my brother, and I was glad to receive it.

Chapter 52

Pete

Text me back, Pete.

Or call me.

Either way, need to talk to you.

I IGNORED HER. WHATEVER she wanted didn't matter. But she didn't stop.

Seriously. This is important.

What do you want?

I have something big I need to tell you. I already told Lucy.

Lucy? This definitely got my attention. What would Charisma have to say that involved all three of us?

"What's going on?" I asked in a curt tone as soon as Charisma answered my call.

"I did something." Her voice was shaky. "I meant it to protect Lucy, but it just damaged both of you."

The swift sinking feeling had me dropping down into my nearest dining room chair. I stayed there as Charisma told me all about Miss Havisham, the messages, and all the putrid social media hate. My skin hurt from rubbing my free hand over my face so much. There was an explosive inside of me rattling around, time just about damn out on it.

"Are you out of your freaking mind?" I nearly shouted at her when she was done. I couldn't allow myself to care about the fact that she was crying so hard by the end that she could barely speak.

"I'm sorry! It wasn't supposed to get as big as it did. I needed to protect Lucy from you. You weren't a nice guy when I knew you, and I doubted that you'd changed in that time."

"So why not just tell her face-to-face? Why almost destroy my career in the process? Destroying my relationship wasn't enough?"

"I didn't mean for it to—" she began, but I didn't let her finish.

I ended the call, gripping my phone tight so as to not throw and potentially shatter it.

How could she do it? How could she sabotage my relationship with Lucy? How could she sabotage my life?

Charisma and I had never been a damn thing to each other, really, other than a good roll in the hay every other day or so. But it hadn't lasted long. I'd also told her I didn't want a relationship. I told every woman I dated that. Until Lucy.

The pain from this brought forth a whole slew of expletives aimed at Charisma even though she wasn't there to take the brunt of it. Even knowing it was her didn't help a single bit. I'd already done everything I could to have it all taken down, even reluctantly recruiting one of the IT guys from the bank to no avail.

Hearing about Charisma's major, public "eff you" to me made me want to call Lucy and talk about it all with her, but I couldn't. I didn't know the words to say outside of this one issue. I didn't know how to navigate any of it. Nothing was going to make me feel better.

I fumed about Charisma and the entire situation for days.

Then something hit me. I was so focused on hating her and blaming her, but Tess continued ignoring me at work and Lucy kept texting such sad words to my phone. Those things were not Charisma's fault. They were mine.

It was me. I was the problem.

I needed to do better. And I knew the perfect woman to start with.

·♥·♥·♥·♥·♥·

"Have a good night," Tess said in her most professional tone of voice, giving me a smile that was never going to reach all the way up to her eyes. At least she'd actually spoken to me. That was a first.

"You, too," I replied. But then I jumped up from my desk and joined her in the corridor.

She continued walking.

"Tess, wait," I pleaded. I adjusted my tie so it wasn't so tight on my neck.

Thankfully, she paused her steps and turned to face me. "What?" she said with a fair amount of exasperation.

I moved just close enough that I didn't have to speak loudly. "We've never had a problem being friends before."

"That was before I showed up in your office half naked and stupidly threw myself at you."

"I'm sorry for that. I'm sorry for all of it."

She closed her eyes for a moment, then she looked up at me. "It's about damn time."

"What?" I asked, taken aback.

Tess motioned for us to walk back into my office. Once we were in, she closed the door. "We're supposed to be friends, Pete. Your constant radio silence to everyone you mess up with is not only hurtful, it's bullshit."

"What did you want me to do?"

"Apologize. Which you've now done."

"How was I supposed to know to do that? You made it clear you didn't want to hear anything I have to say."

"Yeah, because I was wounded and angry after my performance on your desk and your utter lack of enthusiasm."

"You know why I turned you down. It wasn't about you."

"I do know, and it makes sense, but it didn't then."

"So you've been treating me like a stranger out of spite?"

She waited a few seconds before replying. "I guess I have been. I just didn't realize you were so hung up on her."

"I'm not hung up on her. I'm in love with her."

Tess nodded in understanding. "I knew you were falling hard for her. I cheered you both on, then you crashed and burned. I thought that was the end."

"Are you and I okay now, at least?"

Tess slowly nodded. "Pete, I . . ." She stopped and scrunched her eyebrows together. "What I mean to say is, isn't this the kind of conversation you should also have with a certain blonde woman?"

"It's been too long. I had the chance before, but I doubt I still have it now."

"Does she know you love her? Really love her? Or did she ever know it for sure?"

I wanted to say yes, but my fight with Lucy the day of Gwenn's wedding told me otherwise.

"Have you completely given up hope?"

"I think so." And it killed me to say it.

"But you still love her."

"Always. Forever. She's the one."

"So find a way to get her back."

"There's only one thing I can do. *If* she ever gives me the chance."

Chapter 53

Lucy

IN KEEPING WITH LETTING go, Kenzie and I volunteered to drive up to the cabin and pack up all the personal belongings. Gwenn suggested we take out all of our stuff before they began showings. The furniture, appliances, and major outdoor items like the portable fire pit were going to be included in the sale with the building and property.

Since Kenzie was available Saturday and not Thursday like she originally thought, I was able to go without requesting time off. This was a huge relief to me in ways no one else could imagine. No one except Pete.

Kenzie and I had been at the cabin for only an hour or two that morning. I hadn't stepped foot in the place since Pete and I left it in December. There was a churning swell of competing emotions inside me, and I made myself nauseous trying to control them all and keep them from taking over.

The biggest of them all?

The urge—no, the *need*—to say goodbye.

A car pulled into the driveway. We hadn't expected anyone. Well, I hadn't, but based on my sister's reaction, she knew exactly who it was.

I looked out the window to see Charisma coming up to the door, travel bag in hand. Kenzie opened the door for her and let her in.

"What's she doing here?" I asked Kenzie, no longer willing to look at Charisma.

"She's our friend. Your friend. And she's worried about you."

"I messed up." Charisma's voice caught, sounding like she choked up a little. "Maybe I should have done things differently. Handled it better. I thought I was doing the best I could to protect you and get you to know the truth about Pete without hurting you too much. I thought if I just came out and told you, that you might not believe me. I was wrong."

I let this sink in for a few moments while Charisma took a shaky breath. I was much more receptive to this speech the second time around.

"I've said all this already," she acknowledged, seeming to know what I was thinking.

I still couldn't look at her.

"Maybe hearing it again might help," my sister added. "Hear her out, Luce. It seems like she was right about Pete. He totally flaked on you. He could have cheated on you. Doesn't that count for something in Charisma's favor?"

Finally, I looked at Charisma's face. Her eyes were glossy and reddened. The corners of her mouth were down.

"I told Pete what I did." She gasped for breath.

I was desperate to know what he said, but I just couldn't seem to form those words in my mouth. Whether he forgave her was no longer any of my business. It was only in my power whether I forgave her.

"Not talking all these weeks hasn't been easy for me, either," I told Charisma. "You've still had Kenzie and Dom, but I needed you, too."

Charisma nodded, tears dripping down her cheeks.

"I do wish I'd known the truth about Pete months before you and I had our first talk about this. The whole truth, including what he did to you. Anonymous messages can only do so much to help, and they far too often cause nothing but destruction."

"I know. I know that now." She wiped at her face with her hands.

"Maybe I wouldn't have fallen in love with him with that truth," I continued, talking more to myself than my companions.

"You would have fallen in love with him anyway," Kenzie told me. "Not because you're man-obsessed, but because you believe in giving chances."

I knew this was a pointed comment about my friendship with Charisma.

I looked to my friend once more.

"I'm so sorry," she said again. "Kenzie told me about Pete's wager."

"Yeah." I sniffled. "Can you believe that?"

Except, of course, we all did.

"Can she stay?" Kenzie asked.

"You can stay," I told Charisma.

We told her she could take her suitcase down to Dom's old room. He never came up here and wouldn't mind her sleeping in his bed. While Charisma went to her room for the night, I wiped my own damp eyes, took a few deep breaths, and headed to the kitchen to make some tea. Kenzie followed me.

"What would you like to do while we're up here? I know you have favorites from when we stay."

I wasn't sure I could handle my favorite things. I also couldn't stop remembering Pete sharing cocoa with me at the beach, drinking coffee with me in this kitchen, eating dinner with me in the living room, and making love to me in my old bedroom. "Well, it's too cold to swim. A fire would be nice. Can we go to the park and walk around a little?"

Kenzie gave me a kind smile. "Sure."

Charisma rejoined us.

"Care for a walk at the state park?" Kenzie asked her.

"I'm up for anything," she replied. "Though I wouldn't mind hot coffee or tea first if that's okay."

"Already about to put the kettle on," I told her with a smile.

This had her in tears again. She walked over to me, and we quickly embraced. "Thank you," she whispered.

And that was that. I knew I couldn't hold it against her anymore. Yet another thing it was time to forgive, move on from, and not look back at.

Once the kettle was up to boiling and our coffees and teas were ready, we all curled up in the living room with the blankets Pete and I had returned to the storage bench at one end of the sofa before leaving *that* weekend. The three of us wanted to warm up before heading out for our chilly walk.

"How are you? Honestly?" Charisma asked. "I heard you yelled at your kids before break. You never yell at them. You never raise your voice."

"I know. It was awful. I've never had such a rough day at school before. I can't let myself snap at them again. I just can't get Pete out of my head."

"You don't wear yellow anymore, either," Charisma noted.

I looked down at my green sweater and gray leggings.

"People in school have noticed that, too," she continued. "Including the kids. You aren't happy anymore. Is that about Pete?"

I nodded. "Pete loved my yellow. Once he got over the shock," I added with a short, temporary chuckle. "He bothers me even when he's nowhere in sight."

"Maybe we shouldn't go to the park," Kenzie said. "You have a lot of memories with him there."

"I have a lot of memories with him here, too. I have memories with him almost everywhere I go. I can't give up my entire life because of that. I'm already willing to give up this cabin. Besides, I have a lot of memories of here and the park that have nothing to do with him."

I took a breath. "I'm letting go of the cabin. I can let go of Pete, too. I just have to put my mind to it."

"I'm with Lucy," Charisma said. "Pete doesn't deserve having that much power over her."

That settled it. We heated up some soup that Mom sent with us, divided it into stainless-steel containers, gathered eating utensils and napkins, and packed it all into my yellow cooler with the aluminum foil lining like Pete taught me. Then the three of us bundled up in our jackets and were on our way.

At the state park, we started with a short trail hike. I carried the cooler by the strap on my shoulder.

"What are you going to do about Pete?" Kenz asked while avoiding a giant tree root sticking out of the solid ground. Temperatures hadn't been warm enough to start the spring thaw. "Despite all the shit he pulled, I know you still love him."

"I do," I reluctantly admitted, "but there are too many things I can't change. I've never held on to a man as long as I've held on to him. I usually move on so quickly."

"He's hard to get over," Charisma added. "Even after a casual thing. Maybe because the way he ends things is the worst, with zero closure."

I agreed. There wasn't much else to say on the topic.

After lunch in one of the pavilions, we decided to head down to the icy lake. As we walked, we—well, they—talked about nothing in particular. I was too preoccupied to join any of their conversations. Maybe Kenzie was right after all. No matter how many years I vacationed at the lake, all I could think about was the man who hadn't returned my calls and texts in over three months.

At the sound of a squawking seagull, I glanced to my right and saw Pete a short distance away. I froze my steps and blinked a bunch of times. He was really there. He'd even fully grown out his beard again. I could have jumped for joy. Except he had a dark-haired woman with him. She wasn't facing me. Just the side of her was visible, then she turned the other way and walked off.

I yelled Pete's name and waved, catching his attention.

At least, I think I did. He looked like he maybe saw me but didn't look directly at me, and he instantly turned around and began to walk in the opposite direction, the same way that woman went.

"Pete!" I shouted again to no avail, then I raced toward him.

With the snow and ice still on the sand, it was impossible to get any traction. I had to go as slow as a turtle. On a particularly tricky spot, I had to take my eyes off Pete to watch where my feet were going. When I looked up, he was gone.

I heard Kenzie and Charisma behind me, having attempted to keep up with me. We were near a bench by this time, and I swiftly sat down before my legs failed me.

"What the hell was that?" Kenzie asked no one in particular. "Did he seriously just do that?"

My body shook so hard, I couldn't keep still, and it had nothing to do with the outside temperature. "Charisma was right. He ignored me. He ghosted me. He's done with me."

"You can say it, but do you believe it?" Charisma asked.

I didn't answer. "Can we go to the bar? I really need a drink. Something stronger and faster than we have at the cabin. And I need a distraction. Maybe one named Sven." But even saying this, I knew it wasn't true. I wasn't going to hook up like I easily would have done before last June.

Kenzie's phone beeped. "We have to go to the cabin first. Mrs. Merwin says your car alarm has been going off for a while, Luce."

I knew I should have just driven instead of us all taking Kenzie's SUV. "Of course, my day can't get any better. Why would it?"

We headed for my sister's car. I searched for Pete the whole walk there but didn't see him.

By the time we returned to the cabin and I disabled my alarm, I was no longer shaking. However, I was more in need of that drink. First, we had to check around my car to make sure no one or nothing had disturbed it, then we had to listen to both Mrs. and Mr. Merwin complain about the noise.

Nearly an hour later, we were about to head out to our favorite local bar when Kenzie got a call from Mom, who wanted to explain in detail *again* exactly how we should pack the dishes and photo frames into the boxes and why using the blankets to help prevent breakage was the best idea, which we were already well aware of, but Kenzie was patient enough to not remind Mom.

This all took another half an hour. I waved to get Kenzie's attention, but she waved me off. I tapped on my wrist as if I were wearing a watch, but she ignored this, too.

"Let's go," I whispered to my sister.

She rolled her eyes and pointed to her phone.

"Tell her we have to go," I said a little louder than last time.

Ten minutes later, we were finally on the road again. While Kenzie drove, Charisma took control of the music, and I closed my eyes and tried to shut out everything. Nothing in that car or my brain was going to make me better at the moment. Nothing in the bar would, either, but it would be a start.

Once we arrived, the three of us headed straight for the available bartender and ordered drinks. Kenzie went non-alcoholic, Charisma went for wine, and I ordered a shot—well, three shots—I hadn't had since my college days. None of the tables were available, and there wasn't much space at the long bar, either.

"Some business function," the bartender told us. "Who knew mortgage brokers could party so hard?"

I froze yet again. Then my sister, my friend, and I looked at each other with wide eyes. "Are you sure they're mortgage brokers?" I asked.

"Some kind of mortgage work. I didn't ask for specifics," the bartender said before quickly taking an order from two customers who'd just walked up.

"It couldn't be, could it?" Charisma asked my sister and me.

The bartender placed our drinks in front of us then stepped away to help the others. I couldn't drink mine.

"Lucy?"

The voice came from somewhere behind me.

I swiveled around to face Alec. His face was scrunched in confusion, but his eyes spoke more of surprise.

"What are you doing here?" he asked.

"Shouldn't I be asking you that? You said you never usually come up here in the winter. Your last trip is always in October, until summer." *Usually with Pete*, I wanted to add, except I couldn't make myself choke out those words.

"Our company decided to have a retreat up here. Several of us grew bored with the bar at the inn. Too many bosses there."

"Pete's here, too, right?" I forced myself to ask.

Alec looked like he didn't want to answer.

"I saw him at the state park. He ignored me." This I forced myself to choke out, and *choke* was definitely the right word for it. I almost couldn't get it out of my throat.

Something flashed in Alec's eyes and on his face. It looked something like hot anger mixed with sadness. "Pete's outside on the deck," he told me.

I didn't hang around to hear the rest of what he might have to say.

After finding my way to the door that opened onto the patio, I glanced out and saw Pete through the glass. He was with that dark-haired woman again. I hadn't gotten a good look at her before, and now she had her back to me. They were talking in a way that seemed to me meant they were well acquainted. How well, I hated to guess. The smile on his face told me he wouldn't be opposed to closing the gap between them and making things hotter.

And that thought had me hot with anger.

"Pete," I said when I opened the door and walked out. I worked my damn hardest to not be completely weak at the sight of him again.

"Lucy," he said in a tone of surprise. He tried to step back from the brunette.

The woman spun and faced me. Then I recognized her.

The trembling was back. I hoped I could control it enough to talk, only she spoke first.

"Hello, Lucy."

"Tess."

"You two know each other?" Pete asked, his voice rising at the end.

Tess looked at me. "We're familiar. How are you?"

There was no way I could say anything to her. I shook my head.

"I tried to help," she said, lifting her hands in acquiescence. Then she walked away.

"How do you know Tess?" Pete asked.

"Long story. Well, short story, I suppose." I shook my head, trying to make sense of all the thoughts running through it. "Fancy seeing you here after you ignored me at the park."

"After I what?" Except his face told me he knew exactly what I meant.

"Ignored me. Pretended you didn't see me. Turned and walked the other way. How many other ways should I say it?"

"I panicked," Pete began. "Like I always seem to do."

While I heard and understood his words, I wasn't sure I believed them.

I loved despite everything, even when all signs, signals, hints, clues, and omens were telling me—or rather, screaming at me—that something was wrong. I still loved Pete. Seeing him for the first time in months didn't change that. But my love was never going to be enough to get us through.

"Sorry to interrupt," Tess said from behind me.

I whipped my body around to face her—whether I was shivering from the cold since I no longer wore my coat or the adrenaline coursing through me from this situation, I couldn't tell.

"What do you want?" Pete asked before I could. His tone to her was increasingly annoyed.

"Just forgot my stuff." She motioned to the leather shoulder bag sitting on a cleared part of a snow-covered table. But she didn't make a move toward it.

Instead, she turned to me. "I know what I said in that first DM, but you can understand the predicament Pete was in at the time, right?"

She didn't give me time to reply.

"I mean, yeah, it was a dumb bet, and yes, I told you out of anger. But I really—"

"You what?" Pete snapped at her before she could finish.

Neither Tess nor I looked at him, but we both flinched.

"What do you mean you told Lucy? When? How could you do that?"

Still, we ignored him for the moment.

"I meant what I said after that, too," Tess continued over Pete's voice, "whether you read that next message through or not."

I hadn't. I'd ignored anything else from her. Honestly, I'd hidden the conversation so I wouldn't have to look at it anymore.

"Pete *is* a good guy," Tess said.

That quieted him down. I glanced at him, and he silently stared at me, not her.

"He only ever let me down twice in our friendship. You should know which two instances I mean. And honestly, you two were going to have sex anyway. You both wanted to. What difference would the time have made? It isn't like Pete won the bet. He waited the full six months with you."

My chest was tight. My ears were hot. I forced myself to again make eye contact with my ex. He was scrubbing his face with his bare hands.

None of us moved. Then Pete stormed over to the bag, snatched it up, and shoved it out in Tess's general direction. She quickly walked over and took it into her hands.

"Don't forget I'm your friend," she said to him.

"You sure about that?" he asked. His voice was gruff but also strained.

"If I was anything but your friend, I wouldn't still be here talking with your amazing girlfriend."

"Ex-girlfriend," I piped up.

Pete instantly moved his eyes to gaze into mine, but I looked away.

"You and I will discuss this later, Tess. Please go now," Pete pleaded with her, but he still wasn't using a very nice tone.

"See you back at the inn, pretty boy," Tess said in his direction as she turned away. She gave me a sad smile before walking back into the bar.

"Luce, listen—"

Everything in me and on me burned.

"So, who is she?"

"Tess? You said you knew each other."

"Not Tess. Your new girlfriend." I nearly choked on the words.

"I don't have one."

"Tess thought otherwise. Like maybe I already know the new girl."

"How the hell do you even know Tess?"

"She sent me a DM telling me all about the wager with Miles and how Drea kept throwing herself at you when you and I were supposed to be together."

"Did Tess tell you that I turned Drea down every single time? I also turned Tess down when she propositioned me while half naked on my desk."

I rolled my eyes, but Pete moved closer, trying to keep eye contact with me. "What don't you believe about that? Did she not just say she also told you I'm not a bad guy?"

"She did just say that." I choked back a hard cry. "But I didn't want to hear anything she had to tell me after her first message to me. I didn't trust her, and I didn't trust you. I didn't want to know anything else about you and your shitty group of friends."

"Not the whole group."

"Don't start with the semantics right now. Don't you dare."

"There is no other woman. At all. Drea and I are nothing. Tess and I are just coworkers and friends. I don't have any other woman, nor do I want one. I only want you."

"Then why the hell did you so adamantly tell Florence that I wasn't your girlfriend? Why did you drop out of my life?"

Pete put his hands up and stepped closer to me. "Not because of another woman. I swear."

"You expect me to believe that?"

"It's the truth," he said with urgency.

"You never cared to answer any of my messages."

"That's not true. I cared more than you know. I still do."

"Then why did you ghost me? We'd only been a couple for a week before you bolted."

"You made me leave Gwenn's wedding."

"That was not the last time I contacted you, and you know it." I sniffled as my nose began to run. "All those messages and posts about you. All those women. They were right. Charisma was right."

"About the person I was then, yeah. But not now."

"Come on, Pete. I'm not stupid. The first time I see you in months, you're with a gorgeous woman."

"Coworker and friend. I promise."

"She hit on you. You're telling me you never wanted her, too? Or any of the hundreds of other women who would instantaneously drop their panties or even their boyfriends—maybe husbands—for you?"

"I can't help how women feel about me. I only care what you think and feel."

"What I think?" I gave a sharp laugh. "I think you always said how much you stood by your ethical code. That was the reason you gave as to why you never mentioned working with my parents on their mortgage. How does that not spill over into your personal life?"

"Wh—"

"How could you take that bet?" I screamed in frustration.

"I snapped, okay? Miles was being an ass, and I just lost my cool. I also lost the bet *on purpose*. I was not going to let Miles have anything to do with our first time."

I swiped a hand roughly across my cheek. "Except he did. I changed my mind about waiting, remember? I practically begged you. You never would have held me to the six-month agreement if not for Miles and your ego."

"You think I'm proud of myself for that?"

I'd expected Pete's voice to be as booming as mine, but his words come out softly.

He continued before I could reply. "I have hated myself every single day since that weekend I accepted the wager. The weekend we met. I've also loved you every single day since that weekend. I loved you so much, it scared the shit out of me."

I huffed, tears burning my eyes. "It doesn't take a genius to figure out that you're full of nothing more than lies and bullshit." I turned and stormed off as fast as my legs could carry me.

Chapter 54

Pete

"Lucy!"

I ran after her into the bar, but couldn't get through the crowd as easily as I needed to. I'd tried to grab hold of her arm outside, but she slipped away. Alec found me.

"Hey, did you see Lucy?" he asked.

"Yeah. Where did she go? She ran off away from me."

Alec shrugged. "I have no idea, but I'm not surprised. There was fire in her eyes when she asked about you."

"Help me find her?"

Instead, we found Charisma.

"Where's Lucy?" she asked. "She was looking for you."

"She ran off. I was hoping someone saw her come back in here."

"Kenzie," Charisma called.

Lucy's sister walked over.

"The asshole lost Lucy," Charisma told her.

"What happened?" Kenzie asked.

I didn't have time to explain. "Just look for her," I told everyone. "If you find her first, let me know."

Kenzie got on the phone to call or text her. We all split up and moved around to different sections of the building. I soon noticed Tess watching me and hurried over to her.

"Did you see Lucy in here? This is serious," I told her.

"I did. I tried to talk to her, but she wouldn't listen to me. I'm not one of her favorite people, considering what I've told her."

"That's the best you've got?"

"She's angry right now, right? Why would she want to hear anything I have to say? I helped shatter her world."

"But if you'd tried harder—"

Tess heaved a hard breath. "It isn't about *me* trying harder, Pete. Lucy ran out of here about five minutes ago with some guy."

I'd been staring past her, still searching the room, but at this, I jerked my head to look into Tess's eyes. "What guy? Why would you let her do that?"

"He didn't force her to leave, and she wasn't calling for help. He actually helped her put her coat on."

"Why didn't you didn't stop her? Or come tell me you saw her leave?"

"Again, I tried talking to her. And I didn't know where to find you. I didn't realize you two had still been outside."

I rubbed my forehead. This was too much right now. "When you saw her go, you should have said something to me."

"I'm not sure the hot guy she left with would have appreciated that."

"That's not funny." I huffed and pulled out my phone. No signal.

"Pete, relax. It's a joke. I'm sure she's fine. She's never gotten herself into trouble before, right?"

I didn't have time to answer her. Instead, I weaved through people to look for Kenzie or Charisma and found them in close proximity. Both rushed over to me.

"Did you find her?" they asked in unison.

I told them what Tess said about Lucy leaving.

"That's not abnormal for her," Kenzie said. "At least it wasn't before you came along. She'd disappear all the time."

"With men," Charisma said meaningfully. "Gorgeous, single men. You might not want to find her. She's been wishing for serious alone time with Sven."

"Who the hell is Sven?" I snapped. "The guy she went outside with?" I was already having a difficult time breathing, but this had me wanting to throw some furniture. How could she leave with some guy and not even care how much I needed to talk to her? How could she not care how badly I missed having her in my arms?

Where the hell was she?

"There is no Sven," Kenzie said after a few beats as Charisma laughed.

"What?" My voice understandably sounded strangled.

"Maybe not, but she still left with someone. Probably never even asked his name. I mean, I told you she likes leaving with random men," Charisma added. "You should get that. That's how you've always lived your adult life."

I ignored her last comment and ushered them to the front door in hopes of one of us spotting Lucy in the parking lot. Alec came along, too.

She wasn't out there.

I asked Alec for his keys. "I have to find her," I told them.

Kenzie called after me to stop, but I didn't have time for discussions. I was only half a mile down the road when my phone rang.

"I figured calling would be easier than looking for your dumb ass. Good thing I got a signal. Lucy just texted us," Charisma said after I answered hastily. "She's okay. She's at the lake. State park," she corrected herself.

"I'll be there as soon as I can. If you talk to her again, tell her to stay there."

I arrived at the park much faster than I should have and drove straight to the parking lot to find an empty spot, which was pretty easy to do. As I walked toward the lake, I still couldn't get Lucy to answer my calls and texts. Almost immediately, I was beyond the grassy area. My feet hit the sand.

And there she was down by the shoreline, still slushy with ice and snow. From my position, I couldn't tell if her body shook from the cold or from crying. Either way, it was my fault. At least she was alone.

"Lucy?" I said as I ran up to her.

She instantly swiveled around, her hands dropping to her sides. From what I could see, her skin was red and wet with tears.

"Why are you here?" she asked.

Chapter 55

Lucy

"WHAT DO YOU MEAN why am I here? Why are you here?" Pete quickly responded. "Where's Sven?"

"Who?" Then I remembered my joke to Kenzie and Charisma. Pete must have spoken to them at the bar.

"You ran off," he said, by way of reply.

"I needed to get away from you."

"With some random guy?"

"No, with an old friend. He and his wife were in the bar. They were leaving, so they offered me a ride when they saw how hard I was crying. Why are you so worked up about me leaving the bar?"

"I was worried about you." He sounded sincere.

For a moment, it seemed like he wanted to hold me, but it was fleeting. As quickly as he moved toward me, he stepped back again.

We silently stood together as I attempted to dry my still-trickling tears. My heart pounded; my body shook. His amazing baby blues locked on mine, only neither of us smiled.

"Lucy, I—" Pete stopped.

He wouldn't even finish what sounded like maybe an apology.

"What is *wrong* with you?" I bore my eyes into him. "You stole my heart, then you lied to me about it. You bet some asshole that you'd get me to screw you, and you couldn't even follow through with that."

"Luce—"

"Don't 'Luce' me. What the hell happened, Pete?"

"I couldn't handle it anymore."

"Handle what?" I cocked my head in disgust. "The idea of being a grown man in a mature, loving, committed relationship? Because that's where we were headed. I was ready. You said you were, too."

He sighed. "It was too much pressure. I felt pressured to be with you. Even to be happy with you. It just became too much."

"Don't even think for a second you can blame this on me," I said sharply. "You were okay with waiting. I was okay with waiting, too. For the most part. Then you said you loved me. If you felt any pressure, it was all your doing, not mine."

I rubbed my wet eyes, making them burn even more. "You led me on."

"No, I didn't, Luce. You and I genuinely fell for each other."

I ignored this. "Why didn't you tell me the truth? About the bet. About wanting to flake on me. You had many, many opportunities to say something, even after Gwenn's wedding."

"I didn't want to do it over the phone."

I gave a laugh. "I mean, why not? Did ghosting me really sound better than dumping me over the phone? Would being honest with me have been so bad?"

When Pete didn't reply, I snapped. "Give me an answer. Tell me why you chose to do it the way you did. Any honest answer you might have inside of you somewhere. Find it, and let it out."

He gave me an almost remorseful look. "I never planned on dumping you. I did, however, think I should tell you about the bet so you could dump me in person."

"You assumed I would break up with you?"

"I'm well aware I've done something you think is unforgivable."

I ignored this for the moment. "But you never came to see me. You never invited me over."

Pete was quiet.

"Here we are, Petey Boy."

He winced, but said nothing.

Guilt immediately struck me over that last comment, but I continued. "In person. Start talking."

Still, Pete remained silent. He just shifted his feet.

"Why couldn't you have just meant it?" I cried. "Why did it all have to be lies? Why did you just drop out of my life?"

Pete sniffled. "It wasn't lies. I do love you."

"I don't believe you. You are a lying, cheating, selfish coward."

He cocked his head. "Coward?"

"Yes. *Coward*. You professed your love for me even up until the day you started ghosting me. Gwenn's wedding. You didn't bother calling me back after I gave in and contacted you, hoping to make up. Why couldn't you just tell me you weren't interested anymore?"

"I was and I am still interested in you, Lucy."

"You so happily told Florence that I wasn't your girlfriend."

"There was nothing happy about that conversation. Not on my end."

"So why not tell me you wanted out?"

"I don't know!" he practically barked out. "I just— I didn't really want out. I didn't deserve you, and I knew it. You could do better than me. You deserved better than me. I just couldn't tell you that. I couldn't tell you anything."

"And you wonder why I think you're a coward."

"Maybe I am. But Lucy, I swear I didn't cheat. I had many opportunities to and never once wanted to give in. And I didn't lie about how I felt. Not until the month leading up to the wedding. I'd hit my breaking point. The weekend up here with the hot cocoa was not just because we'd reached the six-month point. It was to give myself hope that maybe if I could make you as happy as possible, that maybe I was good enough for you. I honestly don't know what happened after that other than to say it was sheer panic."

I let out a hard breath. Then I waited a few seconds before I spoke. "For future reference, there are some things you don't do when you are unsure about your relationship with the woman you say you love. You don't avoid all contact with her without giving her a reason for your silence. You don't have sex with other women or make her think you have. And you don't keep telling her how much you love her if you don't mean it!"

I nearly screamed the last part and needed to take several breaths.

Pete took this opportunity to speak again. "You're right. I should have been honest with you."

"You were more than happy to blame Charisma's posts, weren't you? I don't need an answer to that one. I know well enough. Why haven't you owned up to your mistakes before now?"

"Will you at least be friends with me?"

This I hadn't expected. Not with the direction our conversation had gone. "You're kidding, right?" I gave a spiteful laugh.

"No, I'm not. If you're done with me, that's my punishment. But I would like to at least be friends again."

I shook my head. "People always say that, but it never happens. Why even bother? It's so pointless."

He looked as if I'd just pummeled him in the stomach. "Please. *Please*. Just say we can be friends." His voice began to crack.

I couldn't agree. I wouldn't have meant it. "Friends only" no longer worked for me. I wanted so, so much more, but the trust was gone. "Life can't only consist of sunny June days. Neither can relationships. I know that. But you've disappointed me in ways I'm not sure I'll ever get over."

Pete silently stared at me, his eyes blurred with tears.

"I want you to have a good life," I said, wiping my own tears. "I want you to be happy."

"You aren't happy, Luce. You don't have a smidgen of yellow on you. Remember when you told me yellow makes you happy?"

I nodded, my eyes still flooded.

"You are so unhappy now, you aren't wearing your favorite color at all. You've lost hope. I'm guessing that has to do with me."

My throat was so tight, my breath so ragged, I couldn't say anything in return.

"You said you wore yellow when you had hope. You don't have any hope for us now, do you?"

"Should I? And how?" I didn't give him time to respond. "I came up here to let everything go."

"Including me?" Pete's voice was strained, and his tears fell as steadily as mine.

There was nothing I could do at the moment except nod. My heart was breaking too much for anything else.

"So this is it?" he whispered hoarsely.

"This is it." I almost choked on my words as I nodded. Then the sobs came again.

I gasped for air as Pete moved closer to me, so close I could smell his spicy cologne. I stepped back, unable to feel him touch me. It would have been too much.

Slowly, I turned and walked away. Cold. Numb. Heartbroken.

"Lucy, wait," Pete called after me.

I paused my unsteady steps, not sure if I could face him again.

"Lucy?"

My chest tightened even more, but still I swiveled around to see Pete watching me. He closed the gap between us.

"This better be good," I told him.

Chapter 56

Lucy

"I screwed up," Pete said.

"And?" I asked.

"I never should have done that. I never should have let Miles get to me." He scratched at his beard for a moment. "He's out of my life now. I don't share any accounts with him. We don't talk anymore."

He still hadn't hit on the deal breaker. "And?"

Pete took a step closer to me, our bodies nearly touching now but not quite. "I'm sorry."

"I get that." But I couldn't say I was ready to accept it just yet.

"You were not wrong for loving me."

There it was. The thing I never thought I'd hear him say. Hot, acrid tears streamed down my face.

"Charisma was right in some ways. The way she went about it was pretty shitty, but she was right about me having been an ass for far too long."

"Have you forgiven her? Will you forgive Tess?"

"I don't care about forgiving them right now. I want to focus on you and me. All right?"

I could only nod in return.

"I don't deserve you, Luce. I don't think I do, anyway. But I want to. It's up to you to give me another chance."

"I thought you just wanted to be friends."

"I don't like being nothing to you. It's too hard." He stopped talking and took a couple breaths. "If you decide you don't want to give me any more chances, I'll stay away. It'll break my heart, but I will leave you alone if you tell me to." Then he sniffled again.

I caught his gaze and saw how damp his eyes were. "If a woman doubts as to whether she should accept a man or not, she certainly ought to refuse him."

"What?" Pete asked, his face crinkled.

"It's from *Emma*."

"I know that. Why are you quoting it now?"

"I'm not talking about marriage or proposals. I'm saying that I have far too many doubts about you. Like you said, you haven't done anything to deserve my confidence."

Pete wiped his face with his coat sleeve. He was starting to look as cold as I felt. We needed to warm up soon. I assumed that meant separating again, and I didn't think I could bear it. Maybe the cold wasn't so bad.

"You don't hate me more than I hate myself." His voice was strained.

"I don't hate you. I tried to, but it doesn't work," I told him.

His body shuddered, and he exhaled sharply. "I love you, Lucy."

"That isn't fair," I cried.

"We can't move on in this conversation without saying it."

"Why not?"

"Because I think if you are willing to try, you'll see that my love for you kept me distant to protect you from me."

"What do you want?"

He leaned closer—his hand tentatively resting on my hip—and whispered in my ear.

Chapter 57

Lucy

HERE I AM AT the state park again. It's been three months since what I consider our official, in-person breakup in March. It's also been exactly one year to the day since Pete and I first met. I couldn't miss the "anniversary." My parents sold the cabin, but with or without that, this is my last trip here.

I've given up on my idealistic fantasy of the lake, of what I thought it had given me. I will always remember the joys from here, but will also never forget the overwhelming pain. I think it might be time to move on to a new dream and a new escape. I can't bear to think about a new love.

Pete is the man I love. No more planning my future with every cute guy who catches my eye. I love to be in love, but I almost hate myself for having been so infatuated so quickly and so often. No "love" I felt before was ever as intense or as deep as what I feel for Pete, even after the demise of us as a couple. Our time together was much shorter than it should have been.

I force myself to turn away from my view of the lake and see Pete not far away, sitting on the sand near the grass by the narrow shoreline, looking at a similar view to the one I just admired, only toward where the lake curves to the south instead of the north. I don't know if he's seen me. He isn't facing my direction. From what

I can decipher in his expression, I clearly see that he is now as much attached to this place as I ever was.

"What are you doing here?" I call, only he is too far away to hear me.

I hurry my feet in his direction.

"Hey," I say when Pete is within earshot. "Why are you here?"

He stands and brushes sand off his hands and bottom. "I know we agreed to meet tomorrow, but I wanted to come up a day early."

We both know the significance of today. It's exactly why I didn't want to see him until tomorrow. Too much pressure. He's already felt enough of that. I didn't want to add to it.

"How often do you come up here now?" I ask. I fidget with the skirt of my saffron-yellow, tie-front sundress.

"Probably more than you. At least three or four times a week, mostly after work."

I wish I'd been up here that much. Then again, I really don't. "You asked for three months. I gave you three months."

"Three months of intentional silence on both our sides has been an adjustment," he says. "I thought it was exactly what I wanted. Then I realized I needed it but didn't want it. I want you."

"When you stopped all contact with me in December, it hurt. You know that. I can't apologize for you being hurt by three more months of silence."

"Six months without you was a long time. At least before March, I could still see your face pop up on my screen and hear your voice, even if I didn't have an answer to your words. Even when the pain in that voice nearly killed me." Pete pulls out his phone. "I want you to see something."

He taps the screen a few times, then holds the phone out for me to take. I oblige.

"What am I looking at?" I haven't moved my eyes to the screen yet. I want to watch his face as much as I can.

"Three months' worth of emails I drafted but never sent. Not quite the same as the letters I used to send you, but just as heartfelt." He pauses. "More so." There is so much meaning in those last two words.

Now I can't look at the screen fast enough.

"It would have been six months' worth, but I deleted all the messages I drafted from December through March before I finished writing them. I could never get past 'I'm sorry,'" he says, his voice a little rough. "Some weeks have more than one email. Some days do, too. I— well, you'll see."

Pete motions to the phone.

He was always so protective of his phone before. So guarded as to what it contained. So secretive.

"Do I get to read all of them?"

"Please. Take it somewhere comfortable to read if you'd like. I'll be right here."

"This is your special place now?"

Pete nods. "Alec has given up trying to get me to go anywhere else. Dom understands, too."

"You've been talking to my brother." This isn't a question. It's more a statement I need to say out loud, mostly because the anger I felt at Dominic for being friends with Pete after Dom hated on him has softened into mild surprise. But then, they always did get along.

"He forgave me after I apologized to him and to all your family. I told him about our fight and our agreement."

"You apologized to my family?"

"I did. The week after you and I saw each other here in March."

"What about Tess and Drea?"

"Drea went with Miles and Corkie. Of the three, Corkie's the only one I miss. Well, pity, honestly. But she chose to stay with Miles. Tess and I still work together, but she won't be half naked on my desk or hers anymore. Well, she might be on hers, but it'll have nothing to do with me, I promise. We are strictly professional at work now. No more flirting. And strictly platonic friends. Both she and Drea thought I was fair game because I never showed them I wasn't."

I can accept that.

"Please read the emails. They say everything I want you to know. Then we can talk."

"You're really letting me take your phone?" I ask. "You've never even let me look at it before."

He nods. "I know, but that was me then. I want you to trust me. I want you to know I've worked hard at earning your trust."

I quickly stand on my tiptoes and give him a kiss on his hairy cheek, then I kiss above his upper beard line so he can feel my lips on his skin. Pete doesn't make a move toward me, but from the spark in his eyes, I can see he wants to.

"I'll come find you when I'm ready," I tell him. I start to walk away, then I reach and grab his arm and slide my hand down to his. "I'm sorry for the horrible names I called you when we fought in March. Especially a certain nickname you despise."

Pete nods.

"No matter how I felt at the time, you didn't deserve that. It was a cheap shot."

"It's okay." He squeezes my right hand and rubs my left arm with his free hand.

While I appreciate Pete entrusting me with his phone, I don't want to leave him without one, so I hand him mine from my bag. He slips my phone into his pocket.

I wander down to the far picnic area and sit in the grass, up against a tree. Here, with a bit of sunlight glistening on my skin, I start at the beginning, back in March. It's time-stamped at three in the morning. He must not have been able to sleep. Then I realize it's dated before our big fight here, not after. Actually, it's a week before, around the time Tess direct-messaged me about Pete's wager with Miles.

Lucy, it begins. Not with "dear" or "hey" or any other type of greeting.

Lucy,

Something happened at work today. Something that, in the past, I'd have said yes to in a heartbeat. I wouldn't have cared that there was another woman out there missing me. I'd have literally jumped at the chance to take what was so willingly and tantalizingly offered. I don't want to give you any more details. You'll probably still hate me with or without them. But please know that all I could think about was you.

It should have been you sitting on my desk. It should have been you wanting me so badly, you'd risk us getting caught. And if I'd only talked to you and told you what was going on with me back in December, it could have been.

I miss you.

I read draft after draft after draft of saved emails with the same vibe of Pete missing me and feeling guilty about it. He really did pour his heart out just as much in these emails as he did when he was mailing me love sonnets, only this time, there was no bet and a possible thousand-dollar "prize" hanging over his head. There was just the gut reactions of a man who seemed to recoil at the idea of connecting with any woman who wasn't me.

Then comes this one:

At the end of these twelve weeks, if I can prove I love you as much as I did the first time I said it, when you were asleep on the other end of the line and never heard me, I'll know that I've done enough to deserve your love in return.

This makes me remove my finger from the screen, not wanting to scroll away from these words.

He told me he loved me before that night at his house when he didn't want to make love to me. Correction—when he *wouldn't* make love to me.

I frantically try to remember when I fell asleep on the phone with him, but it's no use. It could have been any late-night conversation. Yet in his email, he mentions saying it when he knew I couldn't hear him.

After all that time, this was exactly what I needed. Proof he truly did love me. The bet was over long before he wrote this email, and telling me he loved me when I couldn't hear him wouldn't have earned him any sexy-time points. He said it because he meant it and felt safe in me not hearing him. Not at that moment.

I finally begin scrolling again. I also feel the urge to tell him my reaction to every sentence he wrote me. It's a good thing he isn't sitting here with me, though I know he isn't too far away.

The last email is time-stamped from today, only five hours ago.

I know you'll be there. You wouldn't miss it. Neither will I, even if I don't see you. I wanted to be the man you saw in me that day. Now, I think I am. I love you, Luce. If you've made it to this point, you have to know it's true.

I have his phone. I can easily check his texts for any between him and other women. But I don't want to. I don't even have the urge to. Anything Pete said to another before March doesn't count. He's already admitted to letting Tess and Drea flirt with him that whole time. What does count is March until now, and I am certain there are no flirty, "please screw me" texts that exist in that time frame.

The old me would have run to him as fast as I could. I choose instead to casually walk back to the beach. Pete will be there no matter what speed I go. I know I can depend on him.

I find him in the same spot. Just like he promised. He starts to stand, but I motion for him to stay where he is. I sit next to him, allowing the warmth of the sun-baked sand to permeate my skin and my legs to brush up against his. Then I hand Pete's phone back to him. He pockets it and returns mine.

Pete swivels his body in order to face me. "Should we make this our official anniversary?" he asks.

I nod, lean in, and kiss the beautiful mouth of this beautiful man with a beautiful soul. He wraps his muscular arm around me and deepens our kiss. After a few more moments, we pull back, mindful of being in a public place.

"Wherever we are, let's always celebrate this way," I finally reply. "No day in June will ever be as sweet as this one."

Epilogue

Pete

"IT'S TOO CLOUDY TO see anything," Lucy says, waving off my suggestion of attending the Syracuse Falls Starlight Festival on this warm July night, one year (and a few weeks) after Lucy and I reunited last June.

Granted, clouds hadn't factored into my plans as much as they should have. I checked the weather constantly this whole week, and by all accounts, it should be clear now. Lucy is unconcerned by this. I lean closer to where she sits on her sofa. From my seat on her coffee table—the one I replaced for her after we got back together, knowing she'd sold hers—I enjoy our knees rubbing up against each other.

I take her hands in mine and give them a gentle squeeze. "You talk so passionately about these small-town festivals that Syracuse Falls holds. I've never been to any of them."

"Because you were always busy. Or busy avoiding me."

She gives a playful smile after a few beats. I can't be mad at her, knowing full well that while she might be joking, we both know she's also speaking the truth. I'm still working on not being mad at me.

"I'm with you now. I'm available. So can we please go?"

Lucy sighs softly. "I do like the parade. And Kenzie and Hayzel are running the booth for Button's. They're supposed to debut a new ice cream sundae they let Hayzel come up with."

"Is that a yes?"

She nods, then grabs hold of me for me to help her stand. She doesn't actually need my help, but after we got back together just over a year ago, she told me she fully intended to find some way to touch me every day, in those non-platonic but still non-sexual ways we employed during our six-month wait. I smile at the memories of this past year, loving how she kept her promise. I love so many things about her.

We decide to walk down to the park with the gazebo—the main staging area for the festival—as it isn't that far. Though it's late—after nine o'clock—the festival is just getting started. There are booths full of food, a face painter, carnival games, and the parade that will start about an hour from now. Then at eleven, the whole town is supposed to turn out their lights for thirty minutes so we can all savor the dark sky and twinkling stars—only the clouds still linger overhead.

Lucy leads us straight to her sister and niece, much closer to the gazebo this year than they have been in any other, eyeing the menu full of ice cream sundaes and milkshakes available for the fest. She turns to Hayzel. "Chocolate, strawberry, pistachio, and caramel sundae. Am I right?"

Hayzel gives a short laugh. "How did you do that, Aunt Lucy?"

Lucy smiles and motions to the menu. "It's the best one up here."

Kenzie looks from Lucy to me and back. "You guys having fun?"

"We just got here," Lucy says, her blonde hair blowing slightly in the breeze. It gently caresses her neck, and for a few moments, I find myself envying her hair.

"We'll circle around back to you," I tell Kenzie.

When Lucy isn't looking, Kenzie gives me a wink and a smile. So does Hayzel. Little does Lucy know that her sister will be far busier than she expected while I pull her away from this section of town. I think the only thing Lucy doesn't want to try is the face painting. My arms full of stuffed animals she won for her students reminds me of this as we find a spot to watch the parade. An hour has already passed since we left the Button's Diner booth and her sister and niece.

I've managed to keep her over here on this side. Though I can still see the gazebo, I cannot see the other side of it, where I know Kenzie and Trevor have been working nonstop getting everything ready.

"Hey!" Lourdes says as she and Gwenn sidle up to us on the sidewalk. "Mind if we join you?"

Lucy greets them with hugs. "I thought you guys weren't going to make it tonight."

Gwenn shrugs nonchalantly. "Change of plans. Rhett's working late anyway, and won't be home for a while. He's helping a buddy fix a broken driveshaft," she adds quickly, noticing my pointed expression.

The shop where Rhett works closes way earlier than this, and I didn't want Lucy wondering why he'd still be there, because I know that's exactly what she'd do. She even opened her mouth to say something before Gwenn added the rest. When Lucy looks away to speak to Lourdes, Gwenn looks at me and mouths, "*sorry*," like she thinks she almost blew it. I mouth "*it's okay*" and smile in return.

We all sit on the sidewalk to watch the show. I thought of everything with this night, but somehow left the chairs back at Lucy's. She doesn't seem to mind sitting on the concrete, however.

There are no sirens or bands or candy with this parade, but everyone still seems to enjoy all the floats and vehicles wrapped up in lights. After having checked out the town's website on social media, I know that the goal is to emulate the stars in whatever way the entrants interpret starlight to be. I also know Lucy goes gaga for the ones with the white fairy lights.

"So pretty," she whispers as a float full of those slowly drives by.

I'm glad she likes it. I take her hand in mine and kiss it softly, then I wrap my arm down around her waist and let it linger there for the rest of the parade.

When the last parade entrant drives by, I carefully tug Lucy up to her feet. She sweeps her arms around my middle, giving me a squeeze as well as a quick kiss on the lips. Lourdes and Gwenn stand as well. Lucy looks up to the sky.

"Oh well," she says, eyeing those still-lingering clouds. "Guess we should head home."

Both Lourdes's and Gwenn's eyes go wide, but Lucy doesn't see this.

"Why don't we head back to the gazebo anyway?" I say casually to Lucy. Except this question is anything but casual. My heart is already racing, and we haven't even gotten there yet.

Lucy shrugs with her arms still around me, so sweet in her trustfulness. I almost want to prolong this moment, just a little. Just to savor this period before the shift. I have to believe there will be a shift. I have to hope.

"Why not?" she says. "I can at least have that sundae even if I can't see the stars."

I move to take Lucy's hand in mine and walk toward the gazebo. Lourdes and Gwenn follow behind. Then I quickly check my watch—10:57. It's almost time.

Lucy's surprised when we return to the diner's booth and Kenzie isn't there.

"We ran out of ice cream," Hayzel says with a laugh. I can tell she's not very good at lying, which is great, only Lucy looks a little suspicious. "All the ice cream? How did that happen? What's in that cooler right there?"

Hayzel stops her before she can open it. "We ran out of *chocolate* ice cream, and my sundae just isn't the same without it. Will you wait until I can make it perfect for you?"

"Of course." Lucy smiles. She returns to her place with me.

"Hey, let's go sit on the bench by the gazebo for a good view before it's taken," I say as I lean down toward Lucy's ear.

She nods, but not enthusiastically. "Okay, but I'm sure it's already taken. No one leaves that bench empty by this time. Besides, I still say we won't be able to see anything except a little moonlight and a whole lot of clouds."

When I take a quick look behind us, I see we still have Lourdes and Gwenn with us as planned, and Hayzel has joined us, too, Dottie having taken over her place at the booth. Kenzie, Trevor, Kerrick, Nadine, Dominic, my parents, Rhett, Alec, Tess, and even Charisma are around here somewhere, having stayed well out of sight so far. I may not have forgiven Charisma as quickly or as readily as some people suggested I should have, but I also worked my best at making amends to her as well, so that helped aid in my ability to forget what she'd done. She also loves Lucy and wouldn't want to be left out of this.

We make it down the stone pathway to the bench, which is indeed empty.

"Will you look at that?" Lucy laughs. "Who knew?"

I look in her eyes, trying to see if maybe she's figured this out after all. I'd hate for the surprise to be ruined after so much effort. Then again, so long as she's happy, I don't mind either way.

We are about to take our seats on the bench that faces away from the gazebo, when I turn to Lourdes and Gwenn and say, "You know what? Why don't you two sit here? I'm sure Lucy won't mind sitting on the gazebo steps with me."

Lourdes and Gwenn instantly accept my offer and sit. Of course, Gwenn sneaks a smile at me as I turn and lead Lucy to the gazebo, which she is also shocked to find empty of people. I turn her so she can't look inside and instead point out someone I claim to see but who I know isn't there. We haven't quite made it to sitting yet, but we are directly in front of the round wooden structure, facing out into the town.

And there it is. The whole town goes dark.

Well, the whole town is dark except for the thousands of white string lights on the gazebo, some around the posts and some hanging down like sparkling curtains. It isn't abnormal for there to be lights on the gazebo for the festival, Kenzie assured me, but the extra strands might be obvious now. Lucy hadn't paid any attention to it before when the rest of the town lights were on, but now that she's turned around, it's all she can look at.

"What's going on?" Lucy asks. "Why aren't these dark?"

"They will be soon. Not just yet."

"But why?" She quickly turns to face me, searching for an answer, wondering how I know this.

I don't reply. Instead, I gently lead her into the middle of the gazebo. We are surrounded by yellow vases of yellow flowers, mostly daisies and sunflowers, courtesy of Lourdes. I drop down to my right knee. Lucy silently stands before me, her eyes already glassy. Then she begins to sniffle.

I take her right hand into my left one. "Luce, I spent a year thinking I didn't deserve you or your love. I spent another year thinking how lucky I am to be the guy who shares this amazing love with you."

Both our hands begin to tremble. Lucy wipes under her eyes, her smile never fading.

"No matter what," I continue, "I will love you this fiercely forever, but I'm hoping to do it with you by my side as my wife." I slip my free hand into my right pocket and pull out the box containing the diamond engagement ring. It's yellow gold and delicate, but still strong, just like my sweet Lucy. I open the box and hold it up to her. "Will you marry me?"

She nods emphatically, a burst of happy tears coming out of her. "Yes," she practically shouts in joy. "Yes, yes, yes."

I rush to my feet, intending to grab her for a kiss. I haven't even put the ring on her finger yet. But before our lips connect, we are suddenly surrounded by applause and cheers. Then I remember all our loved ones are here. Lucy still has hold of me, but looks around with a laugh as our friends and family step close enough for us to see their smiling faces in the brightness of dozens of fairy lights.

My fiancée and I turn to face each other again. Lucy places her hands on my cheeks and pulls my face to her, leaning up to me at the same time. We kiss with as much heat as those stars I don't care if we get to see. If it weren't for where we are and who we are with, this kiss would have me caressing more than just her back.

As we reluctantly pull away, Lucy asks breathlessly, "How soon were you thinking?"

"The wedding?" I respond, just as heady and out of breath as she is.

She nods.

I pull her left hand off of me for one moment, just long enough to slip the ring on her finger. Then I return it to its place on my shoulder and give her my most loving smile. "I was thinking June."

Lucy nods again, her hand slowly sweeping up onto my neck, then into my hair. We press against each other, our foreheads gently touching. "June days are the best days."

Bonus Epilogue

Lucy

WHEN I PICTURED MY wedding day, either as a little girl or as an adult, never did I expect to worry about capricious geese, yet here I am.

The whole gaggle—at least fifteen of them—will not stop honking, one after the other, never at the same time yet almost overlapping. It's like someone taught them how to sing a musical round, and they are practicing before their big performance. But why here? Why now?

Why me?

As it it wasn't bad enough a few of them decided to turn the large wedding tent into their own personal feast, now we have to listen to this obnoxious noise.

Two hours until the ceremony begins.

Hayzel, my twelve year old niece and only flower girl, joins me at the large bay window facing Oneida Lake. "When will the geese go away?"

"I wish I knew."

"Uncle Pete said that there's–" Then she she stops. "Wait. I can call him Uncle Pete now, right? Even if you aren't married just yet?"

I smile. "Of course."

She grins in return. "Uncle Pete said that there's plenty of time before the wedding for them to wander away on their own, but Grampa's worried the geese might ruin your perfect day. He tried to go shoo them, but Gramma wouldn't even let him out of the house."

Which must be why Mom took Dad back to the rental they're sharing with Kenzie and Trevor across the street, since they aren't needed for any photos yet. Half the guests are over there as well, all hanging out until it's time for the ceremony. But Dad is worried. I know he is, only we can't let him do anything about the geese.

The last thing we need is for Dad to damage his already fragile heart in some way and possibly wind up in the hospital. I'd much rather have to deal with a million ornery geese than for something to happen to Dad.

"Can I help?" Hayzel asks, but there isn't really anything I can think of for her to do.

"Why don't you find your mom? See when she wants to start getting ready."

"She's been ready for a while now, and has already planned out time to freshen up. She said you should start within the next hour."

I nod, having read the stream of texts Kenzie sent a little bit ago. As my wedding planner, she has everything all figured out to the minute. As my sister, she's low-key freaking out that maybe I won't be ready on time.

"No worries," I tell my niece with a genuine smile. "We'll all be ready when we need to be. Maybe you can go across the street and ask Gramma if she needs anything."

Hayzel shrugs. "Sure. I can do that. My dress is over there, anyway," she adds, motioning to the outfit of shorts and a T-shirt she's currently wearing.

She happily goes off across the street, after Pete walks over with her to make sure no cars are coming down the road. I love that I keep getting glimpses of him around the house. He's stayed outside, though. While we might see each other through the windows, we made an agreement that we won't be in the same room together until the ceremony, as a way to give us a little time apart, making us miss each other more.

My besties slash bridesmaids Lourdes, Gwenn, and I are enjoying a quiet coffee break together a little later before all the hustle and bustle begins when we hear a screeching from the backyard. Specifically, Hayzel screeching.

We set our coffees down and rush to the back door, finding Pete and my brother Dominic ushering her to the house, Trevor not far away acting as a sort of shield between them and the geese.

The three of us run out there as Hayzel joins us on the porch.

"What's going on? You okay?" We all ask her immediately.

"I'm fine," she replies, a little out of breath.

"We told you to stay away from those geese," Dominic scolds her.

"I just wanted to help," she answers. "They wouldn't go away, and Aunt Lucy and Uncle Pete don't want them at the wedding."

"So, what happened?" I ask.

"I tried chasing them away. Just gently guiding them to a different area of the yard, but one started chasing me instead."

Trevor walks over. He's been within hearing distance this whole time, but now he's shaking his head. "They're probably best left alone. I'm sure they'll go away on their own once all the guests start filling up the lawn. They won't want to be so close to so many of us. But we can try to get rid of them." He motions to Dom.

Honestly, I'll be happy if they can accomplish this without getting hurt or stepping in goose poo. At least they're still in jeans and shorts, thank goodness. No one is in wedding gear yet, except everyone that's across the street.

Pete steps toward them. "My wedding. My responsibility, too."

Though he looks like he's about to argue, Trevor nods.

"What's going on?" Spence's voice asks. "What are we about to do?"

I turn and see Lourdes's husband as well as our friend Alec walking out onto the porch as well.

My fiancé laughs and motions to the waterfowl littering the yard. "We have a little sprucing up to do."

Now Alec and Spence laugh, too. "We get boots and shovels for this?" Alec asks.

All the guys join Trevor, farther into the yard, to come up with a game plan. The girls and I, meanwhile, head back inside.

"You ready for this, soon-to-be Mrs. Lucy Amundsen?" Lourdes asks, sipping her coffee yet again.

I am. I've been ready for this since I met Pete. When I tell them so, Gwenn and Lourdes smile. They always considered me a hopeless romantic, and maybe I was. Maybe I still am, only now, it no longer feels hopeless. I'm not waiting to find my perfect guy. I've loved him for years.

As the minutes tick by, turning into one hour then two, I wish I could hurry them more, if only to get to that moment. The time when Pete and I are officially husband and wife. Do we have to have a wedding ceremony to solidify our commitment to each other? No, but it's the sweetest frosting on top of our little love cake, one that's only going to get better over the years.

A stylist comes to the house to do my hair and makeup, as well as hair and makeup for Lourdes and Gwenn. As Hayzel told me earlier, Kenzie already did her own. We're all dressed in our finest now, the wedding party in soft yellows. The geese have finally gone, the back lawn a bird-less sea of cheerful yellow tulips, daisies, and roses and white silk among the guests Pete and I invited. It's a small but amazing group of our closest friends and relatives, including his wonderful old neighbor George.

In the moment when I expect my dad to come into the house and talk with me before walking me down the aisle, I turn to find it's Pete walking down the hall to meet me in the living room instead. His eyes are closed, and he's using his hands to guide him toward where he thinks I am.

"You don't have to keep your eyes closed," I laugh softly, stepping toward him so he doesn't run his shins into the coffee table that separates us. "I'm okay with having a first look before the ceremony."

I've teased Pete for weeks that maybe my dress is yellow instead of white, though he doesn't care either way. It's the same for me. I'd marry him in ripped jeans or my favorite pajama set. The puffy white dress just makes it more fun, and yes, it's a little bit about me living out my childhood dream. I'm totally okay with that, and Pete is, too.

My lemon yellow heels click against the hardwood floor as I walk closer, near enough to take his hands in mine. His eyes pop open, and he immediately smiles. "You're gorgeous, Luce," he whispers.

I chuckle. "You haven't looked at my dress yet."

"Don't have to. I know how beautiful you are, and what you wear has nothing to do with it."

"Aren't you afraid it's some feathered yellow monstrosity? It is my favorite color."

He laughs. "This is true, but no. For one, I can see in my peripheral vision that there's a cloud of white down by your feet. Secondly, even if your dress was neon yellow and made of feathers or pompom balls or vinyl, if it made you happy, I'd be happy, too."

Leaning forward on my tiptoes, I give him a quick kiss. "You're pretty damn handsome in your suit, I have to say." He thanks me and kisses me, then I ask, "So, since you walked in here with your eyes closed, you obviously weren't coming for a first look."

"We agreed to keep a little distance, just to make it more poignant when we see each other down in the tent."

"We did."

"The thing is, I have a surprise for you."

"Aww. I thought we decided against doing presents. You are my gift. I don't need anything else."

"You like being on the lake?" he asks, but he already knows the answer.

"Of course. A wedding on the shore of the same lake where we met and reunited is the perfect location."

"I didn't want you to be sad, Luce. I had this feeling that in the ceremony, it might hit you that we're only here for a couple more days before we go home. That this house is just temporary. And I thought that might make you sad since your parents never got another cabin up here."

Truthfully, I hadn't considered it much today, but it's definitely something I've thought about for the past few weeks. "This is only temporary. Our rental agreement ends in a few days. We only have it for a week."

But when I look in Pete's shining eyes, I feel like there's something I'm missing. "What's going on?" I ask him.

"What if this house isn't temporary?"

When I don't reply right away, he adds, "What I mean is, what if it isn't a rental?"

He smiles, his face crinkling with joy. I still haven't been able to say anything yet, because if this means what I think it means, then someone owns this house. And I think that someone is us.

"Happy wedding day, Luce," Pete tells me taking me into his arms for a hug. He's careful not to mess up my hair or accidentally tangle himself in my dress. "This house is for you."

My eyes tear up, and I sniffle. "Happy wedding day." I hold him as tight as I can without hurting him. Then I pull back to see his happy expression again, feeling it mirror my own. "I can't believe you bought us a house. How did this happen?"

"Are you okay with it?"

"Are you kidding? I love it here! You know that." So much so that he's right, I've hated the idea of leaving.

"It's just a vacation house. Not like we can quit our jobs and move here. But I wanted you to have a home on the lake again. I want you to have a place where you can relax by the lake you love so much."

"But I love you so much more," I tell him, cupping his face in my hands and giving him a kiss. It's sweet but short, Pete's choice. I know he's afraid of ruining my makeup and having to listen to Kenzie complain about it.

Then I ask him again how this all happened, while we keep our arms wrapped around each other, his chin gently resting on the top of my head.

"When we decided to marry at the lake, I started forming a plan. I asked Gwenn to look for houses in our price range. She found this one, though it needed a lot of work."

I don't need to glance around to know it's fabulous in here, all clean and bright and looking brand new. Now I understand that it actually *is* brand new. "You fixed up the house?"

"Dom and his crew did most of the work. Lourdes added the flower garden and potted daisies and sunflowers. And I know it isn't a lot of land, but it feels perfect for us."

It really does. This house has everything Pete and I like in terms of architecture and décor, but best of all, it's been a labor of love from him and my loved ones. I fan my hands in front of my face with a laugh, hoping to dry the tears that have decided to stream down to my cheeks. "This wasn't supposed to happen yet."

Pete takes a tissue out of his pocket and carefully dabs at my cheeks and under my eyes. He doesn't tell me not to cry. Never tells me not to cry. He just lets me feel my feelings and stays nearby in case I need him or want him. Right now, he has one arm around my back, keeping me close.

"When we met three years ago, this is the exact life I wanted for us. A sweet home together. Time spent on the lake. Happily in love."

"Married," he adds, before giving me a soft kiss on my forehead.

"I hoped for married, but what I really wanted was a sign that we're meant to be together forever. I wanted a promise from you."

"You have it," he says, hugging me extra tight.

I nod, my hands gripping him as I hold him tight as well, both of us having given up controlling my steady stream of happy tears. "I know we're about to say our vows in a few minutes, but while it's just the two of us, I want to tell you I really am so in love with you, and so happy we're here now."

He kisses me again, warming me even more, despite the slight chill coming through the vents from the air conditioner. "I didn't put it in my vows, but I promise to do my best, to love you in whatever way you need, so that you never spend another day without yellow in your life."

We both know what he's referring to without him needing to speak it out loud. I'm glad to not have to discuss that part of our relationship today. "You are my yellow, Pete. So long as I have you, I'm happy. It doesn't matter what colors I wear."

Our next kiss adds my lipstick to the list of makeup I've now messed up, as well as my hair a little bit, but I'm the happiest woman in the world. There's a knock on the nearby wall, and Kenzie's voice carries over to us. "I wanted to check on you first before sending Dad in here, just in case."

"Still fully dressed," I answer my sister with a laugh, though I feel my cheeks burning as red as Pete's are.

Pete promises to see me outside, kisses the tip of my nose, then heads out to the tent. My dad comes in and gives me sweet words of encouragement, as well as a few funny stories about me pretending to be a bride when I was little. And then it's time. I hold my dad's arm and step out into the sunshine, watching my best best friend as he watches me make my way to him, grateful for our past, our present, and all the days we have ahead in our future.

Bonus: Pete's letters

MARCH

Lucy,

I don't know what to do with this information. I don't want to keep it to myself. I don't want to keep it from you. Only I haven't spoken to you in months. My own doing, I admit. But I need a way to tell you, and this is what I came up with.

You see, something happened at work today. Something that, in the past, I'd have said yes to in a heartbeat. I wouldn't have cared that there was another woman out there missing me. I'd have literally jumped at the chance to take what was so willingly and tantalizingly offered, repercussions be damned.

It should have been you sitting on my desk. It should have been you wanting me so badly you'd risk us getting caught. And if I'd only talked to you and told you what was going on with me back in December, it could have been.

I don't want to give you any more details. It would be beyond unfair for you to know them. If I ever manage to find the nerve to send this to you, or if you somehow find out about this, you'll probably still hate me with or without them. But please know that all I could think about was you.

I miss you.

MARCH
Dear Lucy,

I thought about you again today, but I think about you every day. You call or text, and I look at your beautiful face on my phone's screen and freeze. There aren't words good enough to explain what happened, what I did, and why. There never are. But I hope that maybe one day you might consider forgiving me even. Or at least consider seeing things from my POV.

I miss you so much.

I don't know when I'll see you again. I don't want to say "if" though I can't promise I'll go out of my way to run into you somewhere I know you'll be, only because you deserve better than me. I know this, and you should know it, too. I have never been good enough for you. My past tells me that. My present tells me that, too. If ever there was an ex you should run from, it should probably be me. And yet typing the word "ex" has my heart and stomach so constricted, I'm not sure I'll be able to sleep.

I haven't been sleeping much anyway. Not once in these three months without you have I slept more than four hours. You know that's not typical for me. But every time I close my eyes, you're there. Except you aren't actually here, which is where you should be. Or I should be there with you.

One week.

One week of official boyfriend/girlfriend status.

That's all I gave us before freaking out and bailing on you.

Damn.

Luce, I'll never forgive myself. I don't see how you could ever forgive me.

MARCH
Hey Luce—

I think writing these emails every day is getting easier for me, though pretending I'm talking to you doesn't make things easier. In fact, I think it makes me feel worse in some ways, just because once the letter is done, I have to face the reality that you won't actually be reading this or responding in any way. Yet I continue, because in some ways, it feels like the only remaining connection I have to you.

I talked about you with George today. Other than Alec, George has been my sounding board for all of this mess. He agrees that yeah, I probably haven't done the best in my past and maybe that's a reason to think I don't deserve you. But George also said that if my love for you and your love for me is enough, if our mutual trust and respect is enough, then maybe there's a chance we can make it. I just have to be willing to go to you.

I want to.

I want to so bad the thought of it makes my heart slam around in my chest and my legs itch, desperate to run all the way to your house. If I could just get rid of this damn fear that you'll never accept me back, I might send these.

That's something to think about. Not new, mind you. I ruminate on thoughts like this every day. You occupy more of my mind than my job some days. No woman ever had that effect on me before. Only you, sweet Lucy.

You always acted like I was the hero prince in your eyes. You, sweet Lucy are the princess, deserving of far better than I can give you. But I'm working on it. Apart from a little flirtation with Drea—one I regret every day—I was faithful to you all six months of our friends-only deal. I've been faithful to you since the first official day of us, even after our tragically short relationship's demise.

Miss you. Always.

MARCH
My darling Lucy,

I saw you and froze.

Mentally, anyway.

You weren't supposed to be there. You never go to the lake when it's cold. It makes you sad to see it without all its green summer splendor.

It was a shock to my system, but I couldn't do the one thing my heart wanted me to. I couldn't go to you.

There was no way seeing me was going to do anything but destroy you, and I couldn't bear to see that on your face. I turned and ran like a coward, but a thoughtful one. Then you found me by chance yet again. You hated me. You were angry with me. But you still loved me. You love me, present tense.

How was that possible?

How IS that possible?

All this time, I thought since I'd lost you, I lost every chance of making amends. The look on your face during our fight—our official breakup, as you call it—was something I wish I could forget. Except forgetting means pretending it wasn't my fault, and I can't do that. I caused all of this.

Every second of sadness has been because of me. But you granted me a reprieve of sorts. A chance to make things right. Even though it means three months of intentional silence on both our parts—as excruciating as that will be—I have hope that we will be okay. I can't tell you how incredible it feels to actually have that tiny little flicker, knowing you're out there with love for me in your heart. Then again, I don't have to tell you. You are well aware of how hard this has all been. Seeing that pain on your face, hearing it in your voice, nearly broke me, but I can't say my pain is equal to yours. I was the one who walked away.

I can't wait for the day when I can walk back to you again.

I love you, Luce.

APRIL

Dear Lucy,

I decided to do something I've been thinking about. You and I don't often agree on classic literature, especially those you find so romantic that I just don't understand. But I read Emma *again. It's been years since I forced myself to read Austen. After you quoted Emma's words to me, I considered what it meant to you, both the quote and the book.*

I know you romanticize their relationship and think Emma and Knightley are so perfect for each other, and they are. But I'd also like to add that part of the reason they're perfect for each other is that they themselves are not faultless. While each spends a lot of time trying to fix the other, in the end, they also see that they need to work on parts of themselves first.

I've said this before, but it bears repeating. I need to work on me. I am working on me. Have been for a while now. Aside from you, I haven't slept with anyone since a few months before I met you. You know this already. I've told you in these letters and in person, but it's important to point out again. I can only imagine what you think of me now that you know the whole truth of me and my past, and every scenario I picture isn't good.

It's beyond important that you know without a doubt how I have been faithful to you and even to the idea of you since that first day in June.

At the end of these twelve weeks apart, if I can prove I love you as much as I did the first time I said it, when you were asleep on the other end of the line and never heard me, I'll know that I've done enough to deserve your love in return.

APRIL

Lucy,

I've talked and talked in these letters about love and respect, but how can I expect you to respect me if I'm not completely honest with you? There's one thing I never told you. One thing only Drea knows and Miles suspects, I'm sure. You're aware that Drea and I flirted during our six-month agreement, or you at least suspected it. You were right, but unfortunately, there's more. I shaved my beard because of Drea. I don't mean she shaved it for me. I just mean that the weekend we went camping with them and Alec, she mentioned how my beard somehow equated being tied down to you.

I wish I could say her words rolled right off my back. They should have. But I was floundering in guilt and confusion about us and our relationship and that damn bet. Her words haunted me for two weeks, until I had enough and shaved it off. I even kept my face clean-shaven for two weeks afterward, until you saw me that way. It was like a knife to the gut, not because you expected me to have one, but because a woman who should have had zero influence over me knew something my not-quite-yet girlfriend didn't. I let myself get sucked into her game, and I hated me for it. You should have hated me, too. Maybe you will now that you know.

Maybe the bet in and of itself is enough for you to curse my name for all of eternity. It probably should be. I blamed my ego for taking on that bet with Miles and for not being honest with you about it. I guess it's easier to blame part of oneself when in reality, the brain and body work as a whole. I screwed up. I screwed up so, so much relating to every single facet of the bet, the lies, the secrets.

I'm so sorry, my love. I'm sorry my pride affected so many things I did and ways I behaved. I'm sorry I wasn't honest with you about any of it. I'm sorry I allowed other people to have such strong influence over me. I want your influence in my life again. I know I can be a good man for you. I hope you see it, too.

APRIL

My sweet Lucy,

I hung out with your brother again today. I don't think you know this is going on, and I hate hiding it from you, but we are on our official three months of no contact. And yes, I realize I write these emails at least once every day, but I guess I've been afraid that you'll judge Dominic for being friends with me after all I've done. Dom isn't one to involve himself in other people's situations unnecessarily, so you know I understand how important it is when he reminds me not only how much I screwed up with you and Charisma and all those women, but also how much I have done to make amends for all of this.

I haven't forgiven Charisma yet, but I have apologized in return. I also apologized to one of the women from the social media posts, one who made the bulk of them. It wasn't easy, especially when she refused to listen to me at first. But in the end, though I unintentionally made her cry again, she decided to hear me out. I don't know if she'll forgive me, but she won't come after me anymore. She also removed the posts she made, as did Charisma, which leaves only a few posts that are still public. I can live with that. It feels more like justice at this point as opposed to punishment, and I'm okay with it.

I'm so sorry for how the viral posts about me affected you. That's honestly why I haven't forgiven Charisma. I love you too much to cast aside the fact that her actions hurt you. It's going to take a lot of work to get over how much you suffered because of that situation. I don't care anymore what she did to me. You are the one who matters the most.

MAY

Sweetest Lucy,

I'm at the lake for the fourth time this week. This state park never meant much to me other than a fun camping spot until you showed up in my life. Now you are all I see while I'm here. I don't really talk to people unless my friends are with me. I sure as hell don't flirt with any women like I used to before you.

I can't help but wonder if you still come here.

The cabin already sold. I know you know this, even though we can't talk about it right now. The idea of you losing something you cherished so much is hard for me. You said you were okay with letting it go, that it was necessary to help your parents, and while that is absolutely true, I think about the tears you must have shed, and my stomach clenches.

I am so glad I was able to be there for your family, to help them dig themselves out of that massive hole. Your mom and dad are always so kind to me, always have been, even in those moments when you despised me or tried to. Every time I see them, it's like they know this is not just a passing romance. They don't look at me and think, "Eh, well, they gave it their best shot. If it doesn't work, oh well." I know that was their opinion of all your previous relationships. It makes my heart happy to know they see depth in the love you and I have.

Tess sees that, too. I haven't mentioned her to you in these emails yet because I've spent weeks and weeks trying to figure out how.

She shouldn't have been the one to tell you about the bet. That should have been me. I should have owned up to my mistakes. I never should have made that mistake in the first place. I am so, so very sorry, Lucy. For every single thing related to the wager and how it affected us, both separately and together.

I wish I could say that without the bet, I never would have panicked about our relationship, but the truth is, loving you would have scared me no matter what. We talked about this that day in March when the beach was still frozen and I was terrified that your heart might be, too. But I promised to give you nothing but honesty.

Thank you for loving me through all that. You might scoff when you read this or think it's a little dramatic to say, but genuinely, thank you. If you hadn't, I would have given up on not just us but also me. I would have gone back to living my life the way I did before, having a lot of fun but also feeling empty and unfulfilled as hell.

You made me realize that I could be a whole person, not a screwed-up caricature of one.

I can't wait to hold you in my arms again, if you give me the chance.

I miss you.

JUNE

Darling Lucy,

Today is a special day. It looks to be gorgeous weather, according to my weather app. Much more importantly, it is exactly one year to the day since I met the most incredible woman, who changed my life for the better.

I hadn't expected any of this, to be sure. I saw you, and we hit it off. I thought we'd go back to my tent, or wherever you were staying, and have some naked fun then move on. That was routine for me.

Then you turned me down. A blow to my system, but exactly what I needed. You asked for friendship, and while we definitely developed that, we both fell in love, something I hadn't anticipated.

In a way, I'm glad I didn't see it coming. I'm glad you took me by surprise.

We haven't planned this, but I'm going to our park today. I know with the cabin sold, you might not want to spend more time at the lake than you have to. I know it might be difficult for you, and yet I know you'll be there, too. You wouldn't miss it. Neither will I, even if I don't see you. I'll understand if you ask me to stay away today just to give you more time.

I wanted to be the man you saw in me the day we met. Now, I think I am. I love you, Luce. If you've made it to this point, you have to know it's true. Let me just say that when I do see you this weekend, if you're wearing yellow, I can't promise not to hope that means you still love me, too.

June Days Playlist

"Stuck On You" | Meiko
"Clumsy" | Fergie
"The Sound of Sunshine" | Michael Franti & Spearhead
"Summer Paradise" | Simple Plan
"Over the Rainbow" | Israel Kamakawiwo'ole
"Island in the Sun" | Weezer
"Lovefool" | The Cardigans
"Hopeless Romantic" | Meghan Trainor
"Many the Miles" | Sara Bareilles
"I'm Yours" | Jason Mraz
"Daydreamin'" | Ariana Grande
"Good Day Sunshine" | Haley Reinhart
"cardigan" | Taylor Swift
"Super Duper Love" | Joss Stone
"Brighter Than The Sun" | Colbie Caillat
"Marry Me" | Train
"The Way I Am" | Ingrid Michaelson
"Yellow" | Kina Grannis

Want more Lost Hearts Found?

IF YOU SIGN UP for my newsletter, you'll receive updates on my books, free goodies, and more! Subscribe at https://lisakeiferau thor.com

Do you want more from Lost Hearts Found? Check out another book in the series, **Winter Blossoms**. How does being snowed in during a blizzard sound? That's exactly what Marcy and Alec have to figure out in real time, as a snowstorm traps them in her apartment after she already decided that, despite her very real feelings, he can't possibly be the guy for her. Find the description below!

Alec

I met the woman of my dreams without realizing I was looking for her. She made me nervous in a good way. Things started out well, then inexplicably, Marcy pulled away. So much so that she's even refusing my help now that we are trapped together in her apartment during a snowstorm. I know I'll need to navigate through Marcy's hot and cold feelings toward me to get her to understand our insta-love really can turn into meant to be. I just need her to give me a chance.

Marcy

I never asked for much in a boyfriend. Cute. Smart. Kind. Alec checks all the boxes. He also checks a box that, for me, is a complete nonstarter: Sports. Seems innocuous to most people, but most people have never been abandoned on the side of the road by a guy choosing a game over them. After that, I vowed to never date—let alone fall in love with—another sports fanatic. But with the way Alec looks at me? I don't know how to find the right words to tell him I know he will only break my heart. We can't possibly have a future together. So why does he keep coming back? And why do I want him to never leave?

Acknowledgement

ANG—FIRST AND FOREMOST, I want to thank you—my bestie—for the inspiration. As this book morphed and developed into what it is now, I knew without a doubt that I wanted at least part of you to be the base of it. Yes, Lucy's a little (or a lot lol) spicier than you, but the love she has for her family and teaching both come from you. I sprinkled in as much of your family as I could while trying to be as respectful as possible. I hope you love the end result.

Also, thank you for allowing me to interview you so as to better understand what teaching elementary school is really like—even though I changed some of what you told me to better fit the story. Sorry!

Sonya—thank you so much for the "tamed the flirt" line. I might not have tamed *that* flirt from the campground, but I am grateful for the inspiration. It was too good to not use :)

Sarah—you gave me another fabulous cover! Thank you so much!

Joanne—you are an editor extraordinaire! Thank you so much for all your valuable edits and comments.

Courtney Rapp, at Westcott Florist in Syracuse—thank you for kindly answering my interview questions and giving me great insight into how a floral shop works.

My friends and family—thank you for your own ways of encouraging me. Love you all!

Dear husband—you have supported me and stood by me through so, so much. "Thank you" doesn't seem like near enough, but thanks all the same. Love you!!!

Readers, bloggers, reviewers, and just anyone who gave this book and all my books a chance—from the bottom of my heart, thank you so very much.